Date: 1/7/19

FIC FREETHY
Freethy, Barbara,
When shadows fall /

PRAISE FOR THE NOVELS OF
#1 NEW YORK TIMES BESTSELLING AUTHOR
BARBARA FREETHY

"I love *The Callaways*! Heartwarming romance, intriguing suspense and sexy alpha heroes. What more could you want?"
-- *NYT Bestselling Author* **Bella Andre**

"I adore *The Callaways*, a family we'd all love to have. Each new book is a deft combination of emotion, suspense and family dynamics. A remarkable, compelling series!"
-- *USA Today Bestselling Author* **Barbara O'Neal**

"Once I start reading a Callaway novel, I can't put it down. Fast-paced action, a poignant love story and a tantalizing mystery in every book!"
-- *USA Today Bestselling Author* **Christie Ridgway**

"A very touching story that shows the power of love and how much it can heal."
--***All Night Books*** *for BETWEEN NOW AND FOREVER*

"In the tradition of LaVyrle Spencer, gifted author Barbara Freethy creates an irresistible tale of family secrets, riveting adventure and heart-touching romance."
-- *NYT Bestselling Author* **Susan Wiggs**
on Summer Secrets

"Freethy has a gift for creating complex characters."
-- ***Library Journal***

"This book has it all: heart, community, and characters who will remain with you long after the book has ended. A wonderful story."
*-- NYT Bestselling Author **Debbie Macomber** on Suddenly One Summer*

"Barbara Freethy is a master storyteller with a gift for spinning tales about ordinary people in extraordinary situations and drawing readers into their lives."
*-- **Romance Reviews Today***

"Freethy's skillful plotting and gift for creating sympathetic characters will ensure that few dry eyes will be left at the end of the story."
*-- **Publishers Weekly** on The Way Back Home*

"Freethy skillfully keeps the reader on the hook, and her tantalizing and believable tale has it all– romance, adventure, and mystery."
*-- **Booklist** on Summer Secrets*

"Freethy's story-telling ability is top-notch."
*-- **Romantic Times** on Don't Say A Word*

"Powerful and absorbing…sheer hold-your-breath suspense."
*-- NYT Bestselling Author **Karen Robards** on Don't Say A Word*

"A page-turner that engages your mind while it tugs at your heartstrings…Don't Say A Word has made me a Barbara Freethy fan for life!"
*-- NYT Bestselling Author **Diane Chamberlain** on Don't Say A Word*

Also By Barbara Freethy

To my tennis friends at the Peninsula Tennis Club who not only enjoy a good match but also a good book! Hope you like this one!

WHEN SHADOWS FALL

The Callaways

BARBARA FREETHY

HYDE
STREET
—PRESS—

HYDE STREET PRESS
Published by Hyde Street Press
1819 Polk Street, Suite 113, San Francisco, California 94109

Printed in the United States of America

Cover design by Damonza.com
Interior book design by KLF Publishing

ISBN: 978-0-9906952-9-5

One

—▶▷◀◀—

"Callaway, huh? Which one are you?"

Colton Callaway looked into a pair of angry brown eyes and wondered what the hell he'd done to piss off his new captain, a man who had entered the firehouse only ten minutes earlier.

"Colton Callaway," he said, standing up a little straighter so that he was eye-to-eye with his boss. All he knew about Mitchell Warren, the new captain at Station 36, was that he was in his late thirties, had fifteen years of service under his belt and had a reputation as a well-respected hard ass.

The chatter in the dayroom had come to a crashing halt with the captain's entrance, and Colton could see the other guys watching their exchange with interest.

"I should have figured I couldn't get a firehouse without a Callaway in it," Warren said through tight lips. "You guys think you own the city."

Since he had numerous relatives in the department, including his older brother Burke, who was a battalion chief, his father Jack, who was Deputy Chief of Operations, and his sister Emma, a fire investigator—to name just a few—he wasn't surprised by Warren's comment. Firefighting had always been the Callaway family business in San Francisco. He just wished he knew which one of his relatives had pissed off Mitchell Warren.

"Let's get something straight," Warren continued. "I don't play favorites, especially not with Callaways. You screw up, you'll be out on your ass, and I won't care what your father or your big brother has to say about it. Understood?"

Warren jabbed his finger into Colton's chest, and Colton had to rein in a sudden wave of anger. He'd been proving himself for the last four years, and he was damn sick of it. He'd learned the hard way to keep his mouth shut, but it wasn't always easy—like now.

"Understood," Colton said as calmly as he could. He looked his captain straight in the eye. "We won't have a problem, because I don't screw up—sir." His cocky confidence earned him another scalding look.

"See that you don't." Warren stepped back and looked around at the rest of the crew, who suddenly busied themselves with whatever they were supposed to be doing. Then Warren left the room, heading down the hall to his office.

Colton blew out a frustrated breath, then walked over to the table where his friend Adam Powell was scarfing down a heaping plate of scrambled eggs. Adam was thirty-one with blond hair and brown eyes and had five years of experience on Colton, but since they'd fought their way out of a hotel fire a year earlier, they'd become good friends, and Colton valued his opinion.

"What the hell was that about?" Colton asked, sitting down at the table across from Adam.

Adam shrugged, his laid-back attitude in clear evidence today. "He doesn't like you."

"Yeah, I got that, but why? As far as I know, we've never met."

"Sounds like he has a problem with your last name. I'd forget about it. Do your job the way you always do, and he'll get over it. You're a good firefighter. The captain will see that."

"Yeah," he muttered. "I'm just tired of being judged by everyone who came before me."

"Then you should have chosen another profession."

That was Adam, always blunt and to the point. But Colton couldn't have chosen another profession, because all he'd ever wanted to be was a firefighter like his brothers, his father and grandfather. He just hadn't realized how difficult it would be to make his own name in the world.

Changing the subject, he said, "How were your days off?"

"Good. I took a hot redhead to Carmel," Adam replied with a grin.

Colton smiled back at him. Adam had no trouble picking up women. "Things must be getting serious. You've been seeing her for what—two months now? That's a long time for you."

"Dana is a beautiful woman and really good in bed."

"The perfect combination. When do I get to meet her?"

"We'll see." Adam shoved his empty plate to the side and wiped his mouth with a napkin. "What about you? What did you do?"

"I didn't have nearly as much fun as you. I worked for my Uncle Kevin. He's building a house in Noe Valley and had some work for me. And last night, I helped my nephew Brandon and his brother Kyle build a fort out of blocks while my sister and her husband went to Back to School Night."

"What is wrong with you?" Adam asked, shaking his head. "You used to have much better stories. What about the blonde you were dancing with at the club last weekend? What was her name?"

"I have no idea."

"Does that mean you didn't get her phone number, either?"

"I didn't ask for it. She wasn't that interesting."

"She was blonde, and she had a great rack. How could she not be interesting?" Adam challenged.

"I'm not that shallow," he joked.

"Yes, you are."

"Maybe I'm changing."

"Why would you want to? You're young, single, reasonably good-looking, and you wear a uniform. Use that to your advantage. It's gotten me a lot of phone numbers."

He'd gotten a lot of phone numbers, too, but lately he'd felt like something was missing. "I don't know." He waved a restless hand in the air. "I want someone to knock me over. I want to feel like I've been sucker punched."

"Why on earth would you want to feel like that?"

"Because anything less is boring." He'd been living it up on the single scene the last several years and he was tired of it. Plus, he'd had to watch his older siblings falling in love every other second for the past two years, and he was beginning to want something a little more serious for himself. Although that thought made him a little nervous.

Maybe he was just in a rut, and this momentary feeling of wanting something more with a woman would pass. Because in reality, he was far more interested in building his career than building a relationship. He just needed to date someone who made him want to call her the next morning. That hadn't happened in a while.

He sat up straighter as the alarm went off. His twenty-four-hour shift had barely started. It was going to be a busy day. He quickly rose, donned his gear and jumped on the engine. Their firehouse was one of the larger stations in the city and had an engine, a truck and an ambulance. For this fire, all three were being dispatched.

The trio of vehicles raced across San Francisco with sirens screaming. It was still rush hour in the city, so there were plenty of cars to dodge on their way to the garment district, which housed numerous industrial warehouses. As they neared their destination, he saw billowing black smoke mixing with the early morning fog, casting an eerie glow over the city. The color of that smoke suggested chemicals in the mix.

Every muscle in his body tightened in preparation for what might be ahead. Fires were always unpredictable, and every firefighter learned—usually the hard way—that even the smallest spark could turn into a deadly flame.

When the engine came to a rapid stop, he jumped to the ground, adrenaline rushing through his body, giving him speed, power and strength. He would need all three before the fire was out, because at least one half of the four-story building in front of him was already engulfed in flames.

There were engines and trucks from three other houses already attending to the fire. On his way toward the building, he passed his brother Burke, who was commanding operations on the ground. At thirty-six, Burke was the youngest battalion chief in the department, but then Burke had been setting records ever since he was a rookie firefighter. He was smart, courageous and a natural born leader, and Colton had always respected him, even if he hadn't felt very close to him.

Burke gave him a tense look and a nod, but they didn't speak. They both had jobs to do, and Colton would do his job to the best of his ability, because as much as he didn't want to have to prove anything to anyone, every time he battled a fire, he felt the weight of the Callaway legacy urging him to be the same kind of hero as the men who had come before him.

He and Adam were sent inside the south wing of the building to check for several missing warehouse employees. As they entered the structure, they were immediately blinded by thick black smoke.

Colton had taken the lead, but he could barely see a foot in front of him. The smoke was so hot he expected it to combust at any moment. He could feel the edges of his mask melting against his face. But he pushed on, Adam right behind him.

They were halfway down the hall when they heard a man's muffled cry. Colton tried the door but it was locked. He backed up and kicked it in. He could see flames coming from a collapsed ceiling. It looked like the office furniture from the floor above had come crashing down. A man was on the ground, a huge desk crushing his abdomen, a deep gash on his forehead.

Colton ran to him, dropping down to his knees beside the victim.

"Help me," the man gasped.

He was in his early sixties, Colton thought. There was a pool of blood under his head with more blood dripping down his face, and he was having trouble breathing from the weight on his chest.

"I'm going to get you out of here," Colton said.

"Don't leave me."

"I'm not going anywhere without you." He stood up, grabbing the edge of the desk while Adam went to the other side. They lifted it off of the man and were about one second from setting it safely down when an explosion rocked the building.

Colton felt like a rag doll as he was launched into the air and thrown across the room. Stunned, it took him a second to regroup. He looked through the smoky room to see Adam struggling to his feet in the hallway. Then he looked back toward the man they'd been trying to help and saw he'd been buried by falling debris.

He jumped up and ran across the room. His headset crackled with the voice of Captain Warren: "Abandon the building."

He heard the order but he couldn't follow it—not yet. He turned his head to Adam. "Get out of here."

"We go together," Adam said tersely. "And we're taking him with us."

As usual, he and Adam were on the same page.

They raced back to the victim, digging feverishly through the rubble. Finally, Colton got his hands under the man's shoulders and pulled him free.

The man was no longer conscious, and there was a new stream of blood from another large gash on his head.

Colton pulled off his glove to check for a pulse. There wasn't one. He started to give CPR but the man wasn't responding.

"Callaway, stop," Adam said. "We've got to get him out of here."

Adam pulled the man into a sitting position and then Colton lifted him up and over his shoulder. He moved quickly down the hall. When he got to the stairwell, he realized that the fire was ten times worse than when he'd entered the building. Colton wasn't sure they could still get out. There was fire everywhere, but he couldn't let fear steal his focus. This was what he was trained to do and right now he had one goal—to get the victim out of the building.

As he ran down the stairs in Adam's wake, flames licked the railing, teasing him with the breath of an angry monster, but he made it to the front door. He could see daylight, clean air. He was so close...

One step out of the door and then another explosion ripped through the building, tossing him and the man he was carrying into the air. The victim flew out of his grasp, and Colton landed hard on the pavement about six feet away. A sharp pain ran through his hand and his head, but he pushed the pain away, needing to get up, to find the man he was trying to save.

He stumbled to his feet and staggered forward.

A heavy hand came down on his shoulder. He swung around, looking into Captain Warren's eyes. "Callaway, stop."

He looked toward the victim, thankful to see he was being attended to by paramedics, but he'd promised the man he wouldn't leave him alone. "I have to get to him. I told him I would stay with him."

"He's gone." The captain grabbed his arm, his gaze boring into his with the horrible truth.

Colton breathed in and out, still finding it difficult to accept the man's death. A few seconds might have made the difference between life and death. If he'd moved quicker, maybe he could have saved him.

"You need to go to the hospital, Callaway."

"I'm fine. I just want to get back to work."

"You're not fine. Look at your hand."

He stared down at his left hand in bemusement. His glove was off and his two middle fingers looked crooked and swollen. How the hell had that happened?

Captain Warren motioned for an EMT to come over. "Get him to the E.R."

"Come with me," Robin Kendall said.

"I don't need to go to the hospital," he argued as Captain Warren stepped away.

"You got an order. So did I," she said forcefully. "And I'm not going to talk back to the boss on his first day, so let's go, Colton."

He wasn't going to win this battle, so he followed her over to the ambulance. The man he'd tried so hard to save was being lifted into the back, a sheet now covering his face.

"You can ride up front with me," Robin said, giving him a compassionate smile.

"No. I told him I wouldn't leave him. I'll ride in the back."

"You did everything you could, Callaway."

He wanted to believe she was right, but he couldn't help thinking that if he'd done everything he could, the man would still be alive.

Two

⇢⇒⇐⇠

Three hours later with his two fractured fingers taped together and the added diagnosis of a mild concussion, Colton was released from the hospital.

He would have flirted with the pretty brunette nurse who brought him his discharge papers, but his hand and his head hurt like hell, and he was pissed off at the fact that he'd gotten injured at all. He had a feeling his new captain would just use his injury as a strike against him. The doctor had already told him he wouldn't be able to go back to full duty for at least a week.

His mood only got worse when the nurse forced him into a wheelchair. She wheeled him into the waiting room like a damned invalid. When he got there, he saw half of his family taking up just about every chair. Burke must have told them he'd been injured.

His oldest brother was leaning against the wall, still dressed in his uniform, his face sweaty and dirty from the fire. Standing next to Burke was Aiden, his second oldest brother and a former smoke jumper. Aiden had had far worse injuries than this, so it was difficult to believe he'd come rushing across town. Someone must have made his injuries seem worse than they were.

He saw his parents sitting in chairs against the far wall. Maybe it was his dad who had sounded the family alarm. As Deputy Chief of Operations for the San Francisco Fire Department, Jack Callaway would have been immediately informed of his trip to the hospital.

His gaze moved down the row of seats.

Or maybe it was his sister Emma who'd called the troops together. She worked as a fire investigator, and judging by her navy blue slacks and white button-down shirt, she was also on duty, which meant she'd probably already seen the initial reports on the fire.

And then there was Shayla, who was now walking towards him. She wore a white coat over a floral dress and had a stethoscope around her neck. He hadn't seen her in the E.R. when he arrived, but he knew she was currently on that rotation as she finished off her final year of residency.

"Did you have to call everyone, Shayla?"

She gave him a smile. "I didn't call anyone. I think I was the last to know you were here. I was taking a toy soldier out of a kid's throat when you were brought in. How are you feeling?"

"Like I got blown out of a building."

She frowned. "Don't joke about it. You could have been hurt a lot worse."

"But I wasn't." He paused as his sister Nicole rushed into the waiting room, two little boys hanging on to each hand.

"Colton." She let out a sigh of relief as she saw him. "Are you okay? I got here as soon as I could. But it was early release day at school, and I had to stop there first to pick up the boys."

"I'm fine. You really didn't need to rush over here."

"What did you do to your hand?" Seven-year-old Kyle asked curiously, his eyes immediately settling on Colton's wrapped fingers.

"I broke a couple of fingers."

"Does it hurt?"

"A little."

"Can you still throw a baseball?" Kyle asked.

"Probably not today."

"That's enough questions, Kyle," Nicole said, giving him an apologetic smile. "I'm glad you're all right. Mom didn't have any details when she called."

"So you're the one who got everyone down here," he said to his mother.

Lynda Callaway gave him an unrepentant smile. "What was I

to do when your father calls and tells me you're on your way to the hospital? You know I don't like to get those calls, Colton."

She had to be used to them by now with most of his siblings performing jobs with a high level of inherent danger, but he hated that he'd been the one to put the worry in her eyes. He also hated the fact that he was annoyed with his family for rushing to the hospital when he was damned lucky to have so many people who cared about him. "Sorry, Mom."

"The doctor said you have a concussion," his father put in, giving him a sharp, searching look.

"Mild. I was hit harder playing football."

"You'll come home with us tonight," Lynda said decisively. "I want to keep an eye on you."

"I don't need a babysitter."

"You shouldn't be alone," Shayla said, backing up his mom's idea. "It's always a good idea to have someone around the first night after a head injury."

"I just bumped my head."

"I wouldn't argue," Aiden advised with an empathetic grin. "You're only going to lose, Colton."

"Why aren't you at work?"

"I'm on lunch," Aiden replied. "But I am going to take off now. Rest up, little brother."

"I will. But don't worry. I'm fine." Colton got to his feet, refusing to admit the action made him feel a little dizzy. However, the spark in Shayla's eyes told him he might be fooling everyone else, but he wasn't fooling her—or his mother.

Lynda immediately put a hand on his arm to steady him and said, "Get the car, Jack." As his father left to go to the parking lot, she added, "You don't have to act tough with us, Colton. We're your family. Sit down."

Since he thought sitting down would be less embarrassing than falling down, he did as she suggested.

"I'm going to call Drew and Sean and let them know you're all right," Lynda said.

"And I'm going to get back to work," Shayla put in. "Call me if you need anything."

"Thanks."

As his mom and Shayla moved away, Burke and Emma came over to him.

"You did a nice job today, Colton," Burke said.

His jaw tightened at the hollow words. He met his brother's gaze. "It wasn't a good job. The victim died."

Burke's blue eyes darkened with shadows. "Sometimes that happens. You did what you could. Don't beat yourself up."

"I wish people would stop telling me that," he muttered.

"Yeah, sorry," Burke said, an empathetic gleam in his eyes. "Those words never made me feel better; I don't know why I said them." He paused. "I need to get back to the station. I'm glad you're all right."

"Before you go, what can you tell me about Mitchell Warren?" Colton asked. "He started as my new captain this morning, and he apparently hates the Callaways."

"He hates us?" Emma interrupted. "Why?"

"That's what I'm trying to find out. Captain Warren pulled me aside the second he came into the firehouse to let me know I was not going to get special treatment because of my name or who I was related to."

"Warren," Emma murmured thoughtfully. "Didn't he used to work with you, Burke?"

"We worked together for a couple of months many years ago," Burke said, his voice terse, his words clipped.

"So is his attitude stemming from something that happened between the two of you?" Colton asked.

"Not on the job," Burke replied cryptically.

"What does that mean?"

"It means nothing. Don't let him get to you, Colton. Just do your job."

"I always do my job, but I would like to know what I'm dealing with when it comes to my new boss."

"He's a decent enough firefighter. He knows what he's doing," Burke said. "That's all I can tell you."

Colton frowned, thinking his brother could tell him a hell of a lot more—if he wanted to. But Burke apparently didn't want to. In fact, he was halfway to the door before Colton could even consider asking another question. He turned to Emma. "Is it just me or was Burke acting shady?"

"Acting shady," Emma replied, a thoughtful gleam in her eyes. "I wonder what's between him and your boss."

"Me, too. Burke rarely has problems with anyone. Most people admire the hell out of him," he said. "His reputation as a straight shooter is well-noted in the department."

"Yeah, he has always been a leader among men," Emma said, a dry note in her voice.

He gave her a questioning look, curious about her tone.

"What?" she challenged. "Do you really think you're the only one in the family who has to live up to Burke's reputation in the fire department—or Dad's, or Grandpa's? Because I was a firefighter before you, and I didn't just get shit because I was a Callaway but also because I was a woman."

"I've never gotten shit because of my last name before."

"Then you've been lucky," she retorted.

"I guess my luck ran out."

"If Burke won't tell you what's between them, maybe your captain will. But I'd put all that aside for now and take it easy. I hope you'll feel well enough by Sunday to come to Grandma's birthday party at the Sunset Senior Center. Grandpa wants everyone to be there."

"I hope Grandma remembers it is her birthday."

"So do I. The new medication she's on seems to be helping, but there are still bad days. I just want her to stay with us as long as she can."

He wanted the same thing, but his grandmother had Alzheimer's, and the long-term prognosis was not good. Hopefully, she'd beat the odds. She was a stubborn Callaway after all, and Callaways did not go down without a fight.

"Mom said there's a writer coming to Grandma's party," Emma continued. "She wants to write a book about Grandma and some of the other ladies at the center."

"About Grandma? What on earth would that story be about? She's a wonderful woman, sweet, kind, generous, but I'm not sure her life story would merit a book."

An odd look entered Emma's eyes. "Maybe there's more to her life than we know. Grandma has been trying to say something for a while now, but she can't quite remember what it is long enough to get the words out. Or Grandpa comes in and tells her to be quiet, that she doesn't know what she's talking about."

Colton gave her a doubtful look. "You're imagining things."

"I don't think so. Everyone has secrets, Colton."

"Not Grandma. And, sadly, even if she had a secret, she's probably forgotten it by now."

"I guess we'll see."

Three

---»»«««---

Sunday afternoon Olivia Bennett pulled into the parking lot next to the Sunset Senior Center. The two-story building was directly across the street from San Francisco's Ocean Beach, and from her spot she had a perfect view of the water.

It was a windy day in late September, and the dark blue sea shimmered in the sunshine, not a cloud or a hint of fog anywhere in sight. Several people took advantage of the stiff breeze to launch colorful kites into the air. Others were sharing a late lunch picnic, and a few walkers and runners jogged along the shoreline as the ocean rolled onto the beach with big, crashing waves.

It wasn't the kind of sea too many people were going to venture into for swimming, although there were a few surfers in wet suits attempting to ride the waves. That didn't surprise her. Growing up in San Diego, a southern California city, she'd known a few surfers in her time. In fact, she'd ridden the waves herself, but that was when she was young and stupid, when she didn't think anything bad could ever happen to her.

Watching those intrepid surfers now, she felt nostalgic. She'd missed this California beach vibe. Since going to college at New York University and then later working as a freelance writer and research assistant for a famous biographer, she hadn't been back to California for longer than a couple of days in almost ten years.

Now she was reminded of the days of her youth.

She'd been so carefree as a child and a teenager. She'd had an amazing, wonderful life as the adored only daughter of Elaine and

Hal Bennett, two people who tried to give her the world with every breath that they took. She'd truly been blessed to have such wonderful parents. And even though she'd lost her dad, she still had her mom, and they'd always been close.

As if on cue, her phone rang, her mom's number popping up on the screen. They tried to talk every Sunday. It had been their ritual since Olivia had left for college, and she still stuck to it whenever she could.

"Hi, Mom," she said. "I called you earlier, but you didn't answer."

"I had to drive Will to his sister's house. His car is in the shop."

"How is Mr. Hansen?" She wasn't quite sure how she felt about the budding romance between her mother and her former high school algebra teacher, but the two of them seemed to be spending a lot of time together.

"You can call him Will. He's not your teacher anymore," Elaine said.

"So how is Will?"

"He's a good man. I want you to get to know him better. I was hoping you'd come home on your vacation," Elaine said pointedly.

"I was planning to, but then this potential story came up, and I couldn't resist following up on it. You know I've been wanting to write my own book for years."

"I know. The man you work for is a pompous ass who is taking all of your hard work and making millions of dollars off of it."

Her mom was right about that. Philip Dunston was a world-famous, bestselling author of celebrity and political biographies, and she was more than a little tired of writing his books under the guise of being his research assistant. But he paid pretty well, and she'd had an opportunity to perfect her craft the last few years. Now, however, she was itching to get out on her own.

"What I don't understand," her mom added, "is why you think there's some great story to be found at a senior center filled with ordinary people living ordinary lives. You need to focus on getting a celebrity to talk to you."

"They're only going to talk to Philip. And ordinary people can have extraordinary moments. The letter I received from Molly Harper led me to believe that this group of women did something amazing, something worth writing about."

"That still sounds vague to me. Have you spoken to this woman yet?"

Olivia sighed at the question. "Unfortunately, no. There's been a bad turn of events."

"What happened?"

"Molly Harper had a stroke two days ago. She's in the hospital. I called the other number she'd given me and spoke to the director at the senior center. She said the prognosis is not good."

"Oh, dear. I'm sorry about that, but now I really don't understand why you're in San Francisco. Why don't you take a plane down the coast and spend the week with me?"

Olivia hated to quench the hopeful note in her mom's voice. "I need to follow up with some of the other women. I'm actually sitting in my car in the parking lot outside the senior center. They're having a birthday party today for Eleanor Callaway, one of Molly's best friends. Eleanor was mentioned in Molly's letter as someone I needed to speak to. I figured since I was already in San Francisco, I might as well meet the other women in Molly's group."

"So meet them and then come home. By the way, I ran into Jeff Lawson the other day. He's working as an attorney in his dad's law office now and he's single. He asked about you."

Olivia smiled. Her mom was convinced that the only way she was going to get her daughter back to San Diego was if Olivia came home and fell in love with someone who lived there. She was constantly mentioning old boyfriends or someone's gorgeous son who still happened to be single. Jeff Lawson fell into the old boyfriend category. She'd dated him for six months when she was a sophomore in high school, and all she really remembered about him was that he liked to talk about himself—a lot.

"He's handsome and he has a good job," Elaine continued. "You should definitely reconnect when you come back here."

"Mom, I'm not looking for a boyfriend. Right now I'm just

looking for a good subject for a book."

"Well, Jeff might know someone interesting. He's very well connected in the community down here."

"I'm sure he is, but we can talk about him some other time. I need to go."

"Fine, go, and as soon as you realize there's no fantastic story to be discovered, then come home and spend a few days with me. It's been too long since we actually got to see each other in person, and I miss you, Liv."

"I miss you, too, Mom."

"And I worry about you. I know you want a career, but I don't want you to shut yourself off from the rest of life and miss out on the fun stuff."

"I'm not exactly over the hill," she protested. "I'm only twenty-six. I have time for work and fun."

"I know you're not old, but you are cynical, Olivia. It started when your dad died, and it seems to get worse every year."

Her mom wasn't completely wrong about that, but her cynicism wasn't a topic she wanted to get into right now. "Mom, I have to go."

"Just promise me you'll keep your heart open. There's nothing better than a love that makes your heart pound, and your palms sweat and sends little chills up and down your spine."

"I promise," she said, not really because she meant it, but because she wanted to get her mother off the phone. She didn't understand how her mom could still be a romantic after the tragedy of her own love affair, but somehow she was. "I'll call you later."

"All right. Love you, honey."

"Love you, too."

As she ended the call and slipped her phone into her purse, her gaze fell on the lavender-scented purple envelope lying on the seat.

She picked it up, reminded again that the piece of paper inside was the first letter she'd received by snail mail in—she couldn't remember when. The penmanship was beautiful, the sign of a time gone by, and the words were written with the kind of formality that couldn't be found in an email.

The letter from Molly Harper had been forwarded around the

world for almost three weeks by Philip's personal assistant as Olivia accompanied him on a European press tour for the release of his new biography on Carlton Hughes. Hughes was a man who'd entertained the world as an actor and then risen through state politics to national office, eventually serving as the U.S. Secretary of State for over a decade.

Mrs. Harper's letter had finally reached her at her final stop in London. While Philip had been hosting a party in his penthouse suite, she'd been feeling a little like Cinderella, working on her notes in her small room on a much lower floor. She'd tried not to think about the fabulous party she was missing or all the great lines from the book that Philip would be taking credit for. She'd been hired to do a job, and she would do it, until she could find something better or something of her own. She'd opened Molly's letter thinking it was some type of fan mail to be passed on to Philip.

However, the letter hadn't been addressed to Philip, but to her.

She read it again now, even though she'd already committed most of the words to memory.

Dear Miss Bennett:

I'm seventy-seven years old, and I grew up in a generation where women were supposed to be silent, where the men did the talking for them, but in my life I have met many women who amazed me with their courage in the face of enormous odds. One of them I consider to be not only my best friend but also my savior. Her name is Eleanor Callaway. We met forty years ago, and we were part of a very special theater group.

Now you may not think a theater group is particularly interesting, but I can assure you that it was not an ordinary group. We did something that was pretty shocking and amazing. Sometimes I can hardly believe what we accomplished without getting caught.

It's been a long time, and for years we kept our secrets to protect not only ourselves but others—many others. But we are getting older, and our stories will die with us unless we find someone to write them down, someone with integrity and bravery, a woman who is not afraid to speak up for those who cannot.

We need you, Miss Bennett!

We've read about your work and we believe you are the right person to help us. It's a lot to ask. You're a young woman with a busy job, and you're probably not interested in talking to a bunch of old ladies, but I promise that you won't regret the trip.

There are moments in life when we're each faced with a decision. Sometimes we don't realize the full consequence of that decision until many years later. I should have told my story years ago, but I was too afraid. I am hoping you will have the courage that I did not have.

If you can spare a few days of your time, please come to San Francisco and speak to us. We will be forever in your debt.

Yours sincerely,
Molly Harper

Olivia set the paper down and stared out at the ocean, wondering why Molly's words always seemed to send a shiver down her spine. Certain phrases jumped out of the letter: *We did something that was pretty shocking and amazing. Sometimes I can hardly believe what we accomplished without getting caught.* What on earth had the women done?

And there was something about the way Molly said *we need you, Miss Bennett* that made her wonder again just how Molly had found her in the first place.

Molly had referenced her work, but she was only listed in the acknowledgments of Philip's book as someone who had helped Philip with his research, so why hadn't Molly written to Philip or another well-known writer? Why her?

The question ran around in her mind, but she wasn't going to find the answer sitting in her rental car. She was here. She might as well go inside and hear what the women had to say.

When she entered the senior center a few minutes later, she was both surprised and happy to see the brightly colored lobby. She hadn't known what to expect, but this was not some dreary, dismal old folks home, at least the lobby wasn't. There was no one at the reception desk, so she moved to the double doors on her left, seeing balloons and streamers.

She paused in the doorway, noting a buffet table in the corner that was laden with an enormous punch bowl as well as a large cake, platters of finger sandwiches and bowls of chips. An enormous sign covered one wall with the words: *Happy Birthday Eleanor*.

The large airy room with lots of windows was warm and inviting. There were several card tables in one area and then four large couches around a circular coffee table at the far end of the room. There were a half dozen people sitting on the couches, two men and four women, all of whom appeared to be in their seventies or eighties. At the center of attention was a pretty white-haired, blue-eyed woman wearing a bright red dress with a pair of matching red heels. She laughed at something someone said, and the whole room seemed to follow her lead.

The man sitting next to her had black hair peppered with gray, light blue eyes and a ruddy, weathered complexion. He was dressed far more conservatively in black slacks and a gray tweed sports coat over a white shirt. His handsome features would have made him quite the attractive man in his day, Olivia thought. He had his hand on the woman's thigh in a loving, somewhat protective gesture. He obviously cared a great deal about her.

She was about to go over and introduce herself to the group when a woman came up next to her.

"You must be Miss Bennett," she said. "I'm Nancy Palmer."

The tall, middle-aged, dark-haired woman was the one she'd spoken to on the phone the day before.

"It's nice to meet you," Olivia said.

"You, too." Nancy gave her an approving smile. "I am so glad you decided to come. Molly and the other women have been talking about your possible visit for weeks."

"It took a while for Molly's letter to reach me."

"She wasn't sure it ever would, but somehow it did. She called it a little miracle."

"I don't know if I'd call it a miracle." Again she was somewhat baffled by the intensity of Molly's desire to bring her to the senior center. "Do you know why she wrote to me? Did she tell you how she got my name?"

"She didn't tell me. Maybe one of her friends knows." Nancy paused, her smile fading. "I really wish Molly could be here today. She was so looking forward to meeting you, and of course she wouldn't have wanted to miss Eleanor's party. The two of them have been best friends for a very long time."

"How is Mrs. Harper? Has there been any change in her condition?" Olivia asked.

"Unfortunately, no, but I'm not giving up hope, and I know Molly's friends are praying for her every day. This group of women has been coming here for the last ten years. This center has become their second home, and they pretty much keep it going with their own private donations. They feel it's important to have a place for seniors to go and be with their friends and have some fun. These ladies have about twenty-five years on me, but sometimes I think they have more energy than I do."

Olivia smiled. "That's pretty cool."

"It is. You're going to enjoy getting to know them, although there are some very strong personalities in the group."

"Molly specifically mentioned Eleanor Callaway, and I know this party is for her. Can you point her out to me? Or should I just assume that she's the sparkling blonde in the middle of the group?"

"That would be an excellent guess," Nancy said with a smile. "Her husband Patrick is next to her. He rarely spends time here. He usually just drops Eleanor off and picks her up a few hours later. It's the one place he can leave her where he knows we'll take good care of her. Eleanor suffers from Alzheimer's."

"Really?" Olivia asked in surprise. "She seems so normal, so healthy."

"She has good days and bad days. Today is a good one, thankfully. The rest of her family will be arriving shortly; they're quite a large group. Eleanor has five children, at least twenty-five grandchildren and several great-grandchildren. She and Patrick have created quite a legacy—and not just with their family. The Callaways are very well known here in the city. Many of them are

San Francisco firefighters. At one time Patrick was running the whole department. Of course, he's been retired for some time now. Shall I introduce you?"

Before she could reply, a young woman interrupted their conversation, asking for Nancy's assistance in the kitchen.

"I'm sorry," Nancy apologized. "I'll be right back."

"It's fine. I'll introduce myself." She was used to talking to people. She'd conducted most of the interviews for Philip's books, so she knew how to get people to open up, even if they didn't want to. But Molly had led her to believe that this group wanted very much to talk to her, so she wasn't anticipating any problems.

She was wrong, she realized five minutes later. While Eleanor had squealed with delight after she'd introduced herself, and the other ladies had all perked up in anticipation of their conversation, Patrick Callaway had given her a steely glare that was more than a little intimidating. He hadn't said anything yet, but she could see the storm brewing in his eyes.

"Sit down, Miss Bennett," Eleanor said. She turned to her husband. "Why don't you let Miss Bennett take your seat? Didn't you want to call your niece before it got too late on the East Coast?"

Patrick frowned, then reluctantly stood up. "Yes," he said. "I do need to make that call."

"Sit next to me," Eleanor said to Olivia, patting the now vacant seat beside her. "I can hardly believe you're here."

"Why are you here, Miss Bennett?" Patrick asked. Despite his previous comment that he needed to make a call, he hadn't gone very far.

"Didn't I tell you?" Eleanor asked her husband, a puzzled look coming into her eyes. "I swore I did. Miss Bennett is going to write a book about the old theater group." She looked back at Olivia with a warm smile. "Molly was tickled pink when you said you'd come." Her gaze turned sad. "I wish she was here to meet you."

"So do I. She didn't tell me much, but she said you all had a story to tell, and that I would want to hear it."

"We have lots of stories," Eleanor said.

"You're not doing this today," Patrick interjected, making his words a statement rather than a question. "It's your birthday. The family will be here soon. Today is a day for celebration."

"Well, we have a few minutes, I think." Eleanor turned back to Olivia. "Where should we start?"

"Why don't you tell me about the theater group?" She focused on Eleanor, happy when Patrick finally moved away. She didn't know why he seemed so angry or cold, but he was definitely not happy about her presence here. She couldn't help wondering if he was one of the men Molly had referred to in her letter—one of the men who preferred to speak for his wife, rather than let her speak for herself.

"We were part of the Center Stage Community Theater Group," Eleanor said. We started it in 1975, and it ran for six very successful years. Let me introduce you to the gang." She waved her hand toward the only other man in the room. "Tom Kennedy. He used to build our sets. His late wife, Marjorie, was one of our most popular actresses."

Olivia nodded to Tom, a skinny, balding man whose appearance was brightened by the bold colors of his red and yellow Hawaiian shirt. He gave her a smile and said, "These broads were something else back in the day."

"Tom, no one uses that word anymore," the woman next to him complained. She was a curvy redhead with dark brown eyes and a saucy expression that told Olivia she wasn't that displeased by being called a *broad*. "I'm Ginnie Culpepper. I was the makeup artist for the group," she explained.

No wonder Ginnie Culpepper looked ten years younger than everyone else. She obviously had a sly hand with cosmetics.

"This is Constance Baker," Ginnie added, putting her arm around the shoulders of the thin, quiet woman by her side.

Constance had brown hair with wide streaks of gray and a pair of glasses perched on her nose.

"Tell her what you did," Ginnie encouraged.

"I sold tickets and made up the programs and flyers," Constance said. "I was behind the scenes. Eleanor and Marjorie had all those lines to learn every month. They were always in the starring roles. I never knew how they did it. And Eleanor, with all her kids, had a lot on her plate."

"What about Molly?"

"Molly made the costumes," Eleanor said. "She was a wizard with a needle and thread. She could turn scraps of material into a ball gown."

"That's cool. How did you all meet?"

"Molly and Ginnie and I were friends from the neighborhood," Eleanor said. "Constance and Marjorie and some of the others in our group we met either through school—many of us had children the same age—or through friends of friends. I think at one time we had almost forty people working in the theater. It was a wonderful time," Eleanor said.

"Why did it end?"

Eleanor's mouth curved down into a frown. "There was a fire at the theater. The stage was destroyed. We wanted to try to set up somewhere else, but we couldn't make it happen."

"It was sad," Constance said. "There were a lot of tears the day we realized it was over. Not just for the theater, but because we wouldn't be able to use the money anymore, and that was the worst part."

"What do you mean?" Olivia asked. "What were you using the money for?"

"Oh. Well…" Constance looked at Olivia as if she'd just spilled some big secret and now didn't know what to say.

Her guilty look made Olivia sit up a little straighter. Now she was getting to something. "Molly's letter said that the theater group accomplished something shocking and amazing. Anyone care to explain what she meant?"

"We raised money for a charity," Eleanor said, drawing Olivia's attention back to her. "We were able to help some people who needed it."

"That's very generous," she said, still feeling like she was missing something. There was something sizzling in the air now, unspoken words, long held secrets perhaps…or was her imagination just getting carried away?

"That's enough," Patrick interrupted, as he returned to the group. "It's Ellie's birthday today. You can all talk about the past later. The family has arrived."

Olivia looked up as a large group of people came into the room, many of them carrying birthday presents.

"We'll talk again, dear," Eleanor said, patting her arm. "You're going to stay in town for a while, aren't you?"

"I'm not sure," she said, frustrated that their conversation was ending just as it was getting interesting.

"You have to stay at least a few more days," Eleanor said, some urgency in her tone. "Molly wanted you to know her story. And I wish I could talk to you more today, but we're having a party. Can you come back here tomorrow?"

"All right. I can do that."

Eleanor smiled. "Good. And hopefully in the next few days Molly will wake up and be able to speak to you herself."

"That would be nice."

Olivia got to her feet as Eleanor's family swarmed around the seating area, all eager to give Eleanor a kiss, a hug, and wish her a happy birthday.

As she moved away from the couch, she found Patrick Callaway walking along with her. He followed her into the lobby.

"Miss Bennett?"

She stopped and looked at him, sure she was not going to like what he was about to say. "Yes?" she asked warily.

"You need to leave my wife alone."

She was startled by his blunt statement, but in her research assignments for Philip, she'd often run into reluctant subjects, and she didn't back down just because someone wanted her to. "Your wife wanted me to come and talk to her. She and her friend Molly invited me here." It wasn't completely true. The letter had come from Molly, but as evidenced by Eleanor's recent plea, Eleanor also wanted her here.

"Molly is dying. You can't talk to her, and I'd prefer it if you didn't speak to Eleanor. My wife is ill. She may not have appeared that way today, but she has lapses in memory. Sometimes she has no idea who she is or who anyone else is. She gets extremely upset when she can't remember something."

Olivia didn't really know what to say. She certainly hadn't

seen that side of Eleanor in the past half hour.

"I don't want to waste the good moments Eleanor has left talking about ancient history," Patrick continued. "I want her to stay in the present, to enjoy the life she has now."

She supposed she could understand that, but she sensed there was something more behind his concern than just what he'd stated. "It's really up to your wife," she said.

"It's not up to her. I am in charge of my wife's health, because she can no longer take care of herself." He paused as an attractive blonde woman motioned for him to come back to the lounge.

"Grandpa, we're going to take a picture," the woman said.

"I'll be right there, Shayla," Patrick said, then he turned back to her. "I hope I've made myself clear, Miss Bennett."

"Very clear," she said, watching him return to the party. She knew what he wanted, but what he wanted wasn't her priority; it was what the women wanted. She'd come to hear them speak, to write down their stories, and until one of the women sent her packing, she was going to stick around for a while.

"Miss Bennett, there you are," Nancy said, approaching her with a cardboard box in her arms. "I'm glad you didn't leave yet. I have something for you."

She handed the box to Olivia, and it was surprisingly heavy. "What is all this?"

Molly was putting some things together to give to you when you arrived. "I'm not really sure what's in there, but I know she wanted you to look through the items."

"I will." She hoped there might be something in the box that would tell her why she was here. "I'll bring this back to you tomorrow. Eleanor told me to come back then."

Nancy smiled, relief in her eyes. "That's perfect. Eleanor and the others usually arrive around noon. They have lunch and play Bridge until they get tired."

"I'll come around lunch time. I'm staying at the Union Street Inn. If anything changes with the women or with Molly's condition, I'd appreciate it if you'd let me know. I think you have my cell number."

"Yes, and I'd be happy to give you a call."

"Thank you." She paused. "Eleanor's husband doesn't seem eager for me to speak with her. He doesn't want me to agitate her in some way. Is he being overly protective? Or should I be more careful when I'm talking to her?"

"Patrick Callaway adores his wife. Since she was diagnosed with Alzheimer's, he's become very protective of her. In some ways, he isolates her, and I'm not sure that's a good thing. I know Molly was worried about it, too. But I can't criticize, because I have seen Eleanor when she is having a very bad day. She gets confused and frightened, and it's really unsettling to witness. So, yes, I would tread carefully, but I would also understand that Patrick is simply trying to watch out for his wife."

"Of course. Thanks for helping me to understand. I don't want to do anything to upset Eleanor, but if she wants to speak, I want to listen to what she has to say."

"Good," Nancy said. "That's why they wanted you to come here."

"And you really don't know why they picked me?" she asked again.

"I'm sorry, I don't. Someone must have heard you were a really good writer."

She really wished she knew who that someone was.

As Nancy went to join the party, Olivia headed to the door, eager to take a look through the box Molly had left for her. She could see several bound notebooks through the slit in the cardboard. Had Molly left her journals? Or maybe they were photo albums.

She was so caught up in thinking about what possible treasures might be inside that she barreled through the front door without looking where she was going and ran straight into a very solid male chest. The collision brought forth a grunt of pain from the man she'd just knocked back a foot, and she couldn't help the gasp that escaped her lips when the box went flying out of her hands, bouncing off the man's hand and onto the ground.

"Sorry," she said immediately, stepping backward.

"You should be," he muttered, wincing with pain as he grabbed two fingers that were taped together on his left hand.

She hadn't hit him that hard, but she suddenly realized that the box had hit his hand, and he obviously already had an injury. "I am really sorry. Are you okay? Can I get you something?"

"It's fine," he grumbled. "I think the box got the worst of it."

"I wasn't looking where I was going."

"I wasn't, either," he admitted, leaning over to grab his phone off the ground. "I was checking a text."

She appreciated his candor, and now that he wasn't wincing she could see how attractive he was. His brown hair was thick and wavy, his eyes a deep blue that matched the color of the nearby sea. He had strong features with a defined jaw and chin, and she could see the same muscled definition in his body as a thin t-shirt clung to his broad chest and faded jeans hugged his hips.

Her heart was beating a little too fast, she realized, not knowing why she felt so shaken up. She was the one who'd knocked him over, not the other way around, but there was something about the way he was looking at her, something about his sexy mouth that made her feel lightheaded and dizzy.

She cleared her throat, realizing she was staring. It had been a long time since a man had made such an impact on her. Forcing herself to look away from the knowing smile that was now playing on his lips, she tucked her hair behind her ears and squatted down to collect the items that had come out of the box when it hit the ground.

A couple of small floral-covered journals had years written on them, the dates going back to the nineteen-fifties. Excitement ran through her. Maybe Molly had left her the story in these journals.

"Let me help you," the man said, reaching over to pick up a photograph that had flown down the steps. As he straightened, he said, "Wait a second, this is my grandmother. What is this—some kind of play?"

She got up and moved next to him to see the picture. The photograph in his hand was of three women standing on a stage. "Which one is your grandmother?"

He pointed to the blonde. "That's her. Eleanor Callaway."

"You're related to Eleanor Callaway?" she asked in surprise.

"I'm her grandson, Colton. Why? Do you know her?"

"I just met her. I'm Olivia Bennett. One of your grandmother's friends, Molly Harper, asked me to come and write down the stories of the women here at the center. I'm a biographer." It was the first time she hadn't called herself a research assistant, and it felt right.

"My sister mentioned something to me about a book. Is it going to be about my grandmother?"

"I'm not sure of the focus yet. I'm still gathering information, but this theater group seems to be the point where their lives converged."

He frowned as he looked back at the picture. "I didn't realize my grandmother ever acted on the stage."

"She didn't tell you about the community theater she was involved in back in the seventies?"

"I can't recall her ever talking about that time of her life."

"Maybe you just weren't listening."

"I'm very close to my grandmother, so I think I do listen to her," he snapped.

A different kind of spark sizzled between them now as anger and irritation moved through his deep blue gaze. His expression reminded her very much of his grandfather, Patrick Callaway. Apparently, she was not making a good impression when it came to the Callaway men.

"Okay." She took the photo out of his hand and put it back into the box.

"What is all that stuff? Are those diaries?" he asked.

"I'm not sure. Molly Harper put together some things for me to look through in anticipation of my visit."

"I heard Molly had a stroke."

"Yes. I didn't know that until I got here. But I'm hoping she'll recover quickly. In the meantime, I'm going to talk to her friends and look through what she had already put together. Sorry again about running into you. I hope I didn't hurt your hand."

"It was already hurting."

"How did you break your fingers?"

"I got thrown on my ass when a building exploded."

Her eyes widened. "Seriously? Was it a bomb or something?"

"No, it was a fire. I'm a firefighter."

"Oh, that makes a little more sense. You were lucky not to break more than your fingers."

"So they tell me. But I would have been luckier if I hadn't broken anything at all. I'm probably going to miss at least one shift now."

"You're that eager to get back to work?"

"It's what I do."

"And getting blown out of a building doesn't make you reconsider your career choice?"

"Not for a second."

"How do you do it?" she asked curiously. "How do you choose to put yourself in danger every time you go to work?"

Her question seemed to take him by surprise. "I don't think about the danger. I just look at the job in front of me."

She nodded, thinking he'd repeated her father's answer to the same question pretty much word for word. She hadn't liked the answer when her father said it, and she didn't really like it now. But what this man did with his life was none of her business.

"Whatever," she said, moving past him.

"Hey, wait a second."

She paused on the bottom step, looking back at him. "What?"

"Why did you ask me that?"

"No reason."

"I don't believe you."

"Believe whatever you want," she said, turning her back on him.

As she walked to the car she couldn't help thinking it was just her kind of luck that the first man to make her heart beat faster had to be a firefighter, a risk-taker. She didn't go out with men like that. She'd watched her mom worry every time her dad put on his cop's uniform.

Her father had probably never known how much his wife worried about him, because to him he was just doing his job. But Olivia had seen the fear in her mother's eyes, the same fear she'd started to feel as she got older.

And they'd been right to be afraid—because one day her father had gone to work and never come back.

She opened the car door, put the box on the passenger seat and then slid behind the wheel, her pulse still racing way too fast.

She hadn't thought about her dad in a long time. She tried to keep those painful memories out of her head, but meeting Colton had stirred up the old feelings. He'd been so casual in his comment that he'd gotten blown out of a building, like it was no big deal.

It probably wasn't a big deal to him. He thrived on the danger.

Well, it didn't matter. She wasn't going to see him again. And he could be married or in love with someone, for all she knew. She needed to focus on why she was here, and that was to get a good story. She already had one Callaway breathing down her neck; she didn't need another. She started the car and drove back to her hotel, eager to dive into Molly's journals and find out why she was in San Francisco.

Four

Colton made his way slowly into the lounge of the senior center, his hand throbbing after the unexpected encounter with the beautiful brunette. God, she'd been pretty with her long, thick, curly brown hair falling almost to her waist. And those eyes—her light green eyes had reminded him of a cat, and like a cat, she'd snapped at the least provocation, apparently irritated with him for choosing to be a firefighter.

That was strange. Most women he met liked him even better after finding out he was a firefighter. There was something about the uniform that turned women on, and he'd used that to his advantage on many occasions.

But Olivia Bennett had not been at all impressed. Well, as she'd said—*whatever*. He had bigger problems than a hotheaded brunette wearing a short sexy dress, although that dress had been really nice, clinging to a great pair of breasts and some beautiful curves.

He felt a rush of heat at the thought of those curves. He'd told Adam a few days earlier that he wanted a woman who knocked him off his feet. He hadn't meant that literally, but he couldn't help thinking that fate or the universe had put Olivia Bennett in his path for some particular reason.

"Colton, it's about time."

He looked up as twin sister Shayla and her boyfriend Reid walked into the lobby. Shayla had traded her physician's white coat for a pair of jeans and a light pink sweater. Her long blonde hair was pulled back in a ponytail and there was a sparkle in her blue eyes. But then she always seemed to light up when Reid was around.

Reid was in his early thirties, a former military man who now did something with a private security company. Reid had dark hair and a sharp, commanding expression that set him apart from the crowd. There was a darkness inside Reid that came from his years in the service, but whenever Shayla was around, Reid had a smile on his face and seemed younger, happier.

"Hey, Shayla. Reid, how's it going?"

"Very well," Reid said. "Unfortunately, I have to take off. I just wanted to wish your grandmother a happy birthday before I left."

"Where are you off to?"

"Sorry—classified."

Colton grinned. "You know, I wish I could use that excuse when people ask me what I'm doing."

Reid smiled back. "It does come in handy." He turned back to Shayla. "I'll call you."

"You better."

Reid gave his sister a loving kiss, nodded to Colton and then headed out the door.

Colton laughed at the blush on his sister's face. "God, you look happy."

"I know, right? It's crazy that one man could make me feel so good."

"I'm glad."

Shayla had gone through some rough times a few months earlier, and she deserved all the happiness she could get.

"How's the hand?" she asked.

"It's all right."

"Don't be a hero. Take some pain medication if you need it."

"I don't need it."

"I know you're bummed out about the injury and having to take time off, but it's important to let your bones heal. You're going to need that hand for a long time."

"It's frustrating."

She nodded with understanding. "I know. You hate to have nothing to do but relax. In fact, I don't think you even know how to relax."

"I take vacations."

"And those vacations usually consist of fifty-mile bike rides, climbing a mountain or shooting your snowboard down the steepest, iciest path you can find."

He smiled. "Those are fun trips."

"But not relaxing. You need to learn how to just be still."

"Look who's talking—when's the last time you took a vacation?"

"That's different."

"No, it's not. You may not love physical activity, but you're always in the lab or working on some project. Face it, Shayla, we both like to be overachievers, just in different areas of life."

"Well, I am starting to learn how to have some balance in my life."

"Balance or sex?" he teased.

She blushed and punched him in the arm. "I am not talking about sex with you."

"Good, because I do not want to hear about your sex life."

"Colton," his grandfather said sharply, interrupting their conversation. "I was looking for you."

That didn't sound like a good thing. His grandfather rarely pulled him aside for a private conversation, but he seemed intent on doing that now.

"I need to speak to Colton alone," Patrick said to Shayla.

"Okay."

Shayla sent him a curious look, but all he could do was shrug. He was as baffled as she was by his grandfather's sudden desire to speak to him.

"How are you feeling?" Patrick asked when they were alone. "I heard you had a concussion as well as some broken fingers."

"My head is back to normal. My hand will take a few days to heal."

"So you're off work for the next few days?"

"Yeah, you know I can't even get back to limited duty for five days after diagnosis."

"Exactly what I was thinking. You know my sister-in-law Helene recently passed away," Patrick continued.

That had not been at all what he'd expected his grandfather to say next. "Mom mentioned that." His grandfather had had two older brothers, both of whom had passed away years ago, and Helene had lived in Chicago for as long as Colton could remember. He didn't think he'd seen her since he was in elementary school. "Sorry."

His grandfather brushed his condolences aside. "I'm leaving tomorrow to go to Chicago for a few days. Helene named me as the executor of her estate, and it's a mess. I've got relatives fighting over property and money. I don't want to leave your grandmother, but I need to take care of Helene's estate. I promised her I would do that before she died."

"Okay," he said slowly, trying to make sense of what his grandfather was telling him. "Are you asking me to look after Grandma?"

"No. Don't be ridiculous. I've hired a day nurse and a night nurse to be with her when she's at home, and your mom is going to help out with anything else Ellie needs. I know she'll be well taken care of. But that's not my main concern."

Colton sensed his grandfather was finally coming to the point of this conversation. "What are you concerned about then?"

Patrick looked around the entry, as if to make sure they were alone. "There's a writer who wants to interview your grandmother. I don't want that interview to happen."

"Can I ask why?"

"It will upset Ellie. She doesn't think it will bother her, but I know that it will. I know what is best for her, Colton. I have spent my entire life protecting that woman, and I will continue to do that as long as I am alive."

"I understand that," he said, a little surprised by his grandfather's dramatic words. Patrick Callaway was usually terse and gruff and rarely used two words if he could use one, but he seemed to be quite worked up by the arrival of Olivia Bennett, and Colton couldn't help wondering why.

"I want you to keep your grandmother away from that writer, or the writer away from your grandmother, whichever is easier."

"Uh..." He didn't know what to say. "Maybe Mom would be a better person for the job. She and Grandma are very close."

Patrick immediately shook his head. "Your mother thinks it's a great idea. She's encouraging Eleanor to get her life down on paper before she forgets everything. And your father doesn't want to go against either of them, so he's no help. I need you, Colton."

While he was somewhat flattered to be his grandfather's choice, he really didn't know how he was going to keep Olivia Bennett and his grandmother apart. They both seemed intensely interested in speaking to each other.

"You may have to be subtle or use your wits to come up with a reason why they can't meet," Patrick continued.

"How am I going to do that?"

"Just spend time with your grandmother. If she wants to come here to the center, find a way to persuade her to go somewhere else. If the writer wants to come over to the house, tell Eleanor that you want to spend time with her alone. She hates to disappoint her grandchildren."

"I guess I could try," he said half-heartedly.

"I'm not looking for an attempt; I'm looking for success," Patrick said forcefully. "Can I count on you or not?"

Since his grandfather so rarely counted on him for anything, Colton could hardly say no. "Yes. When are you leaving?"

"Tomorrow morning around eleven. Lynda will be arriving at the house just before noon. Their current plan is to come back here to the center for lunch and Bridge. I'd like you to head them off, get them to change their plans. I'll expect to see you at the house before I leave."

"I'll be there." Getting to the house was the easy part. He had no idea how he would be able to accomplish the rest of what his grandfather wanted.

Relief flashed in his grandfather's eyes. "All right, good." Patrick patted him on the shoulder.

"Hey there," Emma said, interrupting their conversation as she came through the front door with a plate of brownies in her hand.

"I know I'm late, but I brought Grandma's favorite brownies, so hopefully she'll forgive me."

"I'll take them in," Patrick said, grabbing the plate from her hand.

"Okay, thanks." She gave Colton a curious look as Patrick headed back into the party. "What were you and Grandpa talking about?"

"He wants me to babysit Grandma while he's in Chicago taking care of his sister-in-law's estate."

"Mom is going to do that."

"Yeah, but what Grandpa really wants me to do is make sure Grandma doesn't talk to that writer who wants to write a book about her."

"I told you that Grandma has a secret, and I'm not at all surprised that Grandpa wants to keep her from telling that secret. Every time she says something cryptic to me or someone else, he whisks her away."

"But you've been alone with her, Emma. If she really wanted to tell you something, she would have."

"No, it's more complicated than that. I don't think Grandma *wants* to tell the secret; I think it's bubbling up inside of her, and it's only her disease that is threatening to let it out. What are you going to do?"

"Hell if I know."

She smiled. "And you thought you were going to be bored with nothing to do until your hand healed."

"This is not what I want to be doing."

"If you really want to put a stop to this interview, you need to go straight to the source. Maybe the writer will be here today."

"Actually, she just left. I ran into her a few minutes ago. She had a box of Molly Harper's journals and photographs."

"Interesting. I have a feeling those journals are only going to whet her appetite."

He frowned. "You don't even know her."

"I know what it's like to have a job that consists of putting puzzle pieces together. Once you get into it, you can't stop until you're finished. You have to see the full picture. Only then can you walk away."

—➤➤◀◀—

Olivia loved journals. They were a window into someone's past life, a place, a moment captured in time forever. Setting down the box Molly had left for her on the queen-sized bed in her hotel room, she pulled out one of the leather-bound books and ran her fingers across the cover. She felt like she was about to open a treasure chest. Who knew what information was in these books? She couldn't wait to find out.

But first she was going to get comfortable. She walked over to the closet, kicked off her wedge heels and unzipped her dress, letting it pool around her feet as she stepped out of it. She threw on leggings and a long-sleeved t-shirt, then walked over to the small kitchenette to make herself a cup of coffee.

She was still fighting off jet lag from her trip back from London, and she needed a little caffeine to get her started.

As she waited for the coffee to brew, she glanced out the window. She had a fourth-floor room at the Union Street Inn, a boutique hotel on one of San Francisco's most popular shopping streets. Outside her room she could see a busy restaurant across the street as well as an art gallery and a trendy clothing store. A few blocks away, she could see the Golden Gate Bridge and the sailboats bobbing gently in their slips at the marina.

If she wasn't so eager to get into Molly's diaries, she might have taken a walk, but since her time in San Francisco was limited, she didn't want to waste the afternoon. Not that it wasn't tempting to take a little time off; she'd been working a ton of hours the past several months—make that years—and she was a little burned out. She'd put everything else in her life on hold for a long time: family, friends, boyfriends…

At some point she needed to have a *whole* life, not just a work life.

But that wasn't going to happen today.

She turned away from the window, grabbed her coffee and then curled up in the middle of the bed.

The books were dated, and she had never been one to go out

of order. Her mind was too analytical for that. She would start at the beginning, and then she wouldn't have to wonder if she'd missed anything.

Molly's name was scrawled inside the first book, the childish handwriting not at all surprising given the date. Molly had apparently received the diary on her ninth birthday.

Olivia settled back against the pillows and began to read. Three months in, she yawned. Molly's writings were mainly a boring recitation of her daily chores, homework assignments, and a cat named Franco who liked to sleep with Molly at night.

One thing that resonated with Olivia was the fact that Molly was an only child. When Molly complained of being lonely and wishing she had a brother or sister to play with, Olivia felt like she was reading the pages from her own journal. While she'd enjoyed being the center of her parents' world, she'd also been jealous of her friends who had siblings.

As she thought about family, her mind flashed back to the recent party at the senior center and the arrival of the massive Callaway clan. The room had filled with love and laughter as so many of Eleanor's family had come together to wish her a happy birthday. She couldn't imagine what it would be like to be a part of such a large family.

Thinking about the Callaways also took her mind back to Colton. She'd been deliberately trying not to think about him, because he'd left her feeling a little rattled and off balance. She hadn't had such a gut-clenching reaction to a man in a long time. And it had to happen with a fireman. Well, why not? He was good-looking, fit, sexy...the kind of man who didn't run away from danger but rather ran straight into it.

She sighed. She might not choose to hook up with a guy like that, but she was a woman, and she wasn't blind or immune to a charming smile and a hot body. Not that Colton had given her much of a smile, especially not after she banged up his already injured hand and told him she was there to write his grandmother's story. He hadn't liked that idea at all.

Frowning, she couldn't help wondering what the Callaway men were so afraid of.

The fact that they didn't want her to talk to Eleanor or hear her story only made her want to hear it that much more. She'd always been that way. When someone told her she couldn't do something, she wanted to prove them wrong. The Callaways had tried to warn her off, but they didn't realize that warning her away was like waving a red flag in front of a bull.

She smiled at the thought and then gave herself a mental scolding for daydreaming. She was supposed to be reading Molly's journal, but somewhere in between a litany of what Molly had had for dinner and what her best friend was wearing tomorrow, Olivia had allowed herself to get distracted.

She reached for her coffee mug, but it was empty. Then she glanced at the clock on the bedside table. It was only four; too early for dinner and way too early to go to sleep. If she took a nap now, she'd be completely messed up. She just needed to gut out the next few hours so she could get rid of her jet lag and return to her normal schedule.

She forced herself to focus on Molly's writings. She skimmed through the rest of book one and moved onto the second book and finally the third. She was halfway through the third journal, which took Molly from seventh grade to ninth grade, when Molly's world abruptly changed. On the way home from a second honeymoon, Molly's parents were killed in a plane crash.

Today, my parents died.

Olivia stared at the words Molly had written. The ink was smeared, probably from tears.

Olivia flipped the page. The next one was blank, and so was the one after that. She went all the way to the end, thirty blank pages.

No wonder. Molly's world had shattered. And she would have had no words to explain the horror of it all.

Olivia set the journal down, knowing that Molly eventually started talking again, because there were two more journals in the stack, but she wasn't ready to move on yet. She was thinking again of how similar her own life had been to Molly's. She hadn't lost both parents, but she had lost her father, and in the same abrupt manner.

She didn't want to think about that day, but the memories tugged at her brain. The last time she'd seen her dad had been the day of his murder. He was supposed to give her a ride to school, but she hadn't wanted to go with him. She'd wanted to go with her friends, with the boy she was interested in. So she'd said she'd see him later.

And that was that. Later never came.

Moisture filled her eyes, and she drew in a deep breath. It had been nine years, but it felt like yesterday.

The hotel phone rang next to her bed, startling her with the unexpected sound. The only person who knew she was in this hotel was her mother, and her mom would call her cell phone.

She picked up the receiver, thinking it had to be the front desk or housekeeping. "Hello?"

"Miss Bennett?" a male voice asked.

She sat up a little straighter. "Yes?"

"It's Colton Callaway. We met at the Sunset Senior Center, the guy with the broken fingers, remember?"

Her hand tightened around the phone. She couldn't believe the man she'd just been thinking about was calling her. "I remember. How did you know where to find me?"

"You left your information with the director of the senior center. I told her I needed to talk to you, and she passed it along."

"What do you want to talk to me about?" she asked warily.

"My grandmother."

She sighed. "Look, your grandmother is a grown woman. She gets to make her own decisions, and that includes who she wants to talk to."

"She's sick, Miss Bennett. She can't make her own decisions. Can I come up and talk to you?"

She tensed. "What do you mean—can you come up? Where are you?"

"I'm in the lobby. They wouldn't give me your room number. If I can't come up, will you come down?"

She hesitated, debating her options for a long minute. Colton Callaway didn't seem like the kind of man to be put off by the lack of a room number or her reluctance to speak to him. If she didn't talk to him now, he'd probably be hounding her steps all week.

In the end, her curiosity won out. She wanted to know what he had to say. "I'll be down in a few minutes."

"I'll be waiting."

Five

As she hung up the phone, Olivia felt a shiver run down her spine along with a tingle of anticipation. She jumped off the bed and glanced at her reflection in the mirror. She made a face at her appearance, noting the tangles in her hair and the dark shadows under her eyes. She quickly put on a little blush and some lip gloss, ran a brush through her hair and swapped her leggings for a pair of skinny jeans. Slipping on her sandals, she grabbed her handbag and walked out the door.

The hotel had a lobby bar that was warm and inviting, much like being in a living room. Colton sat at a table by the window drinking a beer. Aside from the man tending to the small bar, there was no one else in the room.

She walked across the room and sat down next to him. "Hello."

"Thanks for coming. Can I buy you a drink?"

"I don't know. Will I be here long enough to drink it?"

He suddenly smiled, and it changed his whole face. He went from angry and annoyed to sexy and charming. She had a feeling this side of him was going to be even more difficult to deal with.

"I'm not in a rush. What can I get you?"

"I'll have a glass of merlot, whatever they have."

"You got it." He stood and walked over to the bar to get her drink.

As he did so, she couldn't help but let her gaze follow him across the room. He moved with confidence. He had the kind of walk that said he was a man who knew what he wanted and where he intended to go. She'd always liked a strong sense of purpose in a man, but it scared her a little, too. She liked to be in control and to have the ability to follow her own path, which usually meant she took that path alone.

This wasn't a date, she reminded herself, wondering why she felt so nervous and fidgety. She settled back in her seat as he returned to the table.

He set down her glass of wine, then took a seat. "So, this is kind of strange," he began.

"I'm glad you think so, too," she said, sipping her wine.

"I don't usually do this."

"Do what? Buy women drinks?"

He smiled. "That I do. What I don't do is try to tell people how to do their jobs."

"Then why start with me?"

"Because my grandfather cornered me at the party earlier and asked me for a favor, and he never asks me for a favor."

"I assume that favor has to do with me."

"Specifically you. My grandfather would like you to leave my grandmother out of the book you're writing."

"He told me that as well. I spoke to him right before I ran into you."

"And what did you tell him?"

"That I wasn't going to refuse to speak to his wife. I guess he didn't like my answer, so he decided to bring in backup and send you over here."

"He didn't exactly send me. He asked me to keep my grandmother away from you. I thought it might be easier if I just talked to you about the situation instead of playing a game of keep-away. I prefer to be more direct."

She appreciated his candor. She liked being direct, too, but cynically she couldn't help wondering if his honesty wasn't just part of his plan to disarm her.

"Tell me about your grandmother," she said. "I only spent about twenty minutes with her, but she had so much energy in her eyes and her voice. She lit up the room."

"She's always been that way," Colton said, deep affection his voice. "She has a laugh that warms you from the inside out, like a shot of whiskey. But sadly, she doesn't laugh that much anymore. And some days she has no life in her eyes. She sits in a chair and stares out the window for hours on end. She doesn't recognize her husband of more than sixty years or any of her children or grandchildren. On those days we're strangers to her, and seeing her fade away is one of the worst things I've ever had to experience."

Dark shadows gathered in his eyes, and she could feel the despair within him. "I'm sorry."

"I know you didn't see that side of her today, and I'm happy about that. I keep hoping that the bad episodes will just go away, but realistically I know that won't happen." Colton rested his forearms on the table as he gazed into her eyes.

She licked her lips at the intensity in his gaze. She couldn't remember the last time someone had looked at her with so much purpose. She just wished his purpose wasn't to get rid of her.

"My grandfather thinks that talking about her life will upset my grandmother. He told me that agitation makes her blood pressure go up and that can sometimes trigger an episode."

She nodded. "I don't want to do anything to hurt your grandmother. But I have to ask you something."

"What's that?"

"What are you afraid of? What do you think your grandmother is going to tell me?"

"I'm not afraid of anything. I'm here at my grandfather's request. I told you—it's all about her health."

"I don't think it's *only* about that."

"Of course it is. My grandfather is incredibly protective. That's the kind of man he is. He's fiercely loyal to family and friends, but especially to his wife. She's his life. He adores her."

It was possible that was true, but she'd done too many interviews in the past four years with reluctant family members not to be able to discern between someone who was being protective and someone who had something to hide. Right now the Callaway men, especially Colton's grandfather, were falling into the second category.

"I'm quite capable of talking to your grandmother without upsetting her, and I understand the concerns about her health, but can I be frank?" she asked.

"Can I stop you?" he countered.

"You said you wanted to be direct and not play games," she reminded him.

He didn't look too happy to have his words thrown back in his face, but he nodded. "Go ahead then."

"I don't think you know why your grandfather doesn't want Eleanor to talk to me."

"I know what he told me, and I don't have any reason to doubt him or to think there's some sort of hidden agenda."

"Well, I do think there's a reason he hasn't shared with you."

"What are you basing that on?"

"My instincts. I've been working as a research assistant for a well-known biographer, Philip Dunston."

"Never heard of him."

"Well, a lot of people have. His most recent book just hit the *New York Times* and had the biggest first-sale day of any biography in the past ten years. The subject was Carlton Hughes, former secretary of state, but he's only one of many people I've researched over the last several years. I've become very good at reading between the lines and figuring out what someone's motive is."

"Fine. Maybe you have good instincts, but you've been researching public figures. My grandmother and her friends are lovely women, but I don't know anything that they did that would warrant a book about their lives."

"Just because you don't know doesn't mean there isn't anything. A few weeks ago, Molly Harper wrote me a letter about herself and her friends at the senior center. She told me that they all had amazing stories to tell and that they were part of a generation of women who had been silenced by men, and it was time to tell their story. She mentioned secrets and danger and doing something amazing without getting caught."

"What does that mean?" he asked with a puzzled look in his eyes.

"I don't know yet. Molly asked me to be the person who would give her and her friends a voice before they couldn't speak anymore. And that's what I want to do."

"My grandmother has never had a problem speaking up. If she wanted to say something, she would say it."

Olivia didn't believe that, and she wasn't basing that opinion just on Molly's letter but also on the conversation she'd had with the women and with Tom at the center. They'd exchanged very pointed looks at times, as if they weren't sure how much to say. They were definitely hiding something.

"Did you find anything interesting in Molly's box?" Colton asked.

"I've just started reading her journals. Molly was quite detailed in her writing. Unfortunately, I've only gotten through her childhood and into high school. You called right about the time I found out her parents were killed in a plane crash."

"I didn't know that. That's sad."

"I don't know what happened to her after that. I guess I'll find out tonight. Do you know if Molly has any relatives—a husband, children, grandchildren?"

"Her husband died a long time ago. She has some kids, but I've never met them. They would be my parents' age."

"Maybe I could speak to your parents at some point."

"I'm confused. Is the book about Molly or my grandmother?"

"I don't know yet, Colton. I haven't decided if there's going to be a book at all. It's too early for me to say."

He gave her a thoughtful look. "I'm not going to be able to stop you from talking to my grandmother, am I?"

"Not if she wants to speak me, too."

"You'd think I would have learned by now," he said with a frustrated shake of his head.

"Learned what?"

"Not to think I could change a woman's mind when it's made up," he said with a dry smile. "I have three sisters, a mother, a grandmother, a bunch of sisters-in-law and many female cousins, so I've had a lot of practice dealing with women, but apparently I like beating my head against a wall."

She couldn't help but smile at his words, and she also couldn't help but notice that he didn't mention a girlfriend in his list of females. "Are your sisters younger or older?" she asked, curious to know more about him and all of the Callaways.

"I have two older sisters and one twin sister."

"I've always found twins to be fascinating. Are you similar in personality? Do you have the ability to finish each other's sentences?"

"We're not alike at all. Shayla is a genius, for one thing. She skipped ahead of me in kindergarten and never looked back. She entered college at sixteen and is now a physician finishing up her last year of residency."

"High achiever," she commented.

"Oh, yeah, like most of my family, but Shayla's brain power is amazing."

"And you didn't get any of those smart genes?" She liked the way he'd spoken so admirably of his sister.

"I'm more street smart than book smart, but I hold my own. But we're not just different when it comes to IQ. Shayla has always been organized, studious, efficient and driven. She'd set her mind to a goal and she wouldn't stop until she got there." He paused. "Actually, you remind me of her a little. You have similar bulldog qualities."

"Great. I love being compared to a dog."

He smiled. "I was referring to your tenacity."

"You haven't seen me in action yet."

"I have a feeling I'm going to."

"If the adjectives you used to describe Shayla don't describe you, what words do?"

"Let's see. Impatient, impulsive, restless and determined."

She sipped her wine. "The first three are opposites of your sister, but driven and determined are pretty much the same thing."

He tipped his head. "I can compete."

"I have a feeling that not only can you compete, but you *like* to compete. More importantly, you like to win."

"There's a certain rush to doing something better than anyone else," he conceded. "You sound a little competitive yourself,

Olivia. And determined. And driven."

"I want to build my own career," she admitted. "I've paid my dues. Now it's my turn."

"You need to pick a more interesting subject. You can't go from secretary of state to a bunch of little old ladies who are probably making up half of whatever they're saying."

"You're not going to talk me out of this, Colton." She paused as the bartender came over to their table and asked if they wanted another drink. "I probably shouldn't," she said. "I haven't eaten in a while, and I still have work to do."

"No thanks," Colton said to the bartender. As the man walked away, Colton added, "I haven't eaten either. There's a good Italian restaurant right across the street. My friend's dad is the chef there. They have the best pasta and pizza in the city."

"The desk clerk mentioned that," she muttered, glancing down at her watch. It was almost six—definitely time for dinner.

"Why don't we get something to eat?"

She should really say no. Colton had said what he'd come to say, and she'd told him in no uncertain terms that she was going ahead with her project. What else was there to talk about?

"You're going to have to eat, Olivia. Do you really want to eat alone?"

"It wouldn't be the first time." She'd eaten many meals on her own in Europe. But it wouldn't be such a bad thing to have some company, especially his company. Despite the fact that they appeared to be at cross-purposes, she liked talking to him.

Colton might not be a brain like his sister, but he was intelligent, and he seemed to care a lot about his family. He was also really attractive, which made for quite an interesting combination. But she couldn't let herself think for a second that he wasn't going to use dinner as another opportunity to convince her to stay away from his grandmother.

"Come on, say yes," Colton said impatiently. "It's just dinner."

"Yes," she said, thinking maybe she should add impulsive and reckless to the list of adjectives describing her personality.

His eyes sparked with approval. "Good. Let's go."

Six

Alonzo's had a great vibe, Olivia thought, as they entered the restaurant across the street from her hotel. The dining room had dark hardwood floors, cozy red leather booths and an open-air kitchen. With the smell of garlic in the air, her mouth actually began to water.

The hostess, a cute brunette in her early twenties, gave a little squeal when she saw Colton.

"You're alive," she said, giving him a big hug. "I was so worried about you. Greg said you got hurt in a fire."

"Just smashed a couple of fingers," Colton said, extricating himself from the girl's arms. "Do you have a table for us?"

"I always have a table for you," she said, casting Olivia a speculative look.

"This is my—friend, Olivia," Colton said, stumbling a little over the word *friend*. "This is Theresa Alonzo, daughter of the owner, and sister of Greg, who works with me."

"Nice to meet you," Olivia said, thinking Theresa didn't look all that happy to meet her. She obviously had a crush on Colton.

Theresa muttered, "Hello." Then she led them to a booth at the far end of the room. "Do you want your usual, Colton?"

"Olivia and I will take a look at the menu."

"Papa made a special minestrone soup tonight," Theresa said, handing them menus. "You should try it."

"Sounds good," Colton said. "Can you bring me a beer and a glass of merlot for my friend?"

"I'll tell your waitress," Theresa said. "She'll be right over."

As Theresa disappeared, Olivia smiled at Colton.

"What?" he asked warily.

"Someone has a crush on you."

He immediately shook his head. "Theresa just turned twenty. She's way too young for me, and she's my friend's little sister."

"I don't think either of those facts is a problem for her."

"Well, it's a problem for me. I don't date anyone related to my friends or coworkers. That would be way too complicated."

She nodded. "Because of the whole brotherhood thing?"

"We look out for each other and for our families. What we do requires trust and commitment. We have to be able to depend on each other in a life or death situation, so the less drama we have with each other, the better."

"Right." She really wished she had not asked the question, because she didn't want to talk about his job. She looked down at the menu. "So what's good here?"

"Everything."

He startled her by reaching across the table and covering her hand with his. A jolt of heat ran through her at his touch. "What are you doing?" she asked, her voice a little too breathless. She really needed to get a grip.

"You said something to me earlier about my job, asking me why I did it, and I couldn't help thinking there was something behind your question and something behind the pain that just flashed through your eyes a moment ago. Did you lose someone in a fire? Did you get dumped by a firefighter? What's your deal?"

She hesitated, not really wanting to get into it, but she had a feeling he wasn't going to let go of her hand until she answered.

"My father was a cop. He died in the line of duty," she said shortly.

"I'm sorry," he said, sincerity in his eyes. "I didn't expect you to say that."

"That's the problem with questions. You never know what kind of answer you're going to get." She licked her lips as his fingers tightened around hers. She'd pull away in a second, but just for a moment she'd soak up the warmth and strength of his touch.

"How old were you?"

"I was sixteen, a junior in high school. My father answered a call for a robbery at a convenience store. He was the first on the scene, and the guy came out shooting. My dad died on his way to the hospital." She drew in a shaky breath. "I didn't get a chance to say goodbye."

"That's rough," he said, his gaze filled with compassion.

"It was beyond horrific. And it seemed to go on forever. I just wanted to crawl into a hole and be alone, but for days after his death, cops would come to our house. The funeral was attended by thousands of police officers from all over the state. It was supposed to be comforting to see that sea of blue, but all I could think when I saw all those guys in uniform was—where were you when my dad got shot?" She blew out a breath and pulled her hand away from Colton's. As she sat back in the booth, she added, "And that is really all I want to say about it."

He nodded. "Understandable. But can I say something?"

"I don't know if I want to hear what you have to say. You remind me of my dad. He loved his job. He loved helping people. He had no idea how much we worried about him. Or if he did have an idea, he didn't let on, he didn't act differently. He just followed his dream, and he didn't care that his dream might take him away from us."

"You sound angry."

"I am, or I was," she amended. "I don't know what I feel anymore."

"I hope you can feel some pride along with the anger, because your dad sounds like a hero."

"He was a hero, I know that. And I am proud of him," she admitted. "Since I grew up, I have a better understanding of it all, but I can't completely let go of the sadness. I didn't want a hero; I just wanted a dad, someone who would choose my mom and me over his job. But he didn't do that."

"Do you think you could make that choice, Olivia?"

She stared at him in surprise. "What do you mean?"

"You seem pretty determined to go for what you want, maybe a little like your dad."

"What I want isn't dangerous to me or to anyone else," she said defensively.

"You don't know that. You're in the business of unraveling secrets, and it seems to me that secrets carry an element of danger."

She supposed that was possible, but she'd never looked at her job that way. "I think you're reaching. Most of the secrets I uncover have to do with someone sleeping with someone they're not supposed to be sleeping with."

"And that's not dangerous?"

"It's not the same thing."

"Maybe not. But my point is that you have a passion for what you do, and it's difficult to walk away from your passion."

"I suppose."

"So, change of subject?" Colton asked.

"Please."

"What are you in the mood to eat? I know I mentioned pasta, but if you feel like splitting a pizza, they're unbelievably good."

"Then let's split a pizza," she said, happy to have that decision made.

"What don't you like?"

"I like everything but anchovies and pineapple."

He grinned. "So do I. See, we have something in common."

"Something," she said, sipping her wine as he relayed their order to the waiter.

When they were alone again, Colton said, "Now, I'd like to hear a little more about all those people you caught having sex with the wrong people."

"I didn't catch them. I just happened to stumble on some of their affairs in my research."

"Are we talking about Carlton Hughes?"

"Yes. He had a fling with an intern. It's in the book."

Colton groaned. "He couldn't be more original?"

"Apparently not. But his wife stuck by him—I can't imagine why. Actually I can imagine why," Olivia corrected. "She loved his power, his stature and his money."

"All aphrodisiacs. What other juicy scandals have you

discovered?"

"You're going to have to read some of Philip's books if you want to find out."

"I might have to do that." He paused. "I know I said change of subject, but getting back to my grandmother."

Now she was the one to let out a groan. "Colton—"

"I don't think she had an affair with anyone, but if she did, no one needs to know about it. She's in her eighties, for God's sake."

Olivia smiled. "I like that you're protective of your grandmother, but I'm not a threat to her."

"You just told me you think she's hiding something, so how do you know you're not about to uncover something that could hurt her?"

She met his gaze, seeing the worry in his eyes. "I guess I don't know."

"Exactly."

"You should really talk to your grandfather, Colton. If you can give me a good reason to walk away, then maybe I'll go."

"What kind of reason are we talking about?"

"I won't know until you find one."

"I'm supposed to speak to my grandfather in the morning, before he leaves for Chicago. I'll see what I can find out. Otherwise, I'll be spending the next couple of days trying to keep you and my grandmother apart."

She smiled. "Well, you'll do what you have to do, and I'll do the same. I really don't think you need to worry, Colton."

"You know what I think?"

"I'm afraid to ask."

"I think you're about to lead us into an iceberg, and we're all going to go down."

"If there's an iceberg to avoid, your grandmother probably knows where it is."

"She may not remember," he said heavily.

"Then I'll go home with nothing."

He started at her words. "I forgot for a minute that you don't live here. Where do you live?"

"New York City," she replied, thinking that her apartment

seemed very far away at the moment.

"How long are you planning to stay in town?"

"Until I know whether or not I have a story to tell, but probably not longer than a week, maybe ten days. I'm using some of my vacation time for this project."

"It could be a waste of time, Olivia."

"My time to waste," she said lightly.

Before he could reply, the chef brought out a steaming pizza and set it on the table in front of them. Then he stretched out his arms to Colton.

Colton stood up and gave the older man a hug.

As they broke apart, the man said, "I'm so glad to see you were not badly hurt in the warehouse fire."

"I just had a minor concussion," Colton said. "This is my friend, Olivia. This is Raphael Alonzo, Theresa and Greg's father."

Raphael had dark brown hair and eyes. He gave her a welcoming smile. "It's nice to meet you. It's about time Colton brought a pretty girl in here."

She doubted that Colton had much trouble finding a pretty girl to have dinner with.

"I don't share your pizza with just anyone, Raphael," Colton joked.

"I made a special pie for you tonight," Raphael said. "And it's on the house. Your money is no good here."

"I pay my own way."

"Any man who saves my son's life eats for free," Raphael said firmly. He looked at Olivia. "Colton pulled my son out of a fire two months ago."

"Greg has done the same for me many times," Colton said.

Raphael nodded, then slapped Colton on the shoulder and said he had to get back to the kitchen.

As Colton sat back down, he gave her an embarrassed smile. "Raphael is always a little dramatic. It's the Italian in him."

"He loves you as much as his daughter does."

"He's family."

"You seem to have a lot of family," she murmured, wondering why she suddenly felt so alone. But she had her mom, she reminded herself. And she had friends. She didn't see them very often, but they were around. They were busy, too. Everyone had jobs, and her job kept her on the move. And it wasn't like she had coworkers. She certainly didn't hang out with Philip. And Philip's personal assistant was a fifty-four-year-old woman, who was lovely, but she and Olivia did not have much in common.

Everyone else she spoke to in the course of a day was usually involved in some way with the book they were working on, either with the subject or the publishing house or Philip's agent or Philip's fans.

She frowned, realizing how much of her life revolved around Philip.

"Something wrong?" Colton asked as he slid two pieces of pizza onto a plate. "You're not eating. Is there something on the pizza you don't like?"

"No, it looks great. I was just waiting for it to cool down."

"You're a terrible liar."

"What am I lying about?" she challenged.

"You were deep in thought a second ago. What were you thinking?"

"I don't know. Nothing," she said vaguely. She certainly didn't intend to tell him she felt a little sorry for herself. "Let's eat." She grabbed a slice of pizza and took a large bite. The delicious mix of cheese, tomatoes, garlic and vegetables was amazing, and soon she was keeping up with Colton in a race to see who would get the last piece.

Colton won, but he paused in his moment of triumph, his hand hovering over the one remaining slice. "If you want it, it's yours."

"That's very generous."

"Or we could negotiate."

"What would be the terms? And they can't have anything to do with your grandmother," she added quickly.

"That's no fun."

"What would be fun is if you just give me that piece of pizza because you're a giving person who is here on this earth to make other people happy," she joked.

He smiled. "I thought you didn't like heroes."

"In this case, I might make an exception, because that pizza is really good."

"Fine, it's yours." He dropped the pizza onto her plate.

"And what do I have to do for it?" she asked warily. "Because I know there's no such thing as a free lunch, or in this case—pizza."

"You're cynical, Olivia."

She made a face at his words. "My mom said that earlier, but I don't think that's true."

"Then prove it. Just say *thank you* and enjoy your pizza. No strings attached, because I'm just that good of a guy."

He was enjoying being the good guy a little too much, but since she was still hungry, she decided not to make herself into a martyr. "Thank you," she parroted. "You're such a good guy."

Colton sat back in his seat and folded his arms across his chest. "You are not like anyone I have ever met, Olivia Bennett."

The spark in his eyes almost made her choke on her pizza. She swallowed hard and then took a sip of wine. "How so?"

He gave her a speculative look. "I'm not sure yet. But I think I want to find out."

"Now you're just trying to flirt me out of interviewing your grandmother."

He shook his head. "There you go again, being cynical."

"And you're not? How can you do what you do and not get a little dark inside?"

His smile faded, and he didn't seem to have a ready answer to her question. Then he said, "I try to focus on the positive. But it doesn't always work. The other day—the day I got hurt—I lost someone. He was alive when I got into the room, but he was trapped, and before I could get him out, things got worse."

His words made her feel terrible. "I'm sorry, Colton. I shouldn't—"

"No," he said cutting her off. "Don't apologize. You're right. It's not easy to do what I do and not let the bad stuff get to me. But I have to compartmentalize. I have to focus on the good that gets done. That's not to say that the losses don't hurt, but I have to keep moving forward. And..." He paused. "I've always found a new challenge turns me in the right direction. I go hiking or rock climbing or I run a marathon. I turn my focus towards a goal I can achieve, something that's in my control, and that drives the darkness away."

She nodded, thinking that for a guy who didn't look like he had more than five years on the job, he seemed very philosophical and pragmatic about it all. "Do you really run marathons?" she asked, trying to defuse the tension that had sprung up between them.

"Okay, I was exaggerating. The farthest I've run is a half-marathon. I find running a little boring. But next spring I'm planning to challenge myself in a new way."

"What's that?"

"I'm going to swim to Alcatraz."

"You're going to jump into the freezing cold San Francisco Bay and swim to a deserted island prison?"

He grinned. "Can you think of anything more fun?"

"I can think of a lot of things more fun than that."

"Oh, yeah, care to share? Because I could be persuaded to try something else—if the right woman asked me."

"You are such a flirt." She motioned to the waiter, who immediately came over. "Can we get our check?" she asked.

"Your dinner is on the house," the waiter replied. "Can I bring you anything else, coffee, dessert?"

"No, thanks." She turned back to Colton. "I should get back to Molly's journals."

"I could help you go through them."

"It's a one-person job." She knew that allowing Colton into her hotel room would be an even worse idea than going to dinner with him. He had a way of making her talk, making her reconsider her objectives, and she couldn't let his agenda get in the way of hers. "But thanks for the meal," she said, as she got to her feet.

"It was Raphael's generosity, not mine."

"Well, apparently your hero tendencies made his generosity possible."

They walked through the restaurant and out the front door. Olivia paused on the sidewalk. "Am I going to see you tomorrow?"

"If you see my grandmother tomorrow, you're going to see me."

"Then I guess this is only goodnight and not goodbye."

"Exactly. And just for the record…"

"What?" she asked warily, as he took a step closer. *He wasn't going to kiss her, was he?* Her heart beat a little faster at that thought.

He smiled down at her. "Tonight was fun."

"Yeah," she agreed, licking her lips.

Her gesture brought his gaze to her mouth. His eyes darkened.

She knew that look, and she'd already mixed a little too much pleasure with business. She stepped back.

"It was fun," she said. "But now it's time to work." She might not be a firefighter, but like him, she could compartmentalize when she had to, and this was definitely the time to do that. She couldn't let a sexy man charm her out of going after her story. Men had a tendency to disappear with the dawn, and her story, her career, was the only thing she could really depend on.

Seven

—➤➤◀◀◀—

Olivia spent the rest of Sunday night reading Molly's journals. Mellowed by the wine and pizza, not to mention distracting thoughts of Colton, she'd had a little trouble getting back into the books, but thankfully Molly's story got more interesting as she went along.

After Molly's parents died, Molly was sent to live with her aunt in Bakersfield, California. According to Molly, her aunt was a cold, bitter woman who didn't care much for her but took her in out of a sense of responsibility. Molly couldn't wait until she was old enough to move out. She hated her new life and wished longingly for the good old days, a feeling Olivia could definitely relate to. But like Olivia, Molly had to accept that the past was done and she could only move forward.

Molly didn't have any money, so she had no opportunity to go to college. She took some classes in typing and stenography and went to work as a secretary at an insurance company. After a year she was able to move out of her aunt's house and left Bakersfield to take a new job in San Francisco.

Molly liked being in the city. It felt like a fresh start, but she had trouble making friends, and while surrounded by people, she often felt lonely. She was naturally shy and had trouble reaching out to strangers, so she spent a lot of time reading and daydreaming about a life filled with adventures that she would probably never have.

But eventually Molly met someone, a dashing, handsome man

named Stanley Harper. He told her he was going to take care of her, and she thought finally she was going to be happy again.

Molly didn't write anything more for a couple of years, finally making another entry the night her son was born.

Peter was born at ten minutes past eight. Stan had hoped to be with me for the birth, but he was stuck at work, and he didn't get here until Peter was two hours old. But when I look at Peter, nothing else matters. I feel only love. Being a mother is what I was meant to do. I have a beautiful son now. I have a family again. I just hope I don't screw it up.

There was another big jump in time—almost five years before the next entry.

"It's getting harder to come here and write. My life is so busy now. I have a little girl. Her name is Francine. I can already tell that she's going to be a handful. She cries at every little thing. The noise drives Stan crazy, but she's a baby with a big set of lungs, so what can I do? And I like that she's shaking things up. In a strange way, I feel like Francine is making me stronger. I think maybe she'll bring the light back.

Olivia flipped the page. The next one was blank. She skimmed through the rest of the journal—nothing.

Then she dug through the box, wondering if she'd missed another book. Surely Molly wouldn't leave her hanging like this?

There was a photo album and some trinkets in the box that didn't mean anything to her, but there weren't any more journals.

She sat back on the bed, pondering the contents of the box Molly had left for her. Molly hadn't planned on getting sick, so maybe she'd still been in the process of gathering things together. Because why would Molly give her a bunch of journals that didn't really say that much? Sure, it was nice to feel like she knew Molly better, or at the least the young Molly, but there was no mention of Eleanor Callaway or the theater group or anyone else from the senior center.

There simply had to be more. The last two entries had hinted at something—she just didn't know what, but there had definitely been an undertone to her words. It was as if Molly was waiting for something bad to happen.

Maybe that feeling of uncertainty came from the way she'd suddenly been orphaned. Perhaps being a mother and having the children she wanted had made her fear that it would all get taken away somehow.

Olivia could understand that. Love could be really painful when it was followed by loss.

Still, she was frustrated with the abrupt ending. She stretched her arms over her head and yawned. It was almost eleven o'clock at night. She might as well go to bed. But while she was tired, she didn't feel all that sleepy. She would have to wait until tomorrow to get more information on Molly and her friends, but right now her mind was going in another direction...

On impulse she grabbed her laptop and opened the search engine, then typed in the name Colton Callaway. She was curious about him, and maybe she was acting a little like a stalker, but she wanted to know more about him and his family.

He didn't appear to be on social media, but there were a few articles that came up with his name. She clicked on the first one from a San Francisco weekly magazine. The headline read: *Another Callaway joins the San Francisco Fire Department.* Standing behind Colton were nine strong, handsome men, most of whom were wearing fire department dress uniforms, and one lone blonde woman.

She read through the list of names, noting Patrick Callaway was retired Chief of Department, Jack Callaway currently Deputy Chief of Operations, Tim Callaway retired firefighter, Burke Callaway Battalion Chief, Aiden Callaway, retired smoke jumper, Dylan Callaway and Brody Callaway firefighters and Emma Callaway fire investigator. She assumed that Emma was Colton's sister and the others were brothers or cousins. But whatever the relationship, it was an impressive group.

All of them stood tall and proud as they welcomed Colton into the fold. He certainly did have a legacy to live up to, she thought. That had to put a lot of pressure on him. But with his chin tilted in the air, and a fierce light in his blue eyes, he seemed more than up to the task.

She found herself liking him even more.

She closed her computer and decided to go to bed. But even after she'd turned off the Internet and the bedroom light, she couldn't shut down her brain.

As she drifted into sleep, her dreams were filled with Colton—as they did all kinds of really sexy and reckless things together…

—➤◀—

Colton didn't sleep at all. His fingers hurt when he got in the wrong position. He couldn't seem to get comfortable no matter which way he turned, and he couldn't stop thinking about his grandfather's demands, his grandmother's secrets and Olivia's beautiful green eyes.

He got up around seven and did his usual run along the Embarcadero, but instead of pushing four miles, he stopped after two, grabbed a coffee, a pastry and walked back to his apartment. He lived in a one-bedroom apartment on the fourth floor of an eight-story apartment building on one of North Beach's steepest hills, and he really liked the area. Being on a hill he had a great view of the bay, especially from the rooftop deck, and when he left his apartment he was very close to great restaurants, bars and comedy clubs as well as one of his favorite gyms.

The neighborhood was a mix of people, but there were plenty of young singles and there was always something to do. Most of all, he liked living alone. The past three months had been heaven. After growing up in the chaotic Callaway household, he'd moved into an apartment with three other guys that had felt like he was living in a frat house. And when he wasn't there, he was at the firehouse, which could also sometimes feel like a frat house. So he'd moved out and grabbed a small one-bedroom apartment that was perfect for him. He just needed to find a little time to buy some furniture and decorate.

After arriving back at his apartment, he showered, dressed and then headed across town to his grandparents' house. He got there a little before eleven, just in time to see his grandfather loading a suitcase into the back of a taxi.

"Good, you're here," Patrick said tersely. "I'm counting on

you, Colton. Don't let me down."

"I'll do my best."

"I told you before I don't want your best, I want success. Don't forget that."

He couldn't forget it if he tried. One of his grandfather's favorite sayings was not to try but to succeed. He'd liked the philosophy up until now, when it appeared that a good try might be the best result he could get. But he wasn't going to argue with his grandfather about effort. He had another question to ask. "Is there any reason besides your concern about Grandma's health that is driving your desire to shut down conversation between Grandma and the writer?"

"Her health is everything," Patrick said flatly. "What more is there at this point?"

He had no answer for that question. And if Patrick did have another reason, he certainly wasn't going to share it with him.

"I'll see you in a few days," Patrick said.

Colton nodded, digging his hands into the pockets of his jeans as he watched his grandfather get into the cab. Then he walked up to the front door and rang the bell. A nurse let him in a few minutes later and waved him toward the kitchen.

He found his grandmother sipping a mug of tea at the small oak table in the kitchen. She was working a crossword puzzle, one of her favorite things to do.

She gave him a warm smile. "Colton, what a lovely surprise."

He leaned over and kissed her on the cheek, then sat down in the chair across from her. He looked at her partially filled-in puzzle. "Looks like you're making progress on that."

"Actually, I'm a bit stumped. I've been working on it since yesterday, and I'm a little frustrated. It's a good thing you came, because I'm trying not to cheat by looking at the answers."

He smiled at her candor. "You have always had a lot of willpower when it comes to those puzzles."

"Well, they're supposed to be good for my mind, so I try to keep working them even when I start to feel stupid."

"Besides feeling stupid, how are you today?" he asked lightly.

"I'm fine." She gave him a speculative look. "What are you

doing here?"

"Can't I come and visit my grandmother without an ulterior motive?"

"Of course you can, but you rarely do, and that's okay. You're a busy man, and you have your own life. But you'll have to forgive me for thinking you might have another reason."

"Well, I'm not that busy this week," he said, holding up his hand. He'd redone the tape after taking a shower, and while he'd hoped to see more definite improvement, his fingers were still swollen around the knuckles.

"Is it painful?"

"It's not too bad, but I'm going to have to miss some work."

"They're not going to make you sit at a desk, go on school visits or check out fire alarms? Your grandfather used to hate light duty. I told him he should just try to enjoy it, but he couldn't. He hated to hear the alarm go off and not be able to do his job."

Something he had in common with his grandfather. "I'm sure that light duty is in my future, but with the concussion that I suffered, there's a mandatory five-day wait after diagnosis before I can do anything. I'm on day three, and I'm already restless."

"Do you want some tea or something to eat? I could have Donna make you some food. She's very good in the kitchen."

"No thanks. I was thinking since I have free time today that maybe you and I could take a ride somewhere. We could go to the beach or out to lunch later, whatever you want."

"That's a lovely and generous offer, Colton, but I'm going to the senior center. In fact, your mother should be here soon to give me a ride."

"You wouldn't want to skip it today? It might be nice for you to have a change of scenery. You go there all the time."

"To see my friends," Eleanor said pointedly. "Friends are important, Colton. When you're young, you get busy and life gets in the way, but later you cherish those relationships."

He could see the determination in his grandmother's eyes and felt caught between a rock and a hard place. How on earth was he going to do what his grandfather wanted?

Maybe as he'd told Olivia the night before, it was better to be direct and not play games. He clasped his hands together on the tabletop. "Grandma, I need to talk to you about something."

"The real reason you're here?" she asked dryly.

"I never could fool you."

"So why try?"

"Grandpa asked me to look out for you while he's gone. He's concerned that you'll get tired or upset if you spend too much time talking about the past with that writer Molly invited to town."

The sparkle in her grandmother's eyes faded a bit. "Patrick already spoke to me about that, and I'll tell you, as I told him, that I'm perfectly capable of having a conversation about the past without getting upset in any way. There's really no need for you to babysit me. And frankly, Colton, I'm a little surprised that you would support your grandfather on this. I'm in my eighties. Haven't I earned the right to speak to whomever I want to?"

"Yes," he said. "Of course. I think Grandpa is only acting out of concern for your health."

"I feel good today. Who knows how I'll feel tomorrow? But with my disease, I can only live in the moment."

He nodded, hearing the doorbell ring. The nurse went to answer it, and a moment later his mother Lynda walked into the room. She also looked surprised to see him there.

"Colton?"

"Mom."

"Is something going on?" Lynda asked, her glance darting from him to Eleanor and then back to him again.

"Just checking in on Grandma," he said. "I'm kind of at loose ends today."

"You never did like to be idle," Lynda said with a knowing smile. "But some days you just have to relax."

"Colton will come with us today," Eleanor said briskly.

"To the senior center?" Lynda asked with a raised eyebrow. "Really?"

"Yes," he said, deciding if he couldn't beat them, he'd join them.

Her gaze narrowed speculatively. "Is this about the book?"

"Grandpa—"

"Asked you to ignore your grandmother's wishes," Lynda finished. She turned to Eleanor, shaking her head in disgust. "You know I love Patrick, but he can be so overbearing sometimes."

"He certainly can," Eleanor agreed. "But since I know Colton doesn't want to disappoint Patrick, the only solution is for Colton to come with us." She gave him a pointed look. "Then you'll be able to see that I am just fine."

"Great," he muttered, knowing his first instinct had been right. There was no way he would be able to change their minds. All he could do was go along for the ride. "Can I ask one question?"

"What's that?" Eleanor asked.

"Whose idea was all this—about the book? Was it yours or Molly's?"

"It was Molly's idea, but I agreed with her, and I want to honor her wishes. She's been a dear friend to me for many, many years."

"Is the story you want the writer to hear Molly's story, or does it involve all of you?"

"I guess that will depend on what Olivia thinks is important." Eleanor paused. "Did you meet her yesterday, Colton?"

"Yes. She was on her way out of the center when I arrived." He didn't bother to add that they'd had dinner together.

"She's a pretty girl with her beautiful green eyes and long, curly brown hair, isn't she?"

"I hadn't noticed," he muttered.

His grandmother smiled. "You never could lie to me, Colton, so why on earth would you start now?"

"Fine, she's gorgeous. So what? She's only here for a few days."

"You never know what a few days can bring," Eleanor said wisely. "If I've learned anything in life, it's that."

Eight

On her way to the senior center late Monday morning, Olivia decided to stop by the hospital and see if there had been any improvement in Molly Harper's condition. Upon arrival, the nurse told her there was no change, but she was welcome to sit with Molly if she wanted. So Olivia made her way into the room of the woman whose letter had intrigued her enough to come to San Francisco and use her vacation days to research a story that she still didn't understand.

Olivia paused a few feet from the bed. Molly Harper had short brown hair with at least a half inch of gray along the roots. Her face was pale, her skin so thin it was almost translucent. There was no color at all in her cheeks and no real sign of life. The only sounds in the room came from the machines that appeared to be keeping Molly alive.

She moved a little closer and impulsively put her hand on Molly's wrist. Her skin was cool, another sign that life was slipping away.

"I don't know if you can hear me," she said quietly. "But it's me, Olivia Bennett. I came to see you and your friends, just as I promised." She paused, thinking she was probably just talking to herself, but the words kept coming. "I wish you would wake up, Molly. I have a lot of questions, and I'm afraid you're the only one who can answer them. You told me how much you wanted me to tell your story. I need your help to do that. When you wake up, I'll be ready to listen."

"Who the hell are you?" a male voice demanded.

She turned in surprise to see a man enter the room. He had on a black suit and a maroon tie, and judging by the gray in his hair and the age lines around his eyes, he appeared to be in his fifties or sixties.

"I'm Olivia Bennett," she said, stepping away from the bed. She was glad she'd put on a dress and heels today. She felt more professional in her attire and more confident with a few inches added to her five-foot-four frame.

"Do you know my mother?"

"Your mother?" she echoed. "You're Molly's son?"

He nodded, his gaze narrowing, his expression somewhat stern. "Yes, I'm Peter Harper. I don't think I've ever heard my mother mention your name."

"We haven't actually met. Your mother wrote to me a few weeks ago and asked me to come and meet her. I arrived yesterday only to find out she had had a stroke."

"You're the writer she mentioned."

"Yes. Your mother thought I might be interested in helping some of the women at the Sunset Senior Center write down their stories."

"Why would you be interested in doing that?"

"I'm a biographer. I write books about people's lives." She didn't bother to draw the line between her career goal and what she was actually doing as a research assistant.

"Well, as you can see my mother won't be telling you her story."

"I'm very sorry," she said quietly. Maybe the man's brusque manner was the result of his sadness about his mom's condition. "Is there any chance she'll wake up?"

"The doctors don't know." His gaze moved to his mother. "They're doubtful. This is the third time she's been here, and each time her condition gets worse."

"I'll leave you alone then."

She was almost to the door when he said, "Wait."

She turned around. "Yes?"

"Leave my mother out of whatever you're doing at the senior

center, all right? Whatever those women have to say about her is just their opinion. If she can't speak for herself, I don't want anyone else speaking for her."

"I understand," she said, but as she left the room she realized she didn't understand at all. Peter Harper had had the same reaction to her visit as Patrick Callaway. Why? What were these men so worried about?

Molly's voice rang through her head again...

I grew up in a time when women were silent, when men did the speaking for them.

Well Molly might have grown up in that time, but Olivia had not. And she was now more curious than ever to talk to the women at the senior center.

After arriving at the senior center, which offered a lunch buffet of sandwiches, fruit, vegetables and cookies for a five-dollar fee, Colton grabbed a sandwich and sat down at a table with his mother while Eleanor joined three of her friends for lunch to be followed by a game of Bridge.

There was no sign yet of Olivia. Maybe she'd read Molly's journals and decided there was nothing left to pursue. That thought should have made him happy, but he felt decidedly restless when it came to Olivia. He didn't know whether he wanted her to go or wanted her to stay. Either option seemed problematic in some way, especially the option where he didn't get to see her again, where he didn't have a chance to kiss her.

There had been a moment last night when he'd thought about kissing her, but he'd hesitated, and then she'd left. At the time, he'd thought it was a smart decision not to complicate things with a kiss, but now it felt like the most stupid idea he'd ever had.

Shaking his head, he devoured the rest of his turkey sandwich in two big bites, washing it down with a swig of cola.

His mother was checking her email on her phone while munching on a plate of raw vegetables. "Anything interesting?" he asked, wondering what had gotten her attention.

She looked up at him with a smile. "Nicole just sent me the latest reports from Brandon's new therapist."

"I didn't realize he was going to someone new."

"Dr. Rita Bentley. She's quite good. She has some innovative approaches to autism, and she's been working with Kyle and Brandon together as well as with just Brandon on his own. Fortunately, Kyle is happy enough to come with his brother no matter what the activity. He's such a great little boy. He somehow understands that Brandon needs him to be with him, speak for him. It's that amazing twin connection." Her eyes filled with moisture.

"Hey, don't cry," he said quickly. "This is good news, right?"

She nodded as she pulled tissue from her purse and dabbed her eyes. "Yes, it's good. I just know how long Nicole has been waiting for a break-through, and it seems like it's finally happening. Brandon is starting to make eye contact with people and during his latest session with Dr. Bentley he was able to follow directions and point to appropriate objects as directed. He's slowly reconnecting with the world."

Colton was thrilled to hear that. He still remembered when Brandon had been a perfectly normal little boy—up until the age of two. And then everything had changed. "I'm glad he's getting better."

"Kyle really changed everything, but you probably understand better than anyone the intense connection between twins. You and Shayla had it when you were little. I don't know if you still have it now, but I can remember when you knew what each other was about to say before the other said it. It was kind of eerie."

"That was weird. We're not that close anymore, but we'll always have a connection, a different relationship with each other than with everyone else. At least, that's the way I feel." As he finished speaking, he looked around the room. They'd been at the center for forty-five minutes. Where was Olivia? Had she decided the story wasn't worth anything after all?

"What is going on with you?" Lynda asked.

"Nothing," he said, impatiently drumming his fingers on the table.

She directed her pointed glance at his hand. "It doesn't sound like nothing."

"This is not what I was thinking I'd be doing today, that's all."

"It was your choice to come."

"Not really. Does Grandpa have a reason to be worried about this interview?"

"If I thought he did, I would have supported his efforts, but he couldn't give me a good reason why Eleanor shouldn't write down her memories, and I think it could actually be a wonderful opportunity for her. She's supposed to exercise her brain. I know that Patrick is devoted to her, and I try to respect whatever he wants, but she wants this, and I don't know how much longer she'll be able to speak for herself. While she can speak, I'm going to encourage it."

That made sense. "You're right, but I'm still going to stick around. At least, I can look Grandpa in the eye when he gets back and say I did everything I could do."

"That's true." She slipped her phone back into her purse. "If you're so determined to play bodyguard, I'm going to take advantage of your presence and run a few errands. Eleanor will probably play cards for at least another hour. You can call me if you need me. I won't be too far away."

"Go. I'll be fine. Grandma seems in good condition today," he said, watching Eleanor laugh at something Ginnie had just said.

"She loves being here with her friends. She feels young when she's around them, and I can understand that. When I'm with the women I grew up with, there's a feeling of real understanding and deep friendship."

He nodded. "I get that."

As he finished speaking, he saw Olivia enter the room, and his heart skipped a beat. She saw him almost immediately, and he liked the spark that flashed through her eyes when she met his gaze.

She was here to get what she wanted. And he was here to make sure she didn't. He felt oddly excited about the thought of doing battle with her.

"Is that her?" Lynda asked. "The writer?"

He sat up straighter. "Yes, that's Olivia Bennett."

"She's as pretty as your grandmother said. I only caught a glimpse of her yesterday, and in all the chaos of the party, I didn't even realize that she was the writer Eleanor was so eager to speak to."

He got to his feet as Olivia approached the table.

"Hello," she said tentatively.

"Hey," he said, shockingly happy just to be looking at her.

His mother stood up. "Are you going to introduce us?" she prodded Colton.

"Sorry. This is my mother, Lynda Callaway. This is Olivia Bennett."

Olivia shook his mother's hand. "Nice to meet you."

"You, too. I've been hearing a lot about you."

"I hope at least some of it was good," Olivia said lightly.

"Well, I don't judge until I meet someone."

"I don't, either," Olivia said. "I like to keep an open mind."

Lynda picked up her purse from the table. "I'll be back in about an hour, Colton. I hope you enjoy your time with the ladies, Miss Bennett. They're a fascinating group."

"So I've been told," Olivia said.

As his mom walked away, he said, "Why don't you sit down?"

"I didn't come here to talk to you, Colton."

"Do you really want to interrupt their game?" He tipped his head toward the ladies who had finished lunch and had moved on to their card game. "They're having fun."

As if on cue, his grandmother gave a wave and said, "We'll be done shortly, Olivia."

"Take your time," Olivia said, sitting down in the seat recently vacated by his mother. "Your mom seemed nice and not at all displeased to see me. Does she not know of your grandfather's concerns?"

"She knows. She doesn't care what my grandfather thinks or what I think."

"Interesting."

He tilted his head to one side, giving her a contemplative look. "Let's talk about your family for a change. I know you said your dad died. What about your mom? Is she alive? Is she in your life?"

"Yes, she's alive and well. We keep in touch at least once a week. She lives in San Diego where I grew up, so we don't see each other all that often, but we're still close."

"That's nice. So you're a southern California girl," he mused.

"That I am."

"San Diego has some great surf."

"I know. I used to surf when I was a teenager."

"Really?" He had to admit he was surprised. She didn't seem the type to do something so daring. "You know I'm not talking about body surfing. I'm talking about swimming out a half mile and catching a wave into shore."

She met his gaze head on. "I got my own surfboard when I was thirteen. I went out every weekend after that. My dad was a surfer. He taught me how to stand on a board when I was about five. I loved it as much as he did." Shadows filled her eyes. "I haven't been surfing since he died."

"He'd want you to go back out."

"Probably. And maybe I will—someday."

"Does your mom surf?"

"No." Olivia gave him a smile. "My mother is strictly a sit-on-the-beach woman, and that is usually under an umbrella. She's very fair and burns like crazy. Do you surf?"

"I have, but not for a while. The water is a lot colder up here."

"I wouldn't think you'd let a little cold water stop you."

"Maybe we'll have to hit the beach before you go back to New York."

"I don't think so. I'm here to work."

"Look at those ladies—do you really think they're hiding some juicy scandal?" he asked.

"Like I told your mom, I'm keeping an open mind."

"Does that open mind extend to me?" he challenged.

"What do you mean?"

"You made a snap judgment about me the second you heard I was a firefighter."

"I don't care that you're a firefighter. It doesn't matter to me how you choose to live your life."

"It might matter if you started to like me a little."

She gave him a somewhat nervous smile. "Even if I did like you a little, I'm only here for a few days, and my focus has to be on your grandmother. And knowing that you want to stop me from talking to her, I can't help wondering if your interest in me is really all that pure."

"Oh, it's not pure at all. I've had some pretty dirty thoughts." He laughed at the flood of color in her cheeks. "You, too?"

"Stop it, Colton," she said a little breathlessly. "We're not doing this here."

"Let's do it somewhere else then."

"You are impossible. This conversation is over."

"I think it's just getting started."

"I know what you're doing. You're trying to distract me. It's not going to work." She glanced at her watch. "I need to get the conversation started." She got up and walked over to the game table and waited until the hand was played. Then she said, "Ladies, are you ready to talk to me?"

"Of course we are," Eleanor said. "So sorry to make you wait, but I was winning for a change, and I didn't want to stop. Plus, you and Colton seemed to be enjoying each other's company."

Colton smiled as he saw Olivia's cheeks turn pink at his grandmother's sly smile and perceptive comment.

"It's fine," Olivia said, clearing her throat. "But I would like to begin now if we can."

"Let's move to the couches," Ginnie said, taking charge.

As the women moved from the table to the couches, Colton followed, taking a seat next to his grandmother. It made him feel like he was doing something to protect her, even if that something only amounted to sending Olivia a warning look. Not that she'd heed his look. There was determination in her green eyes. She'd come for her story, and she was going to get it.

His stomach turned over a little at that fierce gleam in her eyes. He really hoped there wasn't a story to be had, or at least not one that would be damning to his grandmother.

But that was ridiculous, he told himself. His grandmother was completely herself today. If she had a secret, she wouldn't reveal it now—would she?

Nine

---»»«« ---

Olivia pulled out a small notebook and a pen and glanced around the group, giving each of the women an encouraging smile. Ginnie Culpepper, the outgoing redhead sat next to the quieter brunette Constance Baker, and Eleanor introduced the fourth woman as Lucy Hodges, another one of the actors from the Center Stage Theater Group. Lucy was an attractive blonde who appeared to be at least seven or eight years younger than the other women.

"We spoke briefly yesterday about your theater group yesterday," Olivia said. "I'd like to know more about it."

"We were very good," Eleanor said with a proud smile. "But we were amateurs until we recruited Lucy, who was a legitimate actress, for our first play, *A Streetcar Named Desire.* Lucy played Blanche, and I played Stella. It was such a dark story with love, sex, desire, and infidelity. It was rather shocking but also exciting."

Olivia could clearly see the passion in Eleanor's eyes as she spoke about the theater.

"I loved being on stage," Eleanor continued. "It reminded me of when I was a little girl in Ireland. I was a child actress until I was ten. My mother was an actress, too. She took me with her to an audition once, and she didn't get the job, but I did. I think that always bothered her." Eleanor looked at Colton. "Did I ever tell you that?"

"No, you did not," he said, giving her a surprised look. "I had no idea you liked performing."

"It was a wonderful time," Eleanor said. "I got to play so many interesting characters. When I stepped on stage, I left my real life behind."

"It was great," Ginnie agreed. "And it was quite a change from our normal boring lives of carpools and bake sales and soccer games."

"Was it ever hard to go back to real life?" Olivia asked.

Eleanor immediately shook her head. "I was a mother with five children. I had a lot of fun playing someone else on stage, but I knew who I was when the curtain went down. Sometimes it took a few minutes to regroup, but by the time I got home I was *Mom* again."

"We only put on the shows during the summer," Constance added. "It was the one time of the year we could justify not volunteering at school. We were all stay-at-home moms with husbands who supported us. We were supposed to be home with the children."

Olivia nodded, thinking about her own mother and how she'd taken for granted that her mom would always be there when she came home from school. She wondered if her mom had ever wanted to step away from that role, if only for a few moments. Maybe she'd have to ask her.

Clearing her throat, she turned her attention back to the group. "What about Molly? Did she enjoy the plays even though she wasn't on stage?"

"Oh, she loved putting those costumes together," Eleanor said. "She used to make her children clothes, but they always had to be a certain way. With the costumes, she could make crazy patterns and shapes and they looked amazing."

"Why didn't you find another place to run the plays after the theater burned down?" she asked.

Her question created a tense silence, and she saw a flurry of looks move around the circle.

"It had just run its course," Eleanor said.

"We were all getting grief from our husbands and families for spending so much time at the theater, too," Ginnie put in. "It would have been difficult to get them to support starting over somewhere else and having to reinvent everything all over again."

"Some things just end," Constance said.

"It was sad, though," Lucy muttered.

Olivia looked around the group, a little puzzled at how the conversation had suddenly fizzled out. They'd been so excited to talk and now they seemed to have no words. "But what about the charity? Surely, your families and friends could support your efforts in that regard?"

"Not really," Ginnie muttered again.

"Ginnie," Constance said sharply.

Ginnie shrugged. "Well, it's true."

Olivia turned to Eleanor, sensing that the other women were not going to tell her anything else unless Eleanor took the lead. "Eleanor? How did you feel about stopping?"

Eleanor shifted in her seat. "I was unhappy that it had come to an end," she said carefully. "I knew there were more people we needed to help, but we weren't going to be able to do it, so we had to accept that."

Olivia sighed. She tried to be a patient person, knowing that sometimes you had to wait for a clue to reveal itself, but she only had a few days in San Francisco, and the clock was ticking.

"Okay, ladies. Here's the deal," she said. "Molly asked me to fly across the country to hear your stories. She told me I'd hear from amazing, courageous women, whose secrets were worth telling. So far I haven't heard one thing that would make me believe she was right. You're a group of interesting women, but you're holding something back. Now, you can either talk to me or I can go back to my job. It's your choice."

The women exchanged pointed glances, and there appeared to be some sort of silent communication going on.

Finally, Eleanor said, "You're right, Olivia. Molly wanted us to talk about something we all did together, something important. It's just been so long since we said it out loud."

"We never said it out loud," Ginnie interjected, drawing accompanying nods from Lucy and Constance.

"What is it?" Olivia asked, beginning to feel like she was finally getting somewhere.

Before any of the ladies could respond, Colton suddenly sat up a little straighter. "None of you has to say a word," he said forcefully. "If you don't want to talk to Olivia, you don't have to. Molly was the one who asked her to come here. It might have been her decision to speak, but that doesn't mean it has to be yours."

Olivia knew he was only protecting his grandmother, but she hated the way he'd put an abrupt stop to what had appeared to be a breakthrough.

Eleanor patted Colton's leg. "Thank you for the reminder, Colton. But actually, what you just said makes me want to talk to Olivia."

Colton frowned and muttered, "Why?"

"Because Molly can't talk, but I still can." Eleanor took a breath, then continued. "You asked about the charity, Olivia. Here's the truth. We used the theater group as a way to raise money to help women who were being abused by their husbands or boyfriends. Forty years ago domestic violence was not talked about the way it is now. And while it's still going on, and there are women still in trouble, there are more resources today. Back then there were very few options."

Olivia edged forward in her seat, anticipation tightening her nerves. "How exactly did you help them?"

"We tried to give them whatever they needed," Eleanor replied. "Every situation was different, but if what they needed was to get out of their home environment, we made that happen."

"You helped women get away from their abusers? How did you do that?"

"We gave them money and helped them plan their escape," Eleanor said.

"You mean, like an underground railroad?" she asked in amazement.

Eleanor nodded. "Yes. It was exactly like that."

Olivia saw the same shock she felt reflected on Colton's face. She'd never imagined that these four old ladies had done something so daring.

"Are you serious, Grandma?" he asked.

"Very serious, dear."

"It started with one person in trouble," Ginnie interjected. "It was a friend of ours. She needed money so she could go to her sister's house. Her husband controlled their bank account. She couldn't access it without his permission."

Olivia couldn't imagine being in that kind of situation, but she was a woman from a different generation.

"Most of us were also on budgets controlled by our husbands," Constance said. "We couldn't take the money out without telling them where it was going."

"And when we did try to tell our husbands, it didn't work," Lucy said. "I told my husband once that I needed to borrow a hundred dollars to help a friend, and he told me to send my friend to the police."

"We realized we had to do something to raise money," Ginnie added.

"I got the idea of putting on plays," Eleanor said. "Molly and I had just volunteered to run a school production, so we knew what was involved. And Constance's brother found us the theater. It all fell into place fairly easily."

"It just seems that way now," Lucy said. "I remember it being a lot of work."

"I suppose that's true," Eleanor said. "But it was for a good cause. We helped two women that first year. The next year it was four and by our fifth year I think we'd helped more than a dozen."

"Not everyone needed a lot," Constance said. "Some just needed help to find a job or bus money to get to their folks' house."

"And others needed more drastic measures," Ginnie said dramatically.

"Like what?" Olivia asked.

"We had to fake one woman's death," Eleanor said. "That was probably the toughest acting we ever did. But if she hadn't *died,* her husband would have hunted her down until he took his last breath."

"I was wondering what the men thought when the women just disappeared," Olivia said.

"I'm sure a few of the men looked for them, but we'd gotten some people to help us with creating false identities," Eleanor said. "Ginnie had a friend who did really good work on driver's licenses and passports."

"So these women started brand new lives." Olivia blew out a breath. "I must admit I am awed and amazed."

"So am I," Colton said. "But I don't understand why this was all done in secret. Why not get the police involved?"

"Most of the times the police weren't interested in helping, or the women couldn't produce any evidence. And if they complained, and their husbands heard about it, they suffered more pain. The women we helped were truly trapped," Eleanor said. "We were the last resort for them. And I can't lie. Sometimes it was dangerous to do what we did."

"What do you mean?" Colton asked. "What happened?"

"I drove a woman to a bus station one night," Eleanor said. "It was almost midnight. Her husband was supposed to be at work. But he showed up. It was just me and his wife on an empty platform. He put a knife to my neck. He told her to get in his car, or he would cut me. She started crying hysterically, and I was terrified. I can still feel that cool metal against my neck." Eleanor put a hand to her throat. "Thankfully, the bus came down the road at just the right moment. I guess the headlights distracted him. He loosened his grip on me, and I kicked him where it hurts the most. I grabbed her arm, and we ran like hell. That time we did go to the police station."

"Oh, my God," Olivia murmured.

"I can't believe you did that, Grandma," Colton said. "Did the guy go to jail?"

"He did," she said. "There were witnesses on the bus who were willing to testify to what they'd seen. That time we got lucky."

"You call that lucky?" Colton asked in disbelief.

Eleanor gave him a smile. "Yes, because she survived and not everyone did. However, after that incident, some of the women in our group got nervous. They were afraid that they would end up in the same situation, and it wouldn't turn out as well. Our volunteer support began to dwindle."

"And our husbands wanted us to be done," Ginnie put in. "At least the husbands that knew about it."

"Did Grandpa know?" Colton cut in.

Eleanor drew a deep breath. "Eventually. Not at the very beginning. I knew he wouldn't like it."

"Did you tell him what happened at the bus station?" Colton asked.

"Later, I did," she admitted. "He was not happy. He didn't want me to risk my life. And he was also worried about our children being in danger. I didn't think that was really possible, but one day when Jack was about eighteen he got jumped by a bunch of older boys. He was beat up and they took his wallet. We thought it was a robbery, but when Jack told me the identity of one of the kids, I wondered if there was a connection, because I'd helped get that kid's mother out of town. But she hadn't taken her son with her, because he was seventeen, and he didn't want to go." She paused. "Jack told me that the boy said something to him about payback, but he didn't know what it meant. I was afraid I did. I realized then that I couldn't jeopardize my family, no matter how good the cause. I was going to quit, but a week later the fire destroyed the theater, and the decision was made for all of us."

Olivia thought about Eleanor's words and a question arose in her mind. "Was the fire deliberately set?"

Eleanor shrugged. "They said it started with a cigarette in the backroom. It was late at night. People used to go back there to smoke. But I always wondered—"

"If someone wanted to stop you," Olivia said.

"Yes, I wondered that. I also wondered if it was the payback the boy was talking about."

"If it was payback, then someone figured out what you and your friends were doing," Colton said.

"It's possible," Eleanor conceded. "But there were too many of us to take out."

"So they took out your theater," Olivia said.

"In some ways, we felt like we were quitters," Ginnie said. "At least I did. I felt guilty about walking away, but we didn't know what else to do."

"We've kept it all secret for forty years," Eleanor said. "Not just because we didn't want to bring danger to our families, but because we had to protect the women that were in hiding. If what we had done was revealed, someone might be able to track them down."

"But Molly thought it was time for us to tell the story," Constance said.

"However, we can't name names," Eleanor said. "We can't even have you use our own names, because then there would be a link between us and the women we saved.

"Is there anyone you helped who might be willing to talk, perhaps someone whose husband has since died?" Olivia asked.

"We thought there might be someone when Molly wrote you the letter," Eleanor said. "But that has since changed. We're happy to tell you everything we know, but we can't give you names."

Which meant she would really have a difficult time getting her book published. She thought for a moment. The ladies had just thrown up a huge obstacle, but there had to be a way around it, because she was quite caught up in the idea of revealing a secret underground railroad that ran through a community theater run by a bunch of housewives. The idea had high concept written all over it. She could probably get a deal on just the tag line alone. But the book would need many more details, and she couldn't promise what she couldn't deliver.

Maybe she could deliver something. Maybe she could do her own investigating, find someone who had absolutely nothing left to lose and convince her to help with the book.

"Do you keep in touch with any of the women?" she asked.

"Oh, no," Eleanor said. "That would have been too dangerous."

"So you don't really know if there isn't someone who might be willing to speak to me?"

"No, but in order to find that out, we'd have to give you their names, and we can't do that."

"Looks like you've hit a dead end," Colton put in.

She frowned at his comment. "I don't quit that easily. I need to think about all this."

"It's a lot to take in," Eleanor agreed. "And we do appreciate you wanting to help tell our stories. As we face the twilight of our years—"

"Twilight?" Ginnie interrupted with a snort. "It's after midnight for some of us."

"As I was saying," Eleanor continued, giving her friend a pointed look. "We've been debating this for some time, ever since Molly brought it up. We never thought to go public, but we know that our time is running out, and if our story would inspire other women to step up, to help, then maybe there's some way to tell it without hurting anyone."

"I don't think there's a way," Colton said, his deep masculine voice drawing everyone's attention to him. "As you said before, it's not just the women you have to protect, it's yourselves. Twilight or midnight or whatever, you're all still alive, and you have families who care about you, and who you don't want to put in any danger or under any kind of spotlight. You were wise to keep this secret for so many years. I don't see why you would want to change that now."

Olivia knew he had a point, but he was thinking like a grandson, and she was thinking like a writer, a revealer of the truth. "It's not your decision," she told him. "Don't you understand that these women have been silenced by men for the last forty years. If they want to speak, they should be able to speak."

"I'm not stopping them from talking. I'm just pointing out the hard truth."

"The hard truth as you see it," she said, anger running through her. "This isn't your business, Colton."

"My grandmother is my business, and my family, too, and I'll protect them, just like they protected everyone else."

She blew out a breath of frustration. It was difficult to argue with someone taking such a high moral ground. But she could turn his words around, she quickly realized. "You run into burning buildings to save people," she reminded him. "You do that at great cost to yourself. You could die trying to protect someone else, and if you did die, your family would mourn you. They would grieve for you." Her words got stronger as the pain of a decade ago coursed through her. "But that wouldn't stop you from doing what was needed for the greater good, right? Why do you think these ladies are any different?"

Her challenge hung in the air—the tense, crackling air that swirled around them.

She could feel the ladies watching their exchange, but her gaze was on Colton's face. His dark blue eyes glittered with anger, and she could see him trying to formulate a rebuttal, but he had none.

"I think she got you, Colton," Eleanor said, amusement in her eyes.

His frown deepened. "She didn't get me. What I do as a firefighter is completely different from this situation."

"Well, you both made excellent points," Eleanor said. "Maybe we need to think about it a bit more."

Olivia didn't know if more thought would work in her favor or Colton's, but hopefully these four women who had risked so much forty years ago would be willing to take another risk now.

"I hope you will think about it," she said. "I don't want to push, but I only have a few days off to work on this, and I know it was important to Molly." She had to play the Molly card, because somehow Molly had convinced them that she should send the letter in the first place. The women had been on board then. They'd just gotten cold feet.

"It was important to Molly," Eleanor said, a little sigh following her words. "I hope she can get better and speak to you, Olivia."

"So do I," she said. "I went through the journals she left me, but they end rather abruptly after the birth of her daughter. I don't know if I'm missing some books or if she just stopped journaling her life, but I do know she gave me the books for a reason. Does anyone know if she has more journals at her house?"

Eleanor stared back to her. "I'm not sure. I know she was putting things together for you, so it's possible. Although it's also possible she got busy and didn't have time to write more."

Somehow she didn't think that was the case. "I know that's a logical answer, but I've been researching people's lives for a while now. I've done lots of interviews. The one thing I know for sure is that the real story begins when people stop talking. And Molly stopped talking in her journals, and I want to know why."

"Maybe she just got tired of writing stuff down," Colton put in. "You're looking for a mystery under every rock."

"And you're not being helpful."

"Good, because I wasn't trying to be," he countered.

Eleanor smiled at them. "You two don't have to be on opposite sides."

From what Olivia could see, that's exactly where they had to be. Colton muttered something under his breath and crossed his arms in front of his chest.

"I know what you need, Olivia," Eleanor said after a moment. "Colton, would you get my purse? It's on the floor by the Bridge table."

Colton got up and retrieved Eleanor's purse, shooting Olivia warning daggers as he did so.

She ignored him. She was here to deal with his grandmother, not him.

Eleanor opened her bag and pulled out a key. "This is the key to Molly's house. You should go there and see what else you can learn about her."

Ginnie cleared her throat. "Are you sure that's a good idea, Eleanor?"

"Molly might not want that," Lucy agreed.

"I think that's exactly what she would want," Constance put in, casting a dissenting opinion. She and Eleanor looked at each other for a long moment. "She wanted Olivia to know the story."

"Yes," Eleanor said. "I think you should go to Molly's place and see if you can find any more journals or anything else."

Olivia got up and walked over to the couch to take the key from Eleanor's hands. "Thank you. I promise not to disturb anything."

"Of course you won't," Eleanor said. "I have no doubt about that."

"Well, I do have doubts," Colton interjected as he rose. "I'm going with you, Olivia."

"That's not necessary."

"I think it is."

And she didn't think she would get very far trying to argue

with him. "What's the address?" she asked Eleanor.

"One-Forty-Seven Halliwell Avenue."

"I'll check it out now, and then I'd like to speak to you all again."

"We'll be here tomorrow afternoon from noon to two," Eleanor said. "And we'll think about what we want to do moving forward."

"I'd appreciate that, and while I realize that you all have something to lose, and I do not, I believe your story would be very inspiring to a lot of people, not only to those who feel trapped, but to those who want to help but are afraid."

"We felt young and invincible back then," Ginnie said, a touch of sadness in her voice. "The years slowly steal that feeling away."

"Only if we let them," Eleanor said, her chin in the air. "We'll think about it, Olivia."

"Thanks."

"Mom will be back soon to give you a ride home," Colton said. "Do you mind if I go with Olivia, Grandma?"

Eleanor smiled. "I think you two will make a great team."

"And I think you all should have your heads examined for opening up this can of worms. But I do appreciate the amazing things you did. So let me do my part by making sure the secrets you've kept all these years are only disseminated in the right way."

"I trust you, Colton," Eleanor said. "I guess I'll see you both tomorrow."

"You'll definitely see me," Olivia said, hoping she could shake Colton in the meantime, but she had a feeling he would be dogging her heels for a while to come.

When they walked outside, Colton stopped on the steps and drew in a long, deep breath. "Holy shit," he said. "That was crazy. My grandmother was running an underground railroad for abused women? She was helping them escape, faking deaths...what the hell, Olivia?"

She had to admit her mind was spinning, too, and she wasn't related to the woman. She could understand why Colton would feel shaken. "If you want to stay here and talk to her about it, that's fine with me."

"No, I'm coming with you. You're not getting rid of me that easily."

"Then let's go."

As they walked toward the parking lot, Colton said, "You'll have to drive. I came with my mom and grandmother."

"I would have driven anyway. This is my deal, not yours."

"I'm making it mine. I'm going to watch out for my grandmother's interests."

She didn't comment as she unlocked the car doors and slid behind the wheel.

Colton got into the passenger seat and buckled up. "Nice car."

"It's a rental."

"What do you usually drive?"

"I don't drive. I live in New York City. I walk and I take subways."

"And you don't miss being in control?"

"Actually, it's the one thing I do really miss, the ability to drive to the store and buy as many groceries as I want, because I don't have to carry them home. But there are so many other advantages to living in the city that it's worth the inconvenience."

"I've never been to New York. What's it like?"

"Very energized," she said. "Everyone is in a hurry to get somewhere. It's a place where people go to make their dreams come true, and you can feel that impatience in the air."

"You paint a nice picture. You must be a writer."

"I'm trying to be. If only I could get one stubborn ass firefighter out of the way…"

"Maybe you should think of me as a partner instead of an opponent. My grandmother thinks we'd make a good team."

"Yeah, well, she probably adores you."

"Give me a chance; I might grow on you, too."

She looked away from his sexy grin, knowing that he was already growing on her, and that was a complication she didn't need.

Ten

Colton smiled as Olivia sped down the street. "I like a woman who isn't afraid of a little speed," he said approvingly.

"I'll bet you do." She shot him a quick look. "So what do you think about what we just learned?"

That was not an easy question to answer. "I'm still processing. I'm having a difficult time seeing my sweet grandmother, who made cookies for me everyday when I came home from school, as the operative of a secretive underground railroad."

"Just goes to show that you never know people as well as you think you do."

"I certainly never imagined she'd been so daring, so bold in her life, and what's even more difficult to understand is how my grandfather let it happen. As long as I've known them, he's been very protective, and I rarely saw her do anything without him."

"Or maybe you just didn't notice."

"Or maybe I didn't notice," he agreed.

"You were a kid. Kids are remarkably self-centered. But as far as your grandfather knowing about the railroad, the ladies were a bit evasive about when the men in their lives knew what they were doing. Maybe your grandfather didn't find out for a while. He might have thought Eleanor was just living out her acting dreams, when she was actually doing something rather dangerous."

"You think?" he asked dryly, still cringing at the thought of his grandmother being held at knifepoint by some crazed maniac. "She could have been killed at that bus stop."

"She could have been, but she wasn't. She's lived a long and happy life, and it sounds like she made it possible for other women to do the same."

"You're right."

"Wow, I never thought I'd hear those words come out of your mouth," she said dryly.

"Don't get used to it."

"Your grandmother didn't get agitated or upset while we were speaking, Colton. She was happy to tell her story, and not just to me, to you. She liked that you were there. She wanted you to catch a glimpse of the woman she used to be."

"It was quite a glimpse. However, I still can't help thinking that the women are embellishing what they did. It was a long time ago. Maybe they got a few women to safe places and just made it sound like more."

"Faking someone's death sounds like a lot more."

"True. But that crowd likes to be dramatic."

"I don't think they were being dramatic. If anything, they were underplaying what they did. Didn't you see how many times they looked at each other, as if unsure of how much to say? I don't think we've heard the whole story yet."

He could hear the excitement in her voice. "You are totally caught up in this."

"Of course I am, and you are, too. You're as curious as I am to know more about their adventures. I'm just hoping there are some answers in Molly's house. She was the driving force behind bringing me here and getting the story down on paper. Hopefully, she was putting together materials at home to further that purpose."

"It would be nice," he said, but somehow he didn't think it would be that easy. "Turn right at the next light and then take an immediate left. Parking is tough in this neighborhood, but hopefully we'll get lucky." He smiled as he said the word *lucky*, thinking that for the past few days his luck had all been bad.

"What is this neighborhood called?" Olivia asked, as she drove slowly down a crowded street of retail shops and cafes.

"This is the Haight and you're coming up on the intersection of Haight and Ashbury, made famous in the sixties for hippies, flower children and the peace movement. While the neighborhood has changed since then, you'll still find tattoo parlors and bong shops amid the clothing stores and bars."

"It's charming," Olivia said, shooting him a smile. "I like eclectic neighborhoods."

"So do I," he admitted. "One reason I love this city so much."

"And you'd never want to live anywhere else?"

"I wouldn't say never, but I'm happy where I am. And I like having the opportunity to protect some of these cool old buildings."

"Is your fire station in this neighborhood?"

"No. I work closer to downtown and the industrial district."

"Skyscraper firefighting must be terrifying."

"It presents a different challenge, but the worse fires are usually in the warehouses where there are more combustible chemicals stored."

"That's how you got hurt," she said, shooting him a quick look.

"Yeah." Wanting to change the subject, he said, "Speaking of cool buildings, see the brick building over there?" He pointed to the right.

She nodded. "Ashbury Studios. Is it famous?"

"I think it will be someday. My brother Sean runs the place. He's a musician as well as a producer and now a business owner. His girlfriend runs a dance studio on the top floor."

"Really? He's a musician? I thought it was all about firefighting for the Callaways."

"Sean never had any interest in firefighting. He was always about the music. I think he felt a little disconnected from the family because of that, but he's come around more lately. And my dad has eased up on him, accepted the fact that he has one son who is not going to follow in his footsteps."

"Did your father pressure you to be a firefighter?"

"There was definitely an expectation that I'd at least consider firefighting, which was fine with me. I was fascinated by what my dad did from when I was very small. I loved hearing the sirens, watching him jump on the truck. I liked the firefighter picnics and the way everyone stood together. Firefighters had their own family and their firefighter family."

"That all sounds good, but I think you've skipped over the danger part," she said dryly.

He tipped his head. "I'll admit that I didn't realize the demands the job would put on me physically, mentally and emotionally. You can't really train for all of that. You just have to live it. But while I love to play the hero firefighter, to be honest, not every day at work is that exciting. We have some slow, boring days, too."

"Really? Even in a big city like San Francisco?"

"Even then." He paused, seeing a parking spot up ahead. "Let's grab that spot. Molly's house is a block away, but I don't know if we'll find anything closer."

"That's fine. I wouldn't mind a little walk around the neighborhood when we're done. But right now I just want to get to Molly's and see if there's anything to be found."

He smiled, seeing the purpose in her eyes as she maneuvered the rental car into the typically small San Francisco parking spot. Olivia was even prettier when she was focused and determined. He wondered if this trip to Molly's was going to pay off in some way. And whether or not that payoff was something he needed to worry about.

If there was nothing to be found at Molly's, maybe that would be the end of it. His grandfather could rest easy. His grandmother could play Bridge with her friends and not think about the past, and he would have done right by both of them.

On the other hand, finding nothing meant Olivia would head back to New York, and he wasn't ready to say goodbye to her yet.

--->>><<---

They walked into Molly's house a little before four o'clock. It was a two-story, two-bedroom home tucked between two large apartment buildings and with the late afternoon shadows, everything about the house was dark. As Colton stepped into the entry, he thought the house smelled like an old person lived there. Thick scents of lavender, vanilla and something he couldn't identify hung in the air. Heavy drapes covered the windows, adding to the depressing atmosphere. It was as if the house had given up hope on the occupant ever coming back.

Maybe Molly wasn't coming back. He felt sad at that thought.

"We need some light," Olivia said, turning on the hallway switch.

Like many San Francisco homes, the building was narrow and a long hallway led from the front door to the kitchen at the back of the house, passing by the living room and dining room on the way.

Colton stepped into the living room first and pulled back the drapes to let in more light. "Better."

"Yes," Olivia agreed, following him into the room. "Although, now I can see just how much stuff there is here."

Olivia wasn't exaggerating. The living room was filled to the brim with antiques, a sofa from another era, an ornate glass-topped coffee table, mahogany bookcases and end tables. There didn't appear to be any sense of design. Molly had just filled her home with things that she liked.

Olivia picked up a pillow with a cat's face on it. "I'm seeing a theme. Cat pillows, cat figurines, cat pictures on the walls...is there a real cat?"

"I don't smell one or see one, but we haven't checked out the whole house. It would be a little surprising if she doesn't have one given her obvious love affair with the furry creatures."

"I've never been that excited about cats. I prefer dogs."

"Me, too. Do you have a dog?"

"No, I live in a very small studio apartment in Manhattan. I can barely fit myself in there. And I often travel for Philip, either to do research or run his book tours, so I'd feel guilty having a pet. Someday perhaps. What about you?"

"Same. Not the right time. I have what is probably a slightly bigger apartment than yours, but my shifts are long and I'm gone for multiple days at a time." He paused, checking out the bookcase. "Molly is a fan of detective and spy fiction. And it looks like she was even thinking about writing her own books."

Olivia nodded, as he pulled out a book on writing. "She's probably had this story in her head for a long time but just couldn't figure out a way to put it on paper." She looked around the room and sighed. "I'm not sure where to start. There are so many things in this room; I can only imagine what the rest of the house looks like."

"It's cluttered, but it is neat. Molly is not a dirty person. You should see some of the places I've been in. It's amazing what conditions people can live in, especially older people, who obviously need help but don't have it." He paused. "But I'm surprised you're confused about where to begin. Isn't this what you do? Aren't you used to going through people's garbage and dirty laundry?"

She frowned. "You like to make my job sound more sordid than it is, Colton. I'm not a tabloid reporter."

"So you've never looked through someone's trash can?"

Her lips tightened. "I wish I could say I haven't done that, but on occasion, yes. This, however, feels different in some way."

"Maybe because Molly isn't a celebrity or a politician or someone famous. This is her private home, her personal life."

"That's true. I am more used to working with people who have a public face, and there's a price that comes with fame. When Philip picks a subject for a biography, the subject of the book knows that they'll get more fame from telling their story, so in those cases I don't feel bad pushing past their reluctance to tell me everything."

"But Molly is different." He liked seeing the conflict in Olivia's eyes. It told him she had a moral code that he could respect.

"Yes, Molly is different. But she wanted me to come to San Francisco and tell her story, so I have to believe she'd be okay with me looking around her home. And I don't think Eleanor would have given me the key if she had any doubts about my motives. So, I need to start figuring out what's important." She paused in front of a wall laden with framed photographs and pointed to one. "I met this guy earlier today."

He crossed the room to see the picture she was referring to.

Molly had her arm around the waist of a young man in a Navy uniform. Judging by Molly's appearance, the photo was at least twenty plus years old. "Who's the guy?"

"Peter Harper, Molly's son. I met him at the hospital when I went to see Molly. He looks a lot older now."

"I didn't know you'd gone to see Molly. Was there any change in her condition?"

"No. She was asleep or unconscious, whatever you want to call it. She looked very fragile, old, pale, and her skin was cold to the touch." She paused. "Her letter to me was so vibrant, so full of hope and desire. It's strange to think she wrote it only a few weeks ago. How quickly everything changed."

"What did her son have to say?"

"He wasn't very happy to see me in Molly's room."

"Why not?"

"Well, apparently your grandfather isn't the only one who thinks a book about Molly's past is not a good idea."

"Her son must have the same protective instinct."

"I guess. I feel like I'm missing something, Colton. It's right here, but I can't see it."

Her words sent an uneasy feeling through his body. "Maybe it's not here, and you can't accept the idea that there's nothing more to find."

"Nice try," she said making a face at him. "But I can't come to that conclusion until I check out the rest of the house."

They walked through the dining room together, which held nothing of personal interest. The kitchen at the back of the house was small and neat; the only thing at all intriguing was the cupboard filled with teas from around the world. Apparently, Molly liked to mix it up when it came to hot beverages.

Leaving the kitchen, they went up the stairs to the second floor, which housed two bedrooms. The smaller room appeared to be a combination guest room and office. The double bed was covered in papers, magazines, and what appeared to be shopping catalogs. Next to the bed was a desk that was stacked high with file folders and bills. It didn't appear that Molly liked to throw anything away.

"There could be something here," he said.

"Why don't you start in this room, and I'll check Molly's room," Olivia suggested. "We'll be able to cover more ground faster if we split up."

It was a good plan, but he felt a little reluctant to let Olivia out of his sight, although he wasn't sure why.

Olivia was gone before he had a chance to suggest they go through each room together. Resigning himself to letting her take the lead, he moved over to the desk and started going through the stacks of folders.

Fifteen minutes later he was about to call it a day, having seen nothing more personal than bills, receipts and retail offers. Molly had discount coupons that had expired three years ago. It was clear that she hadn't gone through anything in a while.

He was down to the last drawer in the desk when he finally found something worth looking at. There was a stack of personal letters, about six in all, held together by a rubber band. What was unusual about the envelopes was they boasted no return address, and the postmarks appeared to be from all over the country. He wondered if these were letters from some of the women they'd helped escape.

His pulse sped up as he thought about his grandmother's story. He'd been trying to tell himself it wasn't true or it was exaggerated, but now he wasn't so sure. Not that he'd even looked at the letters, but there was something about the feminine handwriting and the way Molly had kept them together that told him they were important.

He pulled out the top letter and opened the envelope. The first words confirmed his suspicions.

I know you told me never to write but it's been four years now, and I feel like maybe it's okay. I just want you to know that I'm safe and I'm happy and I've actually met someone else. Yesterday I told him about my past, not any names of course, not anything about you and the other wonderful women, but I did tell him about the man who almost killed me. I was afraid he would reject me or demand a name or something. But you know what he did? He opened his arms to me, and he said he would protect me forever.

That's it. No questions. No worries that he was getting in the middle of something complicated. No comments that maybe I brought it on myself.

You were right, Molly. Everything did turn out okay. Better than okay, and it's all because of you and Eleanor.

I'm sending you this while I'm on vacation. It's coming from a place I've never been and never will be again. I guess I'm still a little paranoid.

Love always,
B.T.

Colton's stomach was churning when he folded the note and slipped it back into the envelope. Here was the evidence that Olivia was looking for. For a split second, he actually thought about not showing it to her. But he couldn't do that. He wouldn't just be betraying Olivia's trust, he would also be betraying his grandmother. She'd given Olivia the key to the house.

But wouldn't he also be protecting his grandmother? She might not be thinking that clearly. And he had made a promise to his grandfather.

Still…the argument was weak. His grandmother had been perfectly clear in her storytelling. And even if he tried to hide the letters, what would be the benefit? There could be more letters. There could be any number of things that they might find in this house.

Taking the letters with him, he went down the hall to Molly's bedroom. The room was empty, but there was a light on in the large walk-in closet. When he entered the closet, he saw Olivia standing on a stepstool, precariously stretching toward a box on a high shelf.

"Do you need some help?" he asked.

He'd barely gotten the words out when the box came tumbling down on Olivia's head, knocking her off the stool.

He caught her around the waist, managing to prevent her from hitting the floor.

"Dammit," she swore, coughing as a flurry of dust surrounded them.

"A thank you would be nicer."

"Thanks." She slipped out of his arms and knelt on the floor to look at the contents that had fallen out of the box.

"More photographs," she said. "I wonder why she tucked them away."

"Maybe she just had too many to display."

He squatted down next to her and reached into the box, picking up a baby bracelet. He read the words aloud, *"Baby Girl Harper, 1988."* He thought about that for a moment. "This couldn't belong to Molly's daughter. She would have been closer to my dad's age than mine."

"Right. I was born in 1988, so this person would be the same age as me. Perhaps it belonged to Molly's granddaughter, Peter's daughter."

"That would make sense." He tossed the bracelet back into the box and watched Olivia skim through some pictures. "Anything interesting?"

"This looks like Molly with her kids. Peter appears to be about eight and Francine about three."

"No one looks very happy," Colton said as she handed him the photo to peruse. "I can relate. When I was a kid I hated taking family pictures. It took forever to get eight kids to stop fighting or crying and look good at the same time."

"I can't even imagine. I'm an only child, so photographs just involved me and my parents."

"Sounds a lot more civilized." He handed her back the photo, seeing a hint of pain flit through Olivia's eye. The family picture probably reminded her of the loss of her father. Here he was complaining about having to take family photos when she'd lost one-third of her family. He felt like an idiot. "Are you okay?"

"I'm fine. This isn't about me. I just need to stay focused."

He wondered if she ever let herself think about her dad or her past. It seemed to him that she'd put all those memories away. Maybe that made it easier, and who was he to judge how to deal with the grief of losing a parent?

Olivia handed him some photos to look through. "You take this stack; I'll take the other."

"Okay," he said, running through the photos, which appeared to be more family shots.

"Do you know what happened to Molly's husband?" Olivia asked after a moment.

"No."

Olivia turned to another photo and then paused. "He was a cop," she said, surprise in her voice. "Look, he's in uniform here."

Colton nodded as she showed him the photo. "My grandfather probably knew him then. Cops and firefighters have always been tight in this town, although the relationship can be adversarial, too."

Olivia stared at him with a question in her eyes.

"What?" he asked.

"If Molly was married to a cop, why didn't she ask him to help the women? Why go around the police force when she had her own personal officer in the house?"

He thought about that for a moment. "Maybe there was nothing he could do. Or maybe he had already passed away? We should check the dates of his death and the running of the railroad."

"Good idea." She gave him an approving smile. "You're actually helping me. I didn't think that was your intention when you volunteered to come with me."

"You know what they say about keeping your enemies close."

Her eyes sparkled. "So now we're enemies?"

"I'm not sure what we are," he said bluntly.

Her tongue darted out and she nervously licked her lips. "It doesn't matter what we are to each other. I'll be gone in a week."

"Yeah, that's what I keep telling myself."

Her gaze clung to his for a long moment, and then she blew out a breath. "We should get back to the photos."

"Do you have a boyfriend, Olivia?"

"Not at the moment. Why?"

"Just curious."

"I've been too busy for dating. What about you? Do you have a girlfriend?"

"No, too busy. We're a lot alike."

"Maybe we're just two people who aren't very good in relationships," she suggested.

"Or maybe we just haven't found anyone worth having a relationship with," he countered.

"So back to work," she said, pointedly changing the subject.

"There's nothing in this stack."

"I don't have anything interesting, either." She dug around in the box to see if there was anything there besides pictures. She pulled out a piece of yellowed paper. "Look at this—a birth certificate."

"For who?"

It says Baby Girl Harper, June 7, 1988." She sucked in a quick breath. "That's weird."

"Why is that weird? It matches the baby bracelet I saw earlier."

She looked up at him. "It's weird, because that's my birthday."

He stared back at her in surprise. "Really? That's an odd coincidence."

"Right—it's a coincidence." Her gaze moved back to the birth certificate. She swallowed hard. "It says the mother's name is Francine Harper. The father's name is blank. So the girl wasn't Peter's daughter. She was Francine's."

He saw her chest heave with her next breath, and her green eyes were suddenly very bright, so bright they reminded him of someone else—of Molly.

His pulse began to race. A crazy thought came into his brain. And judging by the bewildered expression on Olivia's face, she was thinking the same thing. But how could it be possible? Olivia had told him about her parents, about her family. She'd never mentioned...

Olivia suddenly shook her head. "No," she said loudly, forcefully. "No."

"Olivia?" he questioned. "What are you thinking?"

"Something ridiculous and out of this world."

"Why don't you tell me and let me judge how ridiciulous it is?"

She didn't answer for a long moment as emotions ran through

her eyes—everything from fear to anger to shock. "Olivia?" he pressed. "Talk to me."

"I was adopted, Colton. I was adopted when I was two days old, and I've never had any idea who my biological parents are." She blew out a breath. "Maybe I just found out."

Eleven

"Okay, hold on," Colton said. "Just because you were adopted--"

"And I have the same birthday—"

"That still doesn't mean that you're this baby girl." But he had to admit it was a huge coincidence.

He could see the wheels turning in Olivia's head as she pondered the significance of the birth certificate.

"It would make sense," she said. "This could be why Molly chose me to tell her story, why she invited me to come here. I always wondered."

"You're making some big jumps. You've got to slow down and think about this. You're not the only adopted kid born on this day."

"I know you're trying to be logical, Colton, but my gut is telling me that there's a connection between Molly and me."

"Why didn't you tell me you were adopted before this?"

"Because I don't think about it. I was a baby when it happened. I don't know any other life, any other family than the one who raised me."

"When did you find out you were adopted?"

"I don't remember not knowing, so they must have told me when I was really little. My parents tried for twelve years to have a baby, and they said they were so blessed to get me. I had a wonderful childhood filled with love."

"And your mom never told you anything about your biological parents?"

"It was a closed adoption. She had no information."

"And you never thought about tracking down your real mother?"

"Of course I thought about it. Even though I loved my parents, I would wonder now and then about my birth mother. The feeling got stronger as I got older, especially when I was angry with my parents." Raw pain filled her eyes. "Then my dad died, and I thought in some bizarre way that maybe wondering about my real parents was responsible for him dying." She put up a hand as he opened his mouth. "I know my thoughts didn't kill him. But emotionally I felt like I'd betrayed him in some way. And after that, I certainly couldn't leave my mom to go looking for my real mother. She was devastated. She'd lost her husband; she couldn't lose me."

"I get that," he said, admiring her loyalty to the woman who had raised her.

"What I don't understand, though, is if Molly is my grandmother, why wouldn't she just say so? Why would she try to lure me here with a story?"

"She might not have been sure you'd come, so she wanted to pique your interest without putting all her cards on the table."

"Why wouldn't I come?"

"I don't know. If you are this child, and that's still a big question mark, we don't know the circumstances of your adoption. What happened to your mother? Why did she give you up? Why was the adoption closed? Maybe in the answers to those questions, it will all become clear."

Olivia stared at him with a grim look in her eyes. "Do you think Eleanor knows I'm Molly's granddaughter? Is that why she gave me the key?"

He'd wondered that himself. "We could certainly ask her, but you might be better served going straight to someone in the Harper family. Peter should know the details of his sister's pregnancy."

"When I introduced myself to Peter and said I was the writer his mother had written to, he looked at me like he hated me. What if I am his niece?" She paused. "I feel a little sick."

"It's the shock. You need to breathe."

"I can't breathe in here. It's too stuffy."

"We'll take the box and the letters to your hotel room," he said, standing up.

"Wait, what letters?"

"Oh, right." He leaned over and grabbed the stack of letters he'd dropped by the door when he'd caught Olivia. "These letters. I found them in the other room. They appear to be notes from some of the women who were saved by Molly and the others."

Her eyes lit up. "Really? That's amazing. I didn't think we'd find anything about them."

"I only read one. You can go through the rest later."

She got to her feet. "Good idea."

As she finished speaking, she swayed a little, and he instinctively put his hands on her shoulders to steady her. "Easy. You okay?"

"I feel a little shaky."

"Understandable. But try to remember we don't know anything definitive yet. All we have right now is a birth certificate with no baby name and your birth date. That's it. You're going to talk to Peter later and get more information. One step at a time."

She nodded and let out a breath, then stepped away from him. "You're right. Thanks for talking me off the ledge."

"Anytime. Let's go back to your hotel."

"Okay."

They turned off the lights as they went downstairs and out the front door, carefully locking the door behind them.

Once outside, Colton drew in several deep breaths of air and saw Olivia doing the same thing. While he wasn't as personally affected by what they'd found at Molly's house, he had to admit to feeling a little shaken up himself. He was still trying to come to terms with Eleanor's brush with danger trying to rescue an abused woman. Now this birth certificate had just thrown another curve into the story.

"I feel like I'm dreaming," Olivia said, as they walked down the street and paused at the corner for a red light. "Any minute I'm going to wake up."

A loud truck came through the intersection, leaving a trail of exhaust in its wake.

Olivia grimaced and coughed as the smoke swept over them.

"I think that was fate telling you *this* is your real life," he said with a grin.

"I wish fate would have found a less smelly way to do that," she said, wrinkling her nose.

After they crossed the street, Colton held out his hand. "Give me the car keys."

"You're not registered to drive my rental car."

"No one will know."

"They will if we get in an accident."

"We're not going to get in an accident. You're not much of a rule-breaker, are you?"

"I'm really not. And your fingers are broken."

"On my left hand. I can still drive."

"I don't know."

"Olivia, I'm not letting you take the wheel. You're upset. You think you're dreaming. Do I really need to keep arguing with you?"

She reluctantly handed him her keys. "Don't get stopped."

"Don't worry. Everything is going to be fine."

"You're obviously not a worrier, or you'd know that that reassurance means nothing to me. People have been telling me not to worry my entire life. It has never helped."

"Well, I prefer to live in the moment, and I think for at least the next hour or two, you should try to do the same."

"I don't know how."

"I'll teach you."

She sent him a doubtful look. "You're going to teach me how to live in the moment?"

"I am. And I think we should start now. We need a break from Molly and my grandmother and the past, don't you think?"

"I could take a little break," she agreed.

"Good. Instead of heading straight back to the hotel, why don't we get a drink?" He glanced down at his watch and realized he knew just where to go. "It's after five. It's time for happy hour."

"I can't believe it's that late. Where did the day go?"

He shrugged. "We spent the day in the past. Now we come back to the present. And I know where we should go. My buddy

Adam is having a birthday happy hour today. I did promise I would stop by. Why don't you come with me?"

She hesitated, giving him a doubtful look. "I don't know. I'm not really in the mood for a party with a bunch of guys."

"There will be women there, too. And it's not a party, just a few drinks at a bar. It will give you a chance to regroup before you have to make your next move."

"Which is probably to speak to Peter again. I'm sure he'll be thrilled."

"You'll do it tomorrow after you have a chance to think about how you want to approach him."

"I should consider the best way to do that," she admitted.

"So it sounds like for now happy hour is a good idea."

"I guess it is," she muttered as he opened the door for her. "Are you sure you want to take me, though? You could just drop me off at my hotel and go meet your friends. I don't want to intrude."

"Trust me. With these guys, the more the merrier, especially when it comes to beautiful women."

She flushed a little at his comment. "You can be very charming when you want to be."

"I wasn't trying to charm you, just stating a fact. Give me the box. I'll put it in the back."

"That's perfect," she said, obviously eager to hand over the information that had just shattered her life. "I don't want to deal with that for a while."

"You don't have to."

Colton drove a little too fast, Olivia thought, as he took a sharp turn on a corner, but she didn't feel at all nervous with him. He was confident, capable, and completely in control, and right now she felt none of those things. She needed to get a grip, stop the dizzying waves of uncertainty that kept running through her every time the image of the birth certificate flashed through her mind.

Looking for a distraction, she said, "So where is this happy hour at?"

"Brady's Two—as in the number two. The original Brady's Bar and Grill burned down last year. It was owned by a former firefighter, and the department passed a bucket around several times to get enough cash to help Brady rebuild. It's one of our hangouts."

"It's nice that you helped him get back on his feet. Ironic that a firefighters' bar would burn in a fire, though."

He nodded, a grim tightness to his lips. "Yeah, it wasn't so much ironic as deliberate. It's a long story, some of which involved my sister Emma."

"How so?"

"She was the fire investigator on the case. But eventually she learned that that fire, as well as some others around the city, were being set to get her attention."

"Oh, my God, that sounds creepy."

"It was a bad time, but she's okay now."

"That's good." She paused for a moment, then said, "Is it difficult for your sister to be a woman in a job that's primarily done by men?"

"Yes. I can't lie. It's tough on the women, but Emma has never backed down from a challenge. The more you tell her she can't do something, the more she wants to prove you wrong."

Olivia smiled. "Some people say that about me."

"I'll bet they do."

"You're close to your family, aren't you, Colton?"

"I guess I am. There are so many of us that I don't feel like I spend much time talking to anyone for too long. Probably Shayla and I are the closest, because we're twins, and because we were the youngest, so we spent a lot of time with each other."

"What about your brother, the one who is also a firefighter? Or, wait, is there more than one in firefighting?" She tried to remember all the people in the photograph she'd seen earlier on the Internet.

"Right now it's just Burke who's in the department, aside from my dad, that is. Aiden quit smoke jumping and went into construction after he got married and had a baby."

"That's interesting," she said, thinking that it was nice Aiden had quit a dangerous job for his wife and child.

"He quit for himself," Colton said quietly, reading her thoughts. "Not for his family. Sara didn't ask him to quit. She wanted him to follow his heart."

"Well, it sounds like his heart was for her."

"I guess that's true, but smoke jumping is also very demanding. It involves being gone for weeks at a time during fire season. Aiden didn't want that kind of lifestyle anymore. Plus, he banged himself up pretty good in his last fire jump."

She didn't comment, knowing that she did not have an unbiased opinion when it came to this topic.

"We're here," Colton said, turning into the parking lot of the bar. "I have to warn you, Olivia, there's going to be a lot of fire talk."

"I know. I remember when my dad used to get together with his cop buddies. They never left the job too far behind, but I don't care."

"Really?" he asked with a doubtful expression. "You seem to care quite a bit when it comes to firefighters and cops."

"I know I've come off a little strong on that subject, but tonight I'm just looking for a drink or two and some distraction."

"Good. And who knows? You might even have a little fun."

"Let's not get carried away," she said dryly.

He gave her a sexy grin that made her stomach flutter. She'd been so caught up in what she'd learned at Molly's house that she'd forgotten the other dangerous part of this whole adventure—and that part was Colton. It was strange how quickly they'd become friends—or whatever they were. But she'd probably spent more time with him in the past two days than she'd spent with any man in the last year.

"Come on," he said, opening his door.

"I'm right behind you."

The restaurant had brick walls, an open grill along one side and a long bar on the far wall. There were a few booths lining the walls with a dozen or more tables taking up the rest of the space. Flat screen televisions hung in the four corners of the room, each playing a different game.

The room had a great vibe, warm, friendly, the kind of neighborhood place where everyone in the room seemed to know each other. Even if Colton hadn't told her that Brady's was a popular firefighters' bar, she would have guessed that the second she stepped inside, because there were men everywhere. And not the kind of guys she was used to seeing in her New York City bars. These guys wore mostly jeans and t-shirts, some with SFFD insignia on them. They gave off a distinct vibe of being physical, rough-edged and pretty loud.

There were at least a half dozen men standing at one end of the bar watching a baseball game on the flat screen. The other action was in the middle of the room where four tables had been pushed together and another dozen or so guys were sharing platters of ribs, wings and nachos.

There were also four women in the group. She didn't know if they were girlfriends, wives or firefighters, but they seemed to fit right in, and she felt a little out of her element. The nervous feeling intensified when they drew nearer to the table and more than a few people gave her curious looks.

"Colton," a man said, getting to his feet. "You made it. How's the hand?"

"It's better," Colton said. "Happy birthday, Adam."

"Thanks. This is Dana," he said, nudging the shoulder of the pretty redhead by his side.

"Nice to finally meet you," Colton said.

"Likewise," Dana returned.

"So, who did you bring?" Adam asked.

Adam gave her a curious smile, and she couldn't help wondering if there was a requirement that every guy in the San Francisco Fire Department be hot, because Adam was also very attractive with his beach-blond good looks.

"Olivia Bennett," Colton said, putting a casual arm around her shoulders. "This is Adam Powell, the birthday boy."

She shook Adam's hand. "Happy birthday."

He tipped his head. "Thank you. Join us." Adam grabbed two more chairs from a nearby table, and the group made room for them.

"This is Olivia," Colton said as they sat down. "And this is everybody," he added with a wave of his hand.

"Hi everybody," she said lightly.

"Hank was just telling us about the date he had with that woman he pulled out of a car last week," Adam said, tipping his head toward the man across the table.

"Hank—you never learn, do you?" Colton said, shaking his head.

Hank appeared to have about ten years on Colton with brown hair and a square face. "What can I say?" Hank replied. "She wanted to take me out to dinner to thank me for cutting her out of her car. So I said yes. And, by the way, she didn't just treat me to dinner; I got breakfast, too," he added with a wicked twinkle in his eye.

As the group responded with a mix of groans and laughter, Olivia turned to Colton. "Is that common?"

"For women to want to sleep with us after we save their lives?" he asked dryly. "I wouldn't say common, but it does happen. It's the hero thing. We usually don't go out with them, though."

"Why not?"

He shrugged. "It's hard to live up to the image they have in their heads. When we're not being heroes, we're just guys." He paused as one of the men nearby let out a loud burp. "Sometimes obnoxious guys."

"Sometimes?" the woman next to Olivia asked with a roll of her eyes. "I'm Robin Kendall," she added with a smile. "I'm an EMT. I had to force Colton to go to the hospital the other day."

"A couple of broken fingers didn't require an ambulance ride," Colton cut in.

"A concussion did," Robin retorted.

"It wasn't a big deal. I have a hard head." Colton paused as the waitress came over with a tray full of shot glasses. "Now we're talking. Do you want one, Olivia? Or would you prefer wine?"

After the day she'd had? "I'll take a shot."

He smiled. "Shots it is."

As the group toasted Adam's birthday, Olivia tossed back the shot of Jack Daniels, shivering a little as the whiskey blazed a fiery path down her throat. She wasn't a big drinker, and normally she did stick to wine or beer, but finding out she might be Molly's granddaughter had shaken her up.

It wasn't like she didn't know she was adopted. As she'd told Colton, it had been a fact of her life for as long as she could remember. But she hadn't thought about her biological parents in years. When she had thought about them, she'd imagined all kinds of scenarios in which they might meet, but she had never ever anticipated the possibility of discovering what might be her birth certificate in a dusty box at the back of Molly Harper's closet, a woman whose letter she might not have responded to at all. It had just been luck that she'd opened it.

"You're thinking about earlier," Colton said warningly.

"Guilty."

"We're staying in the moment, remember?"

"Right."

"Do you want another shot?"

"Maybe I'll switch to a beer," she said, already feeling a little lightheaded. "And a cheeseburger. That one looks good." She tipped her head to the guy across the table, who was taking a bite out of a thick, juicy burger.

"A girl after my own heart," Colton said lightly.

As he called the waitress over to take their order, she couldn't help wondering what kind of girl would steal Colton's heart. It wasn't going to be her, she reminded herself. She was leaving in a few weeks. She had a life on the other side of the country, a good life, or at least a life that made sense to her. Ever since she'd landed in San Francisco, she'd been faced with one surprise after another.

"So how do you know Colton?" Robin asked curiously, drawing her attention.

"We met through his grandmother."

Robin was an attractive brunette with sparkling brown eyes and a cluster of freckles across her nose. Dressed in jeans and a silky floral top, she appeared to be in her mid-twenties. She gave

Olivia a smile and said, "I never heard that one before."

She smiled back. "It was a first for me, too. I actually live in New York City. I'm just in town for a few days."

"What do you think of San Francisco?"

"I like it a lot. There seems to be an amazing water view everywhere I go. And the weather is great."

"Fall is always good for us."

"So how is it working with all these guys?" Olivia asked. "Do you work out of the firehouse?"

"I do, and it's great."

"Really? You don't run into the occasional male chauvinist?"

"Oh, more than occasionally," Robin said with a laugh. "But I can handle that. There's no question that the guys can be pains in the ass, but they're good men, each and every one of them. I've seen them do amazing things, really beyond courageous. They go where most people would never go. And they don't do it reluctantly. They charge in. They want to save the day."

A chill ran down Olivia's spine at Robin's words. She could picture Colton in action, determination in his eyes, not a speck of fear in his heart.

If she were in trouble, wouldn't she want just that kind of man?

But when she wasn't in trouble…that would be a different story.

"I know it's hard to imagine that this motley group of men is so amazing, but they work as hard as they play," Robin added.

"Do you know Colton very well?"

"Pretty well. We've been working out of the same station the past six months. And I've worked with his brother Burke, too, as well as his cousin Brody. The Callaways are a force in the fire department."

"So I've heard." She debated the wisdom of her next question but then decided to ask it. "Does Colton play hard, too? Does he bring a lot of women around?"

Robin gave her a knowing smile. "You like him."

"Not that way." In the face of Robin's disbelieving gaze she had to add, "Well, maybe that way—a little. But I'm leaving town soon, so…"

"So maybe you'll change your plans," Robin suggested.

"My job is in New York."

"We have a lot of jobs here."

"I wouldn't move across the country for a guy. That would be stupid."

"Ordinarily, I'd agree with you. I wouldn't move for just any guy, but if I were in love…"

"I've known Colton for two days. Don't get carried away."

"Love can be fast."

"You are way off base, Robin." Her gaze narrowed. "Why are you so interested anyway? Are you sure you're not the one who likes Colton?"

"No, I don't date where I work. Colton and I are friends. I actually have my eye on a sexy accountant. And I know what you're going to say—that sexy and accountant don't really go together—but he has that boyish, glasses-falling-off-his-nose kind of charm."

Olivia smiled. "I know that kind of charm."

"We'll see though. We're really just friends at the moment." Robin paused as she sipped her beer. "But you asked whether or not Colton brought a lot of women around, and I'd have to say no. Not that there aren't always a lot of women trying to get his attention when we're all out somewhere, but he rarely actually shows up with anyone, until tonight."

"We were doing something for his grandmother earlier," she said, knowing she really didn't owe Robin an explanation, but she couldn't stop herself from providing one.

"How is his grandmother? I heard she has Alzheimer's."

"Apparently so, but she hasn't had any issues since I've met her."

"That's good news. Her husband, Patrick Callaway, was a legend in the department. He set all kinds of records for heroism, and his son, Jack, followed in his footsteps."

"The younger Callaway men have a lot to live up to," she murmured.

"They're up for the challenge." Robin paused as the guy sitting across from her demanded her attention. He wanted her to settle some sort of bet.

Olivia sat back in her seat as the waitress brought her a beer and a cheeseburger. And for the next few minutes, she just ate and watched the action at the table. While there was good-natured bickering and telling of embarrassing stories, it was clear there was a lot of love and respect within the group.

They were a family, she realized, probably very similar to the work family her dad had had. She'd put those memories out of her head for a very long time, but now bits and pieces of other birthday parties flitted through her mind. Her dad had loved his job and his coworkers, just like Colton, and she felt a bit wistful that she didn't have the same kind of camaraderie at her job. But it was just her, Philip, and Philip's assistant, and while Philip had an office, he was rarely there, and his personal assistant often worked from home, so Olivia had spent a lot of days alone in the small office on the eighteenth floor of a Manhattan skyscraper.

Colton nudged her arm, and she turned to look at him.

"Having fun?" he asked. "You're kind of quiet."

She nodded. "Just observing."

"You do that a lot."

"I guess I do."

"And what have you observed?" he asked lightly.

"That you have a great group of friends. I feel a little jealous. I work pretty much by myself. I don't think I've been part of a team since I played softball freshman year of high school."

"A softball player and a surfer? I'm learning a lot about you tonight. What position did you play?"

"Outfield. I like fly balls over grounders. Did you play baseball?"

"Third base."

"The hot corner," she said with a laugh. "I'm not surprised."

"I like to challenge myself."

"So do I. But apparently I give myself more room to succeed. The balls take a little more time to get to the outfield."

She paused, seeing four older men make their way into the bar. She thought she'd seen one of them the day before at the senior center. "Hey, is that your father?"

Colton turned his head. "Yeah, that's him."

"Who's he with?"

"My Uncle Rob. He's a retired firefighter, and I think the other two are cops."

"I thought this was a firefighters' bar."

"Sometimes we mix it up, and my dad always likes to do that. He thinks it makes for better cooperation between the departments."

"Is your father as gruff as your grandfather?"

"He's decisive, confident, tough when he needs to be, but he also loves to tell stories and have a good time."

"Sounds like he's got a little of Patrick and a little of Eleanor in him."

"I never thought of it that way, but you're right."

Colton had barely finished speaking when Adam said, "Look alive, boys and girls, the brass is here."

Colton seemed to grimace at Adam's words, and Olivia wondered if it bothered him when his dad showed up.

The men sat down at a table on the other side of the room, but when Jack saw Colton, he gave a wave and motioned for him to come over.

"You're coming with me," Colton told her.

"No, you can go on your own. So far the men in your family have not been happy to meet me."

"Well, too bad. You're my date tonight."

"I don't think this is a date."

"It's close enough. And I could use a buffer."

"Why?"

"Because if my grandfather has told my father anything about you and this book, I am going to get shit for being in this bar with you, so the least you can do is come with me."

"Well, since you've made it sound like so much fun," she said dryly. "I guess we're talking to your dad."

Twelve

As they walked across the room hand in hand, Olivia could feel not only the heat of Colton's fingers, but also the tightness of his nerves. She didn't know if he was really worried about being seen with her or if there was more to it than that. Colton had stiffened up the second his dad walked into the bar. Maybe at least some of his tension had to do with the fact that Jack Callaway was in essence Colton's boss.

When they arrived at the table, she could immediately see the similarities between Colton's father and uncle. While Jack had a more stocky build and a ruddier complexion than his brother Rob, they both had dark hair and blue eyes, a dangerously attractive combination that they'd also passed on to Colton.

The other two men at the table were quite different in appearance. One was short and stocky with a square face and a receding hairline. He was introduced as Donald Rand. The other had a long, narrow face, and his dark brown hair and moustache were edged with gray. He was introduced as Keith Fletcher. Both men were detectives in the police department, although according to Jack, they were also both in the running to be the next chief of police.

"Sit down, both of you," Jack said.

"We don't want to interrupt," Colton replied.

"You're not." Jack gave Olivia a speculative smile. "I've been hearing a lot about you, Miss Bennett. You seem to be a bone of contention between my parents and my wife. Now it appears that

Colton is also involved." As Jack finished his pointed comment, he turned to the other men at the table. "Miss Bennett has come to San Francisco to write a book about my grandmother and her friends. My father is not happy about it."

"I heard about that," Rob Callaway said. "I told Dad he should relax and let Mom have some fun."

"It's not quite that simple," Jack said.

"What is the book about?" Donald asked curiously. "I know Eleanor is a beautiful lady, but what's her story?"

"I'm still trying to figure that out," Olivia said. "The book isn't just about Eleanor. I was invited to come here by Molly Harper. Molly said a group of ladies at the senior center would like to share their stories with me."

"Stories about what?" Keith asked.

"Well, they were part of a community theater group," she said, not sure how much she wanted to tell to these men.

Jack smiled. "My mother always had a flair for drama. She also had a ton of friends. She was the queen of the neighborhood back in the day."

"I remember the theater days," Rob said, an odd expression on his face now. "I actually remember Mom and Dad fighting a lot about that theater. I don't really know why. I guess he didn't want her to spend so much time away from home."

Or, Olivia wondered…maybe Patrick hadn't wanted Eleanor to put herself in danger.

"Dad didn't like to share her," Jack said. "But she could be determined when she wanted to be, and she liked putting on those plays."

"Molly was around a lot then, too," Rob said. "She was always bringing her kids over. Francine was cute, but her brother was a pain in the ass. I don't know how Michael was friends with him."

"Michael was a saint even when he was twelve," Jack said with a laugh. "Good training for becoming a priest."

"Did you say that Molly Harper wrote to you?" Donald asked Olivia.

"Yes. Unfortunately, by the time I got here, Molly had had a stroke. I haven't been able to speak to her. I'm hoping her condition will improve."

"That's terrible," Keith said. "I hope she recovers quickly. Will you be able to do the book without her?"

"Maybe. She left me some of her journals to read and other things I haven't gotten to yet. I'm really just getting started." She paused, remembering the picture of Molly's husband in a police uniform. "Wait a second, do either of you remember Stan Harper, Molly's husband? I understand he was a cop."

Donald and Keith exchanged a quick look and then Donald said, "Yes, I knew Stan. He was about fifteen years older than I was so we didn't spend a lot of time together."

"Same for me," Keith said. "I was a rookie when Stan died. It was the first cop's funeral I ever went to. I'll never forget it."

"If you went to his funeral, then you must know how he died," Olivia said, feeling excited at the prospect of getting more information on the Harpers. "Was it on the job?"

"No, it was a fire at his house," Donald said.

"A fire," she echoed, a little surprised. "What happened?"

"I don't remember the details," Donald replied. "It was a long time ago. Do you remember that fire, Jack?"

"I remember that night," Jack said with a nod. "I was away at college, but I came home for the weekend a day early, and the Harper kids were in my room. Mom pulled me aside and told me there had been a terrible fire and Stan had died. It was pretty shocking."

"Is this all going to be in your book?" Rob asked.

"Well, I don't know. I'm just pulling information together." She paused for a moment, thinking that it was surreal to consider the fact that she might be talking about her biological grandparents, which brought her to Francine. "Do any of you know what happened to Molly's daughter, Francine?" she asked, suddenly realizing she had no idea if Francine was alive or dead, if she was married, if she had other children…

"Francine died when she was in her twenties," Jack said, a somber note in his voice. "It was very sad."

"Oh," she said, taken aback by the terrible news. If she was Francine's daughter, she was never going to have a chance to meet her. "How did she die?"

"It was an overdose. Molly certainly suffered more than her share of tragedy," Jack added.

"That is sad," she murmured, thinking how difficult it must have been for Molly to lose both her husband and her daughter. Maybe that's why Peter was so protective over his mother now. His mother was the only one he had left.

"We'll let you get back to your drinks," Colton said.

"What's your part in all this, Colton?" Jack asked.

"Grandpa asked me to keep an eye on Grandma while he's in Chicago this week," Colton replied.

Jack grinned. "Looks like you got your eye on someone else at the moment, son."

Colton tipped his head in acknowledgment. "Olivia doesn't know anyone in town, so I thought the least I could do was buy her a drink. We should get back to the group."

"We should," she agreed, getting to her feet. "If I have more questions, would it be possible for me to speak to you all again?"

"Fine by me," Jack said. "But I don't know much more than I told you, and I think Rob knows even less."

"Jack's right, I probably don't know anything more than he does," Rob said.

"Maybe you two gentlemen might be able to help me learn more about Molly's husband, Stan," she suggested.

Neither Donald nor Keith looked too happy about that prospect, but they both nodded and made polite responses.

"Thanks," she said.

As they moved away from the table, their progress was stopped by the entrance of a large party, many of whom seemed to know Colton, slapping him on the back and saying hello as they made their way over to Adam's table.

"Looks like the party is getting bigger," she commented.

"A little too big for me," he said, his expression turning grim as an older man entered the bar.

"Who is that?" she asked curiously.

"My new boss, Mitchell Warren. He doesn't like me much."

"Why not?" So far everyone she met seemed to like Colton.

He was a friendly, outgoing guy who loved his job, his friends and his family.

"Not really sure," Colton replied. "It has something to do with my last name. He chewed me out about five minutes after we met."

There was no way for Mitchell to get to Adam's group without passing by them. He saw Colton and gave a stiff nod.

"Callaway." His mouth seemed to curl distastefully around Colton's last name.

"Captain," Colton said tersely.

"How's the hand?"

"Better. I shouldn't have to miss more than one shift."

"We'll see." Mitchell looked around the bar. "Your brother here?"

"If you're referring to Burke, no, I haven't seen him."

"Good." And with that odd comment, Mitchell moved past them to wish Adam a happy birthday.

"See what I mean?" Colton asked, turning to her with frustration in his eyes.

"Yeah, he was cold as ice to you. It doesn't sound like he cares for your brother too much, either."

"I asked Burke about him. He alluded to some problems with him, but he wouldn't get specific."

"Maybe you should talk to him again."

"I doubt it would help. Burke likes to tell me to solve my own problems."

"That doesn't sound very generous."

"He's a great guy. He's just very closed off," Colton said. "And that's not all his fault."

"What do you mean?"

"It doesn't matter. Do you want to get out of here?"

"Sure."

"Let me just lay down some cash for our meal and say goodbye."

It took another fifteen minutes to pay their bill and say goodnight, but eventually they made their way back into the parking lot.

"I can drive now," she said.

"Let me. I prefer to be the driver than the passenger."

"Maybe I do, too."

He smiled, and she was happy to see the tension erased from his eyes. "But I actually have the keys in my hand," he said. "Possession is nine-tenths of the law."

"Is that even true, or just an expression everyone likes to use?"

"I have no idea whatsoever."

"Fine. You can drive." As they got into the car, she said, "So Francine is dead. That was shocking news."

He shot her a quick look. "We still don't know if you're Francine's daughter, Olivia. Just because you have the same birth date—"

"I know. I'm jumping ahead. But I can't help thinking that if I am her daughter, I'll never get to meet her."

He frowned. "I don't know what to think about any of this. But I do know that it's been a long day. Why don't we table Molly and the Harpers and my grandmother until tomorrow? We're supposed to be taking a break from all that, remember?"

"I remember, but you should have taken me to a bar where we wouldn't run into any of your family."

"In this town, that's difficult," he said with a smile. "Speaking of this beautiful city, why don't I show you around?"

"I feel a little guilty at not diving back into the research."

"It will still be there in a few hours."

"You're right. Show me your town."

"Okay. Sit back and enjoy the ride."

Thirteen

As he started the car, Colton knew he was heading into dangerous territory. He was spending a little too much time with Olivia, and while he may have started out with the simple intention of finding out what she was up to and protecting his grandmother, his motives had definitely changed.

For one thing, he liked Olivia more than he'd ever anticipated. He'd seen her in action with his grandmother and friends, watched her reel with shock after finding out she shared a birth date with an unknown Harper child and then seen her put her own problems aside to mix in with his friends and relatives. Now, he found himself wanting to show her a lot more than just this city.

But he couldn't go down that road. Olivia was leaving in a few days, and she was still his grandfather's enemy. Even though they hadn't learned anything that could really hurt his grandmother, as far as he could see, who knew what else they would find before this was all over? And if it came down to Olivia or his family, he would obviously choose his family.

As he stopped at a light, he glanced over at Olivia. She had color in her cheeks and her green eyes sparkled as she gazed back at him. He didn't know if it was the alcohol she'd consumed at the bar, the prospect of exploring San Francisco, or if it was being with him that had put the light in her eyes, but whatever the reason, he found himself liking her expression. In fact, he felt the crazy urge to do whatever he needed to do to keep her smiling.

"What are you looking at?" she asked.

"You. You're beautiful, Olivia."

Her lips parted in surprise. "Um, thanks. That's nice of you to say."

"I'm not feeding you a line. It's the truth." He liked her somewhat awkward reaction to his words. It made her even more appealing. "I'm sure guys have told you that before."

"Well, maybe, but usually as a precursor to something else."

"Like sex?"

"It seems to be a popular lead-in," she admitted.

"But so cliché." He put his foot on the gas as the light turned green.

"You've never used the line to soften someone up?"

"Not in a deliberate way—no." He paused and flashed her a smile. "Does it work?"

She folded her arms in front of her chest. "I can't say it isn't always flattering to hear, but sometimes it's clearly insincere."

"Not when I say it."

She gazed back at him. "I think I kind of believe you."

"You *should* believe me. I don't lie."

"Never? Almost everyone tells a lie at some point in their life."

He thought about that for a moment. "I guess I couldn't say never, but it would be a very rare occasion. I don't have time for it. Lies take effort."

"So you're just a lazy honest person," she teased.

"Perhaps that's part of it. But aside from being lazy, I like to stand up for what I believe in. Or if I've done something wrong, I admit it. It seems an easier way to go."

"Easier maybe, but most people have an instinctive urge to protect themselves, so when they're in trouble, they go for the lie. In my research interviews, I've seen that a lot."

"Who else have you researched besides Carlton Hughes?"

"Probably the most interesting person was Stefano Violetti, Italy's most eligible bachelor billionaire."

"And what was he like?"

"Gorgeous, charming and quite good at keeping secrets."

"That sounds interesting."

She tipped her head. "That's what the book description said, and it was interesting enough to sell a million copies."

"What kind of secrets was he keeping?"

"Well, he wasn't actually a bachelor. He'd married a girl when he was eighteen. I found the marriage certificate when I was doing my research."

"How old is he now?"

"Thirty-four. So it had been sixteen years since that marriage when I found the certificate."

"Tell me the story," he encouraged, as they came to another stop.

"Stefano married Yvette St. Moray at the courthouse of a very small town in France during his summer of European travel before he was to start his freshman year at Harvard. They fell madly in love and married in secret just before he left for school in September."

"Why was it a secret?"

"Because his family was very wealthy, and they wanted him to go to the university. They didn't want him to marry a beautiful but poor woman who split her time between waiting tables and trying to be a chef. For two years Stefano and Yvette would travel back and forth between the U.S. and France. Stefano would fly her out whenever he could. But eventually the distance was too great, and they split up."

"But neither one filed for divorce?" That didn't make sense.

"No. When I confronted Stefano with the information I'd dug up, he admitted to me that there was a part of him that still loved Yvette, but he hadn't seen her in over twelve years."

"He must have done something to screw her over."

"Why do you say that?" Olivia asked curiously.

"Because he was rich and he was going to be a Harvard grad. I think Yvette could have hung on until graduation unless she had another reason to get rid of him. So I think he screwed her over."

Olivia nodded. "You're right. Stefano cheated on her, and she found out about it. I got that information from Yvette, who is still single, and still beautiful, by the way. She's a chef now at a small restaurant in the south of France. She's very much a free spirit, but not so free that she could forgive Stefano's transgression. However, I saw something on her face when I first mentioned his name, and I think it was love, maybe a little regret."

"You are really good at this, Olivia."

Surprise flashed in her eyes. "Good at what? Digging up scandal?"

"That—and telling a great story. I am completely captivated by Stefano and Yvette's love story, and I am not a man who usually enjoys a romantic chick flick. I prefer action. But somehow you have spun this story to me in such a way that I want to know if they're going to get back together."

She laughed. "Thanks for the compliment, but Stefano and Yvette's story is not fiction; it's real life. I can't write the ending without them."

"But you probably gave their real-life ending a nudge. I don't believe you just left without trying to do something."

"You are reading me a little too well, Colton. Yes, I gave them a big nudge. I forced them into the same room together."

"And? Don't leave me hanging."

"They looked at each other as if no time had passed. There was love, there was anger, there was everything. And then I left them alone."

"You left?" he asked incredulously.

"I had to move on to Philip's next project," she said defensively. "His story on Stefano was done, and that meant I was done."

"How long ago did this happen?"

"Almost two years now."

"And you never checked up on Stefano and Yvette in all that time?"

"Yes, I did check up on them," she admitted. "And Yvette told me that they are spending time together again, and she thinks they might have their happy ending after all."

He nodded. "Good, you had me worried."

"Worried? Why? You just told me you don't like romantic stories."

"Well, if I have to sit through one, I'd prefer that no one died in the end. It all seems a waste to me when that happens."

"Me, too. So where are we going, Colton? So far all you've shown me is traffic."

"I have a few spots in mind. The road should open up in a couple of blocks."

"It's fine. It gives me a chance to look around the city. The skyscrapers are quite impressive. Not as many as New York, but definitely some with their own unique charm like that one that looks like a pyramid."

"The Transamerica building. It definitely sticks out along the skyline."

Ten minutes later the traffic eased up, and as he got closer to Chinatown, he was able to find a parking spot not far from where he wanted to go. As he shut down the engine, he said, "We have to take a little walk."

"Are you going to tell me where we're going now?"

"Nope."

"Tease," she said back to him, as he met her on the sidewalk.

"It will be more fun this way."

"You're lucky I like an adventure."

"I figured you would. You have a very curious mind, and I have come up with something to show you that is right up your alley—no pun intended."

"Pun?" she queried.

"You'll see." Two minutes later he led her into a narrow, dark lane. "This is Jack Kerouac Alley. I assume you've heard of him."

"Of course. He was in the Beat Generation and wrote the novel *On The Road* in allegedly three weeks, in a frenzy of alcohol and drug-induced ramblings. At least that's how the story goes."

"I did not know that. Actually, I don't know much about him at all. However, my mom is a fan of his work. She's an avid reader, and she showed me this alley when she took me to the City Lights Bookstore, which we just passed. Apparently, Kerouac used to hang out there."

"Interesting."

"But the cool part of this alley are the plaques on the ground." He was happy to see there was enough light from the surrounding buildings to be able to see the plaques. But he took out his phone just in case and switched on the flashlight feature as they neared the first plaque in the ground. "Can you read it?" he asked.

"Yes. It says '*Poetry is the shadow cast by our streetlight imaginations,*'" Olivia read, finishing with the author's name. "Lawrence Ferlinghetti." She paused. "I've never heard of him, but I like the quote."

They walked further down the alley. "How about this one?" He paused in front of a large circular plaque that almost covered the width of the alley and read the words aloud: "'*The air was soft, the stars so fine, the promise of every cobbled alley so great...*' That was by Kerouac." He looked at Olivia. "I wonder if he wrote that one when he was boozed up?"

"Who knows? A lot of genius writers seem to have been inspired by the bottle. I like this quote. '*Love lights more fires than hate extinguishes.*' Ella Wheeler Wilcox."

He laughed. "I haven't seen too many fires started by love. Gasoline and matches are another story."

"Some love stories are filled with gasoline and matches in a figurative sense. One person is the spark, the other is the fuel. Together they burn."

Her words were as mesmerizing as her eyes and her lips, her really, really inviting mouth...

She put her hand on his arm, and Colton started, realizing he'd lost all sense of time and place. Had he been looking at her for a minute or five minutes? He actually had no idea, and it was a very disconcerting feeling.

Olivia's eyes sparkled in the shadowy light. He could hear the traffic a short ways down the alley and laughter coming out of a second story apartment over one of the businesses that backed onto the lane, but the rest of the world still felt very far away.

"Colton?" she murmured, a question in her eyes.

He had no idea how to answer that question, except with a kiss. He could feel the pull between them, and while his mind was telling him to resist, his body was saying, go for it!

Before he could move, Olivia's hand fell from his arm. She stepped back. Cool air flowed between them.

He had the strangest feeling he'd just missed his chance, and he didn't like it.

"Thanks for bringing me here," she said. "Where shall we go next?"

His apartment came to mind—or maybe her hotel room. Any place with a bed. Any place they could be alone.

When he didn't answer, she said, "We should go someplace that means something to you. This alley was for me. As a writer, you knew I'd appreciate it. So where do firefighters go—besides the local firefighters' bar?"

He cleared his throat, trying to get his brain back on track. "Coit Tower is a special place. It's a monument that resembles a fire hose, and it was built to honor the firefighters who fought to save the city after the 1906 earthquake. Unfortunately, the tower is closed at night. It's too bad, because it has one of the best views of the city."

"Maybe we can go another day."

"If you haven't left yet," he said, reminding himself that she would be leaving soon. A few days from now, she might be completely gone from his life.

"If I haven't left yet," she echoed softly. "So no tower, but there must be other places in this hilly city that have a great view."

"My apartment building has a rooftop deck. It's what sold me on the rental. There's rarely anyone there, so I often go up to think or just have a beer and unwind."

She stared back at him, indecision in her eyes, then she said, "I'd like to see that view."

He almost asked her if she were sure but then he decided he didn't want to give her a chance to back out, so instead, he said, "Let's go."

They were just going to look at the city view, he told himself as they walked back down the alley. Nothing else had to happen at his apartment. Nothing was going to happen. He could exercise some self-control—as long as she could.

Fourteen

—⇒⇒⇐⇐—

Olivia had second and third thoughts on the way to Colton's apartment. The sparks between them had been heating up all night and now she was going to his place alone, ostensibly to see the view, but she couldn't help thinking that neither one of them was as interested in a moonlit view of the Golden Gate Bridge as they were in seeing each other naked.

The thought made her shiver, and she shifted in her seat, crossing her arms in front of her chest. That didn't help because the movement made her breasts tingle. She was a mass of sensual nerves right now, and she needed to get over it.

So she was attracted to Colton? Who wouldn't be? He was good-looking, incredibly fit, sexy as hell, charming and outgoing, and a man's man as well as a woman's man.

What she needed to do was stop thinking about all that was right with him and focus on his flaws. He was a firefighter. That was a check against him. She didn't want to end up in a relationship with a man just like her father.

And aside from that, Colton didn't want her to do her job. In fact, he was only with her to stop her from doing her job, finding the story that could launch her career as a biographer.

Okay, that wasn't completely fair. She'd put the brakes on her investigation as soon as she'd stumbled over that birth certificate.

The memory of that piece of paper gave her another reason not to get involved with Colton. She didn't know who she was anymore. And she couldn't be with him if she didn't know who she was—could she?

She rolled her neck around on her shoulders as her mind continued to shoot off question after question. That was her problem. She thought too much. She over-analyzed everything. She tried to predict possible consequences, and in protecting herself from the potential of any painful or embarrassing moments, she tended to do nothing at all. She was very different from Colton, who was adventurous and brave. She was pretty much an analytical coward, especially when it came to men.

She wanted love. She wanted to be in love. But she didn't know how to get there. She didn't know how to risk her heart. She'd retreated after her father's death.

After losing the most important man in her life, she'd put her heart away and swore not to let anyone close to it again. Until tonight no one had. But Colton was chipping away at her armor.

He might not want love. In fact, she was pretty sure all he wanted was sex. But she wasn't very good at separating the two.

She wanted to throw caution to the wind. She'd been trying to do that all night, but how far could she really go before her cautious brain put the brakes on?

She was about to find out.

Colton pulled into an underground garage, and they took the elevator to the fourth floor of his building.

"We can stop in my apartment and get some wine," he said. "There's a picnic table on the rooftop deck where we can sit."

"Sounds good." She forced herself not to consider whether or not he had another reason for wanting to stop in his apartment. "I'm curious to see where you live," she added.

"It's not impressive," he said with a dry smile. He unlocked the door and waved her inside.

He was right. His place was not at all impressive. In the living room there was a mismatched brown recliner and a black leather sofa behind a round oak coffee table that looked like a wagon wheel. The only thing on the wall was an enormous flat-screen TV. There were no framed pictures, no family photographs, no personal items whatsoever.

"Well," she murmured, hands on her hips. "Did you just move

in, Colton?"

"A few months ago."

She raised an eyebrow. "Too busy to hang pictures?"

"Too busy to buy any. I haven't had much time to spruce up the place, and I pretty much just sleep here."

"And watch television."

"I do like to watch sports on the big screen."

"Don't you have a couple of sisters in that big family of yours who'd be willing to help you decorate?"

"No doubt, but I prefer to keep my sisters out of my life as much as possible. With their help usually comes unwanted advice. I'm going to grab some wine out of the kitchen. Feel free to look around, not that there's much to see."

What she saw were the signs of a man who didn't care much about material things and wasn't at all self-conscious about his living conditions. She didn't know whether that was confidence or plain old laziness. Not that the place was sloppy. It was in fact pretty neat; it was just sparse.

She really shouldn't be criticizing, though. She wasn't much of a decorator either, but she had taken time to put some art on her walls and buy furniture that matched.

While Colton was getting the wine, she ventured down the short hallway, poking her head into the small bathroom, which was also neat and fairly clean. All the towels were hung on their racks and the sink looked freshly scrubbed.

Her next stop was Colton's bedroom. Like the living room, the furniture was minimal, just a king-sized bed and one nightstand with a lamp. There was, however, a ten-speed bike along one wall, a set of golf clubs in the corner, and a couple of ten-pound hand weights next to a jump-rope.

"Find anything interesting?" he asked, appearing in the doorway with a bottle of wine in one hand and two glasses in the other.

"I thought it was interesting that you made your bed."

"I grew up in a big family. We were taught from a young age to pull our weight."

"And I was a spoiled only child who still doesn't like to make her bed. It makes little sense to me considering I'm just going to get back in it."

"Now you've surprised me." He tilted his head, giving her a thoughtful look. "I would have taken you for very organized and neat."

"In my business life I am, and in the kitchen I'm pretty good, but when it comes to the bedroom, I can be a little sloppy."

"I like that," he said with an approving nod. "People who are perfect are boring."

"I am definitely not perfect."

"Neither am I."

And she didn't think he was boring, either. In fact, standing here alone in his bedroom was raising the heat level between them, and she was very conscious of how close the bed was, and how much she really wanted to mess up those neat sheets and covers.

Colton's smile faded as he stared at her, and she had the crazy idea he could actually read her mind. Or maybe his mind was just on the same track.

She cleared her throat. "We should go up to the roof. See that view you were bragging about."

"Yes, let's do that." He turned and walked out of the bedroom with a brisk stride.

She wasn't quite sure how she felt about his easy acquiescence. Maybe he hadn't been thinking about taking her to bed. Maybe the attraction was all on her side.

No, that wasn't possible. She wasn't that much of an idiot. She knew when a man was attracted to her. But for whatever reason, Colton was not acting on that attraction, and she needed to follow his lead.

She followed him out of the apartment and up the stairs to the roof. Colton flipped on a light, illuminating the deck.

She was surprised to find the view just as awesome as he'd suggested. She moved quickly to the waist-high railing that ran around the flat roof and gazed out at the lights of the city and the Golden Gate Bridge. Colton's apartment building was on a hill, and she could catch glimpses of different parts of the city from every direction.

Colton set the bottle and glasses down on a nearby picnic table, and while he was opening the wine with the corkscrew he pulled out of his pocket, he said, "So, was I lying?"

"No, you weren't even exaggerating."

"I told you it would be worth the trip." He poured her a glass of wine and handed it to her. Then he poured himself a glass. "I know this isn't a New York view, but it's not bad, right?"

"It's beautiful. I feel like all my problems are way down there."

"That's how I feel when I come up here." He raised his glass. "A toast, I think."

"What shall we drink to?"

He thought for a moment, then said, "Let's drink to Molly."

She hesitated, his words bringing her problems up to the deck. "Really?"

"She is the reason you're here. And I'm glad you're here, Olivia."

"You didn't feel that way earlier today."

"A lot has changed since then."

He wasn't kidding about that. "It's strange. I feel like I've known you for years, Colton, but I just met you yesterday."

His gaze met hers. "Sometimes you have a connection with someone that happens instantly."

She shivered at the husky note in his voice, the gleam of desire in his dark blue eyes and the five o'clock shadow that darkened his jaw. "Yeah, I know what you mean," she murmured.

"I've changed my mind," he said. "I don't want to drink to Molly; I want to drink to you." He clicked his glass against hers. "Cheers."

"Cheers." She lifted her glass to her lips and took a sip. "Nice."

He nodded. "My brother Aiden's friend is a winemaker in the Napa Valley. He makes a good merlot."

"He does." She turned away from Colton, because her pulse was racing a little too fast. She moved back to the rail and set her glass on the ledge.

Colton came beside her and did the same thing. Then he

turned and put his hands on her hips.

Her heart jumped in her chest at the purposeful look in his eyes. "What—what are you doing?"

"I can't wait any longer," he said, lowering his mouth to hers.

He wasn't asking for permission, nor was he giving her time to answer or to move away. He was going to kiss her, and she couldn't wait. She parted her lips as his mouth came down on hers.

The heat flowed between them with the first brief pass, firing up as he settled in for a longer ride, his tongue pushing past her lips, sliding inside in a delicious kiss. She could taste the wine on his tongue, the black cherry, the currants, and with that taste came a heady, dizzying spin of desire.

She put her arms around his waist, moving in closer, wanting to give as well as to take. She'd never had such an incredibly perfect kiss, and she wanted to keep it going as long as possible.

Eventually they had to breathe.

Colton lifted his head, his hands dropping from her waist as he took a step back. The heat of their breath mixed with the cool night air, surrounding them with whirling whispers of lingering passion. He looked at her for a long time, and she had no power to drag her gaze away from his. She could see the hunger in his eyes, but she couldn't read the other emotions, and there seemed to be a lot of them.

"That was—nice," he said.

She nodded, thinking *nice* was a huge understatement for what had been a fairly spectacular kiss, at least in her experience.

"I've been wanting to do that since I met you, Olivia."

"I don't think that's true. I hurt your hand when I ran into you at the senior center."

"Okay, about five minutes after that then."

"No, you wanted me to go away. You can't rewrite history, Colton."

"I wanted you to go away, because I instinctively knew you were going to be dangerous."

"To your grandmother?"

"To me."

She drew in a breath as she shook her head. "I'm not quite sure where you're going with all this."

"I'm not going anywhere. We're just living in the moment, remember?"

"I remember," she said, wishing the last moment was still going on. But with the space between them had come a return to sanity. She didn't want to start something with Colton that she couldn't finish, and she was only going to be in San Francisco for a few days. The last thing she wanted to do was go back to New York with a broken heart. While a kiss wasn't going to break her heart, she had a feeling anything more might, because she liked Colton way too much.

She picked up her glass of wine, took a sip and then moved away from the rail to sit down at the picnic table.

Colton joined her a moment later, sitting across from her.

"Is this better?" he asked with a teasing smile. "A nice big table between us."

She smiled back. "I wouldn't say better, but maybe safer. I can't start anything with you, Colton. It would be stupid."

"We've already started, Olivia."

"Let's talk about something else then."

"Whatever you want."

She thought about his open invitation and realized she had no idea what she wanted to talk about—certainly not Molly or the Harpers or his grandmother. She would leave those topics for tomorrow. "Tell me about your siblings. Start at the top and work your way down."

"Really? I'm going to put you to sleep."

"I doubt that. If they're anything like you, I suspect they all lead interesting lives."

"All right, if you insist. I told you about Burke already. He's a firefighter, overachiever from when he was a small child. He was top of his class, valedictorian, star athlete, class president; he set the bar really high."

"He must have some flaws."

"He can be moody and judgmental, but I suspect that's because he has the same high expectations for everyone else that he has for himself." Colton paused. "He's also very private. I don't really know if anyone in the family knows him very well anymore. He and Aiden used to be closer when they were younger, but they had a lot of conflict and competition between them. And Burke changed after his fiancé died."

"When did that happen?"

"Several years ago. She died in a car accident; her vehicle was smashed by a drunk driver." His lips tightened. "Burke was working that night. It didn't happen very far from the station."

"Oh, no," she said, her stomach turning over. "He didn't--"

"Yeah, he was first at the scene."

"My God! Was she already—"

"I'm not completely sure if she died in his arms or on the way to the hospital. I never wanted to ask. But it was rough. He was in bad shape for a while. He's the kind of person who doesn't accept help from anyone. The family, of course, tried to support him, but he pushed just about everyone away. Since then he's started to reconnect, but there always seems to be a part of himself that he holds back."

"And he's still single?"

"Yeah. I don't know if he'll ever be able to love anyone again."

"I hope he will be able to do that. It would be too sad otherwise." She paused. "Okay, who's next?"

"Aiden, former smoke jumper. He's married to Sara, who grew up next door to us and was friends with my sister Emma. They have a baby girl, Chloe, who has Aiden wrapped around her finger. She's a super cute kid, and my rebel of a brother is completely tamed."

She smiled. "It sounds like they're a happy family unit."

"Disgustingly so. Next in the lineup is Nicole. She's a teacher and married to her high school sweetheart, Ryan. Ryan is a commercial pilot. They have a seven-year-old son Brandon, who is autistic, and that has made for some rocky times in their relationship. They adopted Brandon and recently discovered that he has a twin brother who is not autistic. The boys have been reunited, and Brandon is finding a new connection to the world through his brother."

"That's cool. So does Brandon's twin live in San Francisco?"

"He does now, and his adoptive mom Jessica is actually involved with my brother Sean."

"The musician and the dancer," she said. "The ones who share the studio, right?"

"That's right. You've been paying attention."

"I love big families. As an only child, I yearned to be part of a family like yours. I used to make up stories in my head. I'd give myself brothers and sisters. It was fun."

"Maybe more fun than actually being in a big family."

Despite his cynical words, she didn't think he meant them. "You love it."

"It's all I've ever known, but I do love my family, at least most of the time."

"Okay, keep going," she said, sipping her wine.

"Let's see, Drew is next. He's a former Navy pilot turned Coast Guard pilot. He flies helicopters. He got married a few months ago to Ria who gives sailing lessons and runs charter tours in the bay. They're guardians to Ria's eighteen-year-old niece Megan, who is currently in college. After Drew is Emma, the fire investigator. She's married to Max, a homicide detective. I told you about Sean and Jessica, and then there's my twin sister Shayla."

"And your twin is a doctor."

"Finishing up her residency. Now your turn. Tell me about your mom."

"Her name is Elaine. She was a mom and a homemaker for twenty-five years, and then a few years after my dad died and I went to college, she returned to school. She had originally studied art and was a good illustrator, but she'd never done anything with it except to provide artwork for flyers for my school and that kind of thing. But now she is tech savvy and provides graphics for a web designer."

"Good for her."

"She's also dating my former algebra teacher, which is kind of weird. But I do want her to be happy, and I know she's been lonely with me living so far away."

"At least she's not alone. That should make you feel better."

"It does make me feel less guilty for staying on the other side of the country."

"Do you think you'd ever come back to California?"

"I don't know. That is not a question for a person who is trying to live in the moment."

"Point taken. Tell me more."

"That's really all the family I have."

"Then tell me about your friends."

"Why so curious?" she challenged.

He grinned. "I'm trying to distract myself from moving to the other side of this table."

"Maybe I should go back to my hotel."

"No, let's keep talking."

"Okay," she agreed, because she didn't really want to leave.

As they talked, the moon rose higher in the sky and the air grew cold. Just before midnight they moved their conversation back to Colton's apartment. He handed her a blanket, and she cozied up on the couch while he made popcorn.

And then they talked some more.

At some point, she mentioned going back to her hotel again, but Colton's car was at his grandmother's house, and he would need to collect that, and she would need to find her way across town, and in the end she stretched out on the couch, the length of the day finally catching up to her as she drifted off to sleep.

Colton watched Olivia's eyelids close. He smiled, realizing she'd fallen asleep in mid-sentence, but she was exhausted. He was tired but also wired. They'd been together for hours, but he hadn't wanted her to leave, hadn't wanted her to stop talking. He couldn't remember the last time he'd stayed up until—he checked his watch—two o'clock in the morning just talking to a woman.

He got up and pulled the blanket over her shoulders. She didn't stir. Her lips were parted slightly, her cheeks a soft pink, her lashes long and black. Her hair fell over her shoulders in beautiful waves, and he had to fight back the urge to run his hands through her hair, to wake her up and kiss her again.

He could still taste her mouth on his lips, and he wanted more. He liked her—a lot. But she was leaving in a few days, and that he didn't like. He'd always thought of sex as simple, but being with Olivia felt complicated.

He'd like to think that tomorrow might bring clarity to the situation, but he had a feeling once they returned to Olivia's book project, the complications were only going to multiply, and he still had his grandmother's interests to protect.

He got up and headed down the hall to his bedroom, hoping that there wasn't going to come a point when he would have to choose between Olivia and his grandmother. Hopefully, they would all stay on the same side...

Fifteen

Olivia woke up with a pain in her neck. She stretched and yawned, taking a sleepy minute to realize she was on the couch in Colton's apartment. The sun was shining brightly through the windows, and a glance at her watch told her it was almost nine.

She shot up into a sitting position. She hadn't slept this long in forever. She was usually up by seven. The long night of talking had taken its toll. Glancing down the hall, she saw that Colton's door was ajar, but she couldn't hear anyone moving. Was he also still asleep?

She got up and used the bathroom in the hall. She splashed cold water on her face and ran a brush through her hair, then made her way back into the living room just as Colton came through the front door.

He wore running shorts and a t-shirt that clung to his muscled chest and abs. His face was sweaty, his hair damp and curling from his run. Butterflies danced through her stomach. Was it possible that he actually looked more attractive after a workout than he had the night before? She swallowed back a knot in her throat.

"Hey," he said with a warm smile. "You're up."

"I slept in longer than I usually do."

"We were up late."

"Not too late for you, obviously. How far did you run?"

"Not far—three miles."

She smiled. "What do you consider far?"

"Ten or more."

"Seriously?"

"I have to keep in shape so I can do my job. And while I might be grounded for a week because of my hand, I can still run. You weren't taking off, were you?"

"I need to get back to work. Do you want me to give you a ride to pick up your car?"

"That would be great. Can you wait while I take a quick shower?"

"Sure. Do you have coffee? Or should I run out and find some?"

"Coffeemaker is in the kitchen with plenty of coffee in the cupboard. Help yourself."

"Thanks." She turned toward the kitchen, then paused. "Last night was fun, Colton."

His eyes sparkled at her words. "I thought so, too."

They looked at each other for a long moment, and then she forced herself to drop her gaze.

Coffee, she told herself. Coffee, then work. No more fooling around with Colton.

But as she made her way into the kitchen she couldn't help thinking that she'd let an opportunity slip through her fingers. She could have done a lot more than talk to Colton last night, but as usual she'd been unable to let her guard down.

Well, whatever happened, at least she wouldn't be going back to New York with a broken heart—at least she hoped not.

———

A half hour later, Olivia was back in the driver's seat, following Colton's directions to his grandmother's house. "Do you think I could speak to your grandmother this morning? I know I'm supposed to meet her and the other women at the senior center at noon, but I'd like to talk to her before then." She glanced over at Colton when he didn't immediately reply and saw indecision in his expression. "You're not thinking about trying to keep me from speaking to your grandmother, are you?"

"I am supposed to be keeping the two of you apart," he said

with a sigh.

"Aren't we past that, Colton?"

"We are."

"Good, because I need to ask Eleanor about the birth certificate we found. I also want to find out what she knows about Francine's baby." She paused. "I realize I'm more concerned now about my personal ties to the Harpers, but I have to figure that out first so I can focus on the rest of the story."

"The abused women and the underground railroad."

She nodded. "Yes."

"I guess I should be happy that for now you're concentrating on the Harpers."

She smiled. "So we can talk to your grandmother before she goes to the senior center? Because I would like any discussion of Francine and her daughter to be done away from the rest of the group."

He nodded in understanding. "Okay, we'll see if Grandma is up and willing to talk."

"Great."

"Can I ask you something, Olivia?"

"What's that?"

"What do you want the answer to be? Do you want Molly to be your grandmother?"

That was a complicated question. "The truth is—I don't know. I guess part of me wants to know where I come from, and this is the first and only lead I've ever had as far as my biological parents are concerned. But another part of me isn't quite ready to go down that road."

"What are you afraid of?"

"I'm not sure, but considering the way Molly contacted me, I can't help but feel a little wary. My gut tells me that there are minefields ahead, and I should be careful where I step." She paused and gave him a quick look. "You probably think I'm being overly dramatic."

"Actually, I don't. Hopefully, my grandmother can clear the path of some of those minefields. Turn left at the next corner."

As she drove slowly down a pretty tree-lined street of

Victorian apartment buildings mixed in with what appeared to be single home residences, she said, "Have your grandparents lived here long?"

"At least fifteen years. They used to have a big three-story house in the Marina, but they downsized a while back. Looks like there's plenty of parking today. You got lucky."

"I hope my luck continues," she said as she parked the car.

A few minutes later, they rang Eleanor's bell. A middle-aged woman wearing what appeared to be a nurse's uniform opened the door.

"Hello, Donna," Colton said. "Is my grandmother awake and up to seeing me?"

"She's just finishing her breakfast, but I'm sure she'll be happy to see you," the nurse said with a smile. "She's been having some good days lately. Come on in."

Olivia followed Colton into the house. His grandparents' home was beautiful and tastefully decorated in warm, rich, vibrant colors. The rooms were quite a contrast to Colton's sparsely furnished apartment. "You should get your grandmother to help you decorate," she murmured.

"She's never been in my apartment. I think she would be horrified. She's always liked antiques and art."

"I can see that. She has excellent taste."

"My grandfather does, too—surprisingly, or maybe my grandmother just rubbed off on him after sixty years."

She couldn't imagine being married that long to anyone. Their relationship was certainly an amazing testament to their love.

Colton opened the door to the kitchen. Eleanor sat at a small round table. She'd pushed her empty plate to one side and was perusing a magazine while sipping a cup of tea. She looked up and gave them both a happy smile.

"Oh, my, isn't this a lovely surprise," she said.

Colton gave his grandmother a kiss on the cheek, and Olivia found the moment endearing. Every time she turned around, Colton seemed to show her another side, and each side was more appealing than the last.

"I hope you don't mind us interrupting your breakfast," Olivia said. "I wanted to ask you a few questions before we meet later with the rest of the group."

"Of course, please sit down. And, goodness, you're not interrupting anything. I love to have company."

Olivia sat down at the table across from Eleanor with Colton taking the seat next to his grandmother. She could see that Colton was giving her the lead, she just didn't know what to do with it. After a moment of indecision, she decided to just jump right in. "Colton and I went to Molly's house yesterday, and we found some interesting items."

"Really?" Eleanor asked, curiosity in her blue eyes. "What did you find?"

"A birth certificate for a baby girl born on June 7, 1988. The only name filled in was for the mother, Francine Harper."

"Molly's daughter," Eleanor said with a nod. "Francine was a troubled girl. Molly was very upset when Francine got pregnant, because Francine didn't have the means to raise a child, and even if money weren't an issue, Francine had a lot of emotional problems. In the end, Francine decided to give the child up for adoption. It was a very sad time."

Knots tightened in Olivia's stomach. "Do you know what happened to the child?"

"No. It was a closed adoption. I believe that's the right term." Eleanor paused. "Unfortunately, after she gave up her baby, Francine went into a downward spiral, and she ended up overdosing a year later. It was just as well the baby went to a loving family." Eleanor looked at Olivia with a question in her eyes. "What did I say, Olivia? You look a little upset."

"My birthday is June 7, 1988, Eleanor. And I was adopted. I'm wondering if there's a chance that I'm that baby girl—if I'm Francine's daughter and Molly's granddaughter."

Eleanor's eyes widened. "Oh, my goodness. That's really your birthday?"

"It is. And I wondered if Molly wrote to me because she knew I was her granddaughter."

"She never said that to me, Olivia. Not one word. In fact, we haven't spoken of Francine's daughter in twenty years."

Eleanor's clear blue eyes were completely without guile, and Olivia had to accept that Eleanor was telling her the truth. "Okay," she said, not sure where to go next.

Eleanor frowned. "You're upset."

"I'm just confused. I'm trying to figure out if there's a connection between me and Molly or if my having the same birth date as Molly's granddaughter is just a coincidence."

"I can see how that would be upsetting. It is a bit odd. And..."

"And what?" she prodded.

"Your eyes do remind me of Molly," Eleanor mused, giving her a long look. "I suppose it's not completely impossible that Molly had her own reasons for contacting you. Do you have any information about your biological parents?"

"I don't. Do you think Peter Harper would know anything?"

Eleanor frowned for the first time since they'd arrived. "Peter would probably be unwilling to speak to you. He was a sullen boy who grew up to be an angry, bitter man. He's been terrible to his mother and barely civil to me, and I've known him since he was a toddler."

Eleanor's words certainly corroborated what Olivia had already seen in her brief meeting with Peter.

"However," Eleanor continued. "It's possible that Peter knew something about where her baby ended up."

"How did Molly end up with such screwed-up kids?" Colton asked. "Was it because their father died?"

Eleanor's lips tightened. "Their father was not a good person."

"What can you tell me about Stan, about his death?" Olivia asked, seeing dark shadows gather in Eleanor's eyes. "And when did he die? Was it before you started the theater group or after? I assume it was before Francine got pregnant."

"And how did the fire start?" Colton asked. "Where was Molly at the time?"

"I—I don't. I can't. I..." Eleanor's face paled and her eyes darted around the room.

Olivia didn't know if they'd confused her with the barrage of questions or what, but Eleanor seemed suddenly very agitated.

"Patrick? Where's Patrick?" Eleanor questioned, shifting

nervously in her chair. "Patrick says not to talk. Bad to talk."

Olivia sat straighter in her seat, taken aback by Eleanor's now rambling and cryptic words.

"Secret. Must keep secret." Eleanor nodded her head up and down as her gaze flitted around the room.

"What secret?" Olivia asked.

"Can't tell. Can't tell. Can't tell."

"Grandma," Colton cut into her chant. "It's okay, you don't have to talk."

"Who—are you?" she asked in alarm, shrinking from Colton as he tried to put a hand on her shoulder.

"Olivia, get the nurse," Colton said sharply.

She nodded, jumping to her feet. It was the first time she'd seen evidence of Eleanor's illness, and it shocked her at how quickly it had come on. The happy, cheerful woman who had offered them tea had completely vanished.

Olivia found the nurse knitting in the living room. "Mrs. Callaway needs you."

"Oh, dear," Donna replied as she stood up. "She's been having such a good run lately, I was hoping it would continue."

Olivia followed Donna back into the kitchen. She stood just inside the room as Donna attended to Eleanor, talking slowly and quietly, trying to get her to focus on her. Eleanor seemed to be calming down, but her gaze was completely blank. It was as if her soul had left her body.

"You should go," the nurse told them.

Colton hesitated, but then gave a nod. They walked out of the kitchen and down the hall, not stopping until they were outside.

As they paused in front of Eleanor's house, Olivia could feel the anger and frustration building inside Colton.

"I'm sorry," she said.

"I shouldn't have let you go in there. I should have done what my grandfather asked me to do—keep the two of you apart. But I didn't listen. And I didn't just sit there, either. I asked her questions, too. I upset her. Damn." He waved a hand in the air. "What the hell was I thinking?"

She didn't know how to answer that. She supposed she should

be glad he wasn't putting all the blame on her. On the other hand, she felt bad for him. He was kicking himself hard, and what had happened was in fact more her fault than his. "I talked you into it," she said. "You were trying to help me."

"I just hope she can bounce back."

"Does she usually recover quickly? Or does it take a while?"

"It depends. I don't know." He blew out a breath. "My mom is coming here this morning. I'll stick around until she gets here. You can go."

"Okay." She didn't really want to leave, but she didn't think her presence was going to help anything. "I hope your grandmother will be all right. Will you call me later and let me know?

"Sure."

They exchanged numbers and then she returned to her car.

Sliding behind the wheel, a dozen emotions ran through her. She felt guilty for her part in upsetting Eleanor. But she was also intensely curious about the secret Eleanor had mentioned and still unsure of whether or not she was Molly's granddaughter. Eleanor hadn't been able to confirm their relationship, so she would have to try someone else, and the only person left was Peter Harper.

Sixteen

—➤➤◄◄◄—

After returning to her hotel, Olivia got on her computer and searched for information on Peter Harper. It wasn't difficult to find since Peter was vice president of the Cormellon Financial Group, a group of apparently incredibly profitable venture capitalists who were building a new hotel in downtown San Francisco.

She found a picture of Peter and the mayor wearing hardhats at a construction site with a headline reading: *Winthrop Building Gets A New Life.*

She scanned the article to discover that Peter's financial investment group was razing the remains of a badly destroyed building in order to build a new hotel. The building had been in disrepair for almost a decade, having been destroyed by a tragic fire that took the lives of two firefighters. Apparently the construction of the original building had not been up to code and subsequent lawsuits had bankrupted that company. The site had been left untouched until the Cormellon Group decided to get involved. The city of San Francisco was thrilled to have the blight on its skyline removed.

Peter Harper looked happy in the photograph, and why wouldn't he? He was doing something wonderful for the city.

Maybe he was a good man. Eleanor hadn't really led her to that conclusion, and her own first impression had not been a good one, but perhaps she'd judged him too hastily. Peter's mother was dying. It was only normal for him to be angry and upset. She grabbed her phone and punched in the telephone number before she could change her mind.

A woman answered, "Cormellon Group".

"Is Peter Harper available?"

"No, I'm sorry, he's out of the office. Would you like to leave a voicemail?"

"No, thanks, I'll call back." She ended the call and set her phone on the bed. She wondered if Peter Harper was at the hospital visiting Molly. It might be worth making another trip down there. She'd probably get further with him in person than on the phone anyway.

Jumping off the bed, she went into the bathroom and turned on the shower. She needed to refresh, change her clothes, and then attack the day.

–⟫⟪–

Olivia got to the hospital just before noon on Tuesday. She'd changed into dark jeans and a tank top under a bright pink sweater and had pulled her long hair into a thick ponytail. She was ready to face whatever came next.

When she saw Peter Harper sitting in a chair beside his mother's bed, she felt both relieved and nervous. Peter was reading something on his cell phone, and Molly appeared to be in the same condition she'd been the day before.

Olivia hesitated in the doorway, quite sure she would not get a warm welcome, but she was here, and the man she needed to speak to was also here so she was going in.

She'd never been a coward when it came to research and asking tough questions of reluctant people, but this story had taken a turn when she'd found herself quite possibly in the middle of it.

Peter looked up and saw her, taking the decision out of her hands. He got to his feet, and walked over to her as she stepped into the room.

"I thought I made it clear that my mother is in no condition to have visitors, especially people she's never met before."

"She wanted to meet me, Mr. Harper. She asked me to come here."

"Well, that was before she had her stroke."

"I know, and I really wish I'd been able to come sooner, but your mother left me her journals to read, and—"

"What?" he interrupted, anger flashing in his eyes. "What did you say?"

"Your mother wanted me to write a story about her life. She left me her journals, some photographs and a few other items to go through." She decided not to explain that some of those items had been acquired during her visit to Molly's home.

"You'll return them immediately," Peter said, obviously infuriated at the idea that she had anything belonging to his mother. "Those belong with the family."

"I will, of course, return them, but I need to ask you a few questions."

"I have no interest in your questions. My mother's life has always been private, and it will remain so. You need to leave."

She stared at him, seeing the determination in his eyes, but she didn't quite understand where it came from. Was he trying to protect his mother from her? Or was there something else he was trying to protect?

She'd have to figure that out later, because she was quickly running out of time. She had no doubt that Peter Harper was about two seconds away from calling security and having her thrown out.

"Miss—"

"I think I might be Francine's daughter," she blurted out.

His jaw dropped, his eyes widening from the shock of her words. "What—what did you say?"

"I found a birth certificate for a girl born to Francine Harper on June 7, 1988, which happens to be my birthday. I was adopted when I was two days old. The adoption was closed. I had no information on my biological parents, until possibly now."

She could see the pulse beating rapidly in his neck as he processed the information. His gaze raked her face with new interest, as if he were looking for similarities between her and his sister or someone else in the family.

"Do you know what happened to Francine's child? Do you know who adopted her?"

"I have no idea."

"And your mother never gave you any indication that she might be contacting me for another reason than just a desire to tell her story to a writer?"

"She didn't tell me anything about you until the day she had her stroke," Peter replied.

"What did she say then?"

"Not much. She was excited you were coming. I didn't really understand what she wanted you to write about. I started asking her questions, but before she could answer, she collapsed."

"She never suggested that I might be her granddaughter?"

"No." His lips tightened. "Look, I don't know what your game is, but my mother doesn't have any money, so if you're thinking you're in line for an inheritance, you can forget it. My money is completely separate from hers. And she's been living on a fixed income for a long time."

"I don't want money." She stiffened at his ugly suggestion. "And I'm not running a game. I came at Molly's request, and I'm trying to honor my promise to her."

"What promise?"

"That I would tell her story. Did your mother tell you about the underground railroad for abused women that she was involved in? It was tied to a community theater group she participated in back in the seventies."

"I know she sewed costumes for the theater, but my mother and her friends loved to make up stories. Most of them were not true."

"Your mother's friends were quite convincing."

"Well, they're good actresses. You need to stop the book project."

"Why?"

"Because you don't know what you're getting into."

"Then enlighten me," she challenged. "Because so far no one has been willing to tell me why I should leave all this alone."

"My mother is dying. She can't tell you her story. So that's it."

"Some of the other women are alive, Eleanor Callaway for one."

Anger flared in his eyes. "Eleanor Callaway is not anyone you should be talking to. She acts like she was my mother's friend, but she wasn't. She messed up my mother's life."

She was surprised at his intense dislike of Eleanor, a woman that everyone else she had met seemed to adore. "How did Eleanor screw up your mother's life?"

"It doesn't matter. I don't want to talk about that woman."

"Then tell me about Francine. Did she tell you who the father of her baby was? Do you know why she gave her daughter up for adoption?"

"No. She told me nothing. My sister was a disaster. She suffered from depression and anxiety, and she self-medicated with drugs and alcohol. I have no idea who fathered her kid. As for why she gave it up—it was probably the smartest thing she ever did in her life, at least for her daughter. For herself it was another story. She couldn't get herself out of the darkness or over the loss of her child. A year later, she was dead. Is that the kind of mom you're looking for?" he asked.

"I'm not looking for a mother; I have a good one. The woman who raised me gave me everything. She was wonderful, and my dad was amazing, too. Unfortunately, he died when I was in high school. But the years we had together were all anyone could have asked for in a childhood."

"Then you were far luckier than Francine," he said tightly. "You have nothing to gain here, Miss Bennett. If you don't want money, then what's left? Even if by some remote chance you are my sister's child, what does it matter? Francine is dead. My mother is on her way to join her. And I'm not interested in acquiring any more family. I have had more than enough family problems in my life. I sure as hell don't need anymore. So go home. Go back to the people who raised you and count your blessings that my sister gave you away."

She didn't know what to say, but even if she had known, she didn't have a chance to speak. A doctor and a nurse came into the room, and Peter was immediately drawn into conversation about his mother's health and what tests they wanted to run.

With Peter Harper and the medical professionals encircling

Molly's bed, she felt very much on the outside. She didn't even know if she was Molly's granddaughter, and here she was intruding on what might be the last moments of a woman's life.

Shaking her head, she turned and walked out of the room and ran straight into a solid male chest.

Colton!

He caught her by the waist.

"We have to stop meeting like this," he said lightly.

"What are you doing here?"

"Looking for you. I figured you'd want to talk to Peter, and he was probably here."

"You were right. I just spoke to him." She tipped her head toward Molly's room. "I told him about the birth certificate and that I thought I could possibly be his niece. He wasn't receptive to the idea. In fact, he was quite rude about it. He accused me of being after his mother's money. When I said I wasn't, he told me I should be glad I was adopted, that Francine was a drug addict, and that I was better off without her."

Colton's gaze narrowed. "What you really need to do is find out for sure if you're a Harper. You need a DNA test."

"Which I'm sure would require Molly's consent, which she can't give, and I doubt Peter would be interested in making it happen."

Colton thought for a moment. "Maybe we can figure out another way to get a sample. We still have the key to Molly's house. Perhaps we can get her DNA off a hairbrush or a glass she recently used."

A tingle ran down her spine. "That's actually not a bad idea."

"Why don't we go there now? Peter is still with Molly, so he won't be at the house."

"All right." As they walked down the hall, she added, "I told Peter I had his mother's journals, and he flipped out, demanding that I return them immediately."

"Interesting over-reaction."

"I thought so."

They took the elevator to the lobby, then made their way into the parking structure.

"Do you want to follow me to Molly's?" Colton asked. "I'm parked right over there."

"Sounds good." He started to walk away, but she called him back.

"Colton? Why did you come looking for me? I thought you'd be angry with me after what happened with Eleanor."

"I told my grandfather I'd keep my eye on you."

"Is that really the only reason?"

His expression turned more serious. "No."

She waited for him to explain, but he didn't say anything else. He just gave her a long look and then headed to his car.

Seventeen

---→≫≪←---

Olivia thought about Colton on the way to Molly's house. She was happy that he'd shown up at the hospital and relieved that he wasn't blaming her for his grandmother's setback. They'd been practically inseparable since they met, and yet during the few hours they'd been apart, she'd actually found herself missing him. It was so strange. She was used to working alone. In fact, she'd always thought she preferred to be on her own. But this week was different.

Maybe it was because Molly's story had taken a personal turn for her. It wasn't just about writing a book anymore; it was about finding out who she was and what story Molly wanted her to tell.

Or perhaps Molly didn't want her to *tell* the story but rather to *hear* it, to know where she came from.

Or maybe she was completely off-base, and she wasn't related to Molly at all. She needed to find out for sure.

A few minutes later, she was unlocking the door to Molly's house. Being back in her home reminded Olivia of all the things she had yet to look at, the stack of letters that Colton had found and the rest of the contents in the box she'd pulled down from the closet. She wasn't usually so slow to follow up on potential clues or to walk away from a job when she was right in the middle of it. But that's exactly what she had done the night before, when she'd allowed Colton to convince her to live in the moment and leave the past behind. Well, that moment was over, and it was back to business.

"I'm going to get some plastic bags out of the kitchen," Colton told her. "We'll need something to put Molly's hairbrush in."

"I feel kind of sneaky," she said, following him down the hall. "Is this right?"

"We're not hurting anyone."

"But even with a sample, how am I going to get a DNA test? Will it be difficult to find a lab that will do that?"

"No, because I have a sister who's a doctor. I'll get Shayla to help us."

"Will she do that?"

"I'm ninety-nine percent sure." He opened Molly's cupboards, located a box of plastic bags and then headed back down the hall and up the stairs.

Colton was definitely a man on a mission, she thought. And it was kind of nice to let him take charge of this. While Colton was gathering samples from Molly's bathroom, Olivia returned to the bedroom closet.

She'd been so shocked by her find yesterday that she hadn't looked beyond that one box. Maybe there was more to be discovered.

Molly had quite a few clothes in her closet, many of which appeared to be costumes, probably from her theater days. As Olivia looked through the dresses and coats, she couldn't help thinking about the fact that she didn't even know how to sew. Her mom didn't sew, so there had been no one to pass on that tradition. If she'd grown up with her biological family, would she have different skills now?

She reached the end of the rack and realized there was another box on the floor behind all the costumes. She dragged it out and pulled off the lid. The box was filled with thick yellow envelopes stuffed with what appeared to be bills and tax returns. However, what was most interesting about the receipts were the dates. She would have expected the information to be recent, the past few years, but the envelopes went back to the mid-seventies, the time during which Molly had been working with the theater group.

"Did you find something?" Colton asked, startling her.

She stood up and waved her hand toward the envelopes. "I'm

not sure. These look like bills and tax returns, but they're from forty years ago. It seems strange that she wouldn't have thrown them out by now."

"Some people keep things forever."

"In their closet? And where are her current files?"

A puzzled look came into his eyes. "Okay, now you're making me more curious. Let's take the box with us."

"Really?"

"We can't stay here, Olivia. We don't know how long Peter Harper will be at the hospital, and if there's something here linking you to his mother, and he wants to cover that up, this apartment is going to be his first stop."

"Why would he want to cover it up? Molly is sadly dying and Francine is already dead. What does it matter if I'm his niece? Why would he care?"

"You ask a lot of good questions. Maybe the answers are in that box." He walked over and handed her two plastic bags in which he'd put a hairbrush and a toothbrush. Then he picked up the heavy box. "Anything else we should take?"

She sighed, feeling guilty that they were taking anything at all. But since she'd already tried the straightforward approach with Peter and that hadn't worked, she was going to have to be more devious. "This is all I saw in here. Peter is probably going to file charges against me for stealing this stuff. I hope you're willing to bail me out of jail."

"I'll probably be in the cell next to you. But speaking practically, Peter may not notice anything is gone. It's not like we're taking expensive jewelry, cash or electronics—just a bunch of old papers."

"You're right. Let's take everything to my hotel. We can go through the papers there."

"Sounds like a plan."

—➤➤◄◄—

"Where shall we start?" Olivia asked, as Colton set the box down on the small round table in her hotel room twenty minutes later.

"Why don't you read the letters to Molly?" Colton suggested. "And I'll dig into this paperwork. But before we do all that...what about lunch?"

Her stomach grumbled at his question. She could definitely eat something. Since she'd left Colton's house earlier that morning, she had yet to grab any food. "I am hungry."

"There's a deli down the block. I'll grab us some sandwiches. Any requests?"

"Turkey is fine. I'm not picky; whatever comes on it is great."

"You got it. I'll get plenty of snacks. I have a feeling we're going to be here a while."

After Colton left, Olivia sat down on the bed and picked up the letters. She slipped the first one out of the stack and pulled two sheets of paper out of a pink envelope. Then she began to read...

Dear Molly,

I know we're not supposed to keep in touch, but it's been almost two years now and I wanted to reach out and let you know that I'm doing so much better. I've made some friends here in Houston and the kids are starting to do well in school. Joey Jr.'s nightmares finally stopped about two months ago, and I don't think they're going to come back. His personality has completely changed now that he's not living with daily threats of violence. We've all been reborn, Molly. It's an amazing thing.

I can't thank you and Eleanor enough for helping me to change my life. If you hadn't come to me with such understanding in your eyes and also such determination, I am quite certain I would not even be alive right now. But I am alive and I am well and happy. It's been difficult to have no contact with my family, but I know the complete break was absolutely necessary. I hope one day I'll be able to see them again, but my first priority is the kids, and I'll do whatever it takes to keep them safe and to keep me safe so that I can be a good mother to them.

Love always,
Gracie (I actually feel like Gracie now, too. You couldn't have

picked a better name for me.)

Olivia wondered when the letter had been written. There was no date but the pages were yellowed, and if Gracie had been one of the women helped by Molly's group, then her escape had probably been forty years ago. Little Joey Jr. was probably a man in his fifties by now, and his mother Gracie would probably be in her seventies or close to Molly's age. She wondered if their good fortune and happiness had continued after this letter; she really hoped so.

She moved on to the next letter.

Dear Molly,

You were right. The first step is always the hardest. You told me I deserved better, and it took me almost dying to actually realize that. I hope all is well with you. I think of you and Ellie often and send you my prayers and love. You are two of the strongest women I've ever met. You both risked your lives for me. No one could have given me a greater gift, and even though we may never see each other again, I want you to know that you're always in my heart.

Yours truly,
Kelly

Molly and Eleanor had certainly changed lives, Olivia thought, as she read through several more letters that expressed similar sentiments. With each letter, she felt more proud of what Molly and Eleanor and their friends had accomplished. They'd stepped up when so many others had probably turned away. And even if they'd only been able to do it for a few years, they'd made a huge difference in the lives of many women, and not just the women but also their children.

A knock came at her door, and she got up to let Colton in. Seeing the two large bags in his hand, she suspected he'd gone overboard at the deli.

"They had a lot of good food," he said, answering her

unspoken question. "I probably bought too much, but we won't go hungry."

"It looks wonderful." She moved the box off the table and helped Colton set out the food. "I have a small refrigerator, so you can leave the leftovers here."

"If there are any leftovers. I'm starving." As they sat down to eat, Colton added, "So did you start looking through the letters?"

She nodded as she took a big bite of her turkey sandwich. Swallowing, she said, "The ones I read were all thanking Molly for getting them out of whatever terrible situation they'd been in. One alluded to the fact that she'd changed her name and had had no contact with anyone in her family for almost two years, but that her children were doing really well without living under the threat of violence."

Colton shook his head, a grim look in his eyes. "I don't know what kind of man hurts his wife and his kids."

"I don't either." She paused. "Have you ever seen that kind of violence?"

"Once. We responded to a residential fire where a man had locked his wife in the bedroom and set fire to the place."

"Oh, my God." She set down her sandwich, losing her appetite. "That's horrible. What happened? Were you able to save her?"

"Yeah, we saved her. And he went to prison."

"At least there's some justice in the world. I know that's not always the case, especially when it comes to domestic violence." She paused for a moment, popping the top on a can of soda. "I wonder how your grandmother and her friends were able to stop. They were obviously doing a tremendous amount of good, so how did they walk away?"

"The danger got to be too much for them. I think their cover was blown and what they'd been able to do in secret, they couldn't do anymore."

"That's true."

"They had to look out for themselves and for their families. I'm actually a little more curious as to how they got started versus how they ended."

"They must have seen a need. One of the women who wrote one of those letters was probably the catalyst."

"Which makes that box of paperwork interesting, too," Colton said, tipping his head toward the envelopes they'd taken out of Molly's house. "I wonder if we'll find the details of their rescues."

"I have to think we will. It's a long time to keep paperwork unless it's important in some way."

"Very true. By the way, I called my sister Shayla while I was waiting for the sandwiches, and she said she has a friend in the lab who can run a DNA test for us."

"Really?" she asked, her heart jumping at that thought.

"They'll need a sample from you to compare to what they can take off Molly's personal items. Of course it would be helpful to also get a sample from Peter."

"Yeah, I don't think he's going to do that."

"Agreed, so we'll start with what we have."

She ate silently for a moment and then said, "Is it weird that I'm not sure I want to find out?"

He gave her a thoughtful glance. "No. I'm not sure how I'd react if I were in your situation. But I always think in the long run, no matter what the question is, it's better to know the answer, because not knowing is worse." He crinkled up the paper wrap from his sandwich and put it back in the bag. "Time to get to work."

She finished her sandwich as he took the box over to the bed. "I'll put the rest of the food in the fridge in case we get hungry later."

"Good idea."

He opened the first thick envelope and shook the contents out on the bed. "These looks like medical bills."

"That would make sense. Some of the women obviously were hurt before they ran. Maybe Molly helped them get medical care."

"Possibly."

After putting the food away, Olivia wiped the crumbs off the table and threw the discarded wrappers into the trash. When she glanced at Colton, he appeared to be studying a black and white photograph. She couldn't see it clearly from her vantage point, but it appeared to be a woman's leg.

"What are you looking at?" she asked curiously.

"Some really bad bruises," he muttered. "Someone was collecting photographic evidence of their abuse."

She walked over to the bed, wanting to see what he was looking at. He handed her the first photo, which showed a woman in profile from the hips down. She wore what appeared to be bikini bottoms and there were large purple bruises on her upper thigh.

"Damn," Colton said, as he flipped through two more pictures.

"What?"

He gazed up at her. "I think I know why Molly and Eleanor got in the business of saving women from violence."

Her stomach turned over at the look in his eyes. "What are you talking about, Colton?"

He handed her the photo in his hand. The focus of this picture was on a woman's face. One eye was swollen shut. The other eye was black and blue. Her nose was crooked, and her lip was split open and puffy.

"That's Molly," Colton said.

"No," she said in disbelief.

"It is. I'm sure of it."

She didn't want it to be true, but the longer she looked at the picture, the more she saw the similarities between the woman in this photograph and the woman she'd visited at the hospital earlier.

When she turned the photo over she saw a neatly typed label: Molly Harper, November 1973. Her heart stopped.

Molly had been abused. By who? By her husband? By the man who was probably Olivia's biological grandfather?

She felt sick to her stomach. "You're wrong, Colton. Sometimes it's better *not* to know the truth."

Eighteen

—>≫≪<—

Olivia's legs felt weak. She sat down on the edge of the bed, unable to drag her gaze away from the horrific evidence of abuse.

"Are you all right?" Colton asked.

She shook her head. "No. Who could look at this and be all right?" She paused. "Molly was the catalyst for the charity group. She was the one who was being hurt. They must have gotten together to help her." She looked over at Colton, who had a contemplative expression on his face. "What are you thinking?"

"Still processing."

"It seems so obvious now—Molly's letter telling me that her voice had been silenced and that she'd never had the courage to tell her story, but she hoped I would be brave enough to do it. She didn't want me to write just about the underground railroad, she wanted me to write about her."

"Or at least to know about her," Colton said. "If you're her granddaughter, it makes even more sense."

"It does." She looked down at the photo again. Molly couldn't have been more than late thirties in this shot. It was a long time to keep such damning evidence, especially since Molly's husband was dead. "The fire," she said abruptly. "Molly's husband Stan died in a fire." She sucked in a quick breath. "Do you think Molly's friends set the fire? Or maybe Molly did it herself?"

"Or it was an accident," Colton said.

"Could you get me information on that fire?"

"I could ask Emma. She would have access to that

information. Although it was a long time ago."

"It's still worth a try. Could you ask her now?"

"Yes."

"Good. While you call Emma, I'm going to get on the computer and see if I can find any information there."

"I could also have Emma talk to Max," Colton added. "Since Stan Harper was a cop, there would have been a police investigation."

His words sank in. "He was a cop," she echoed. "That's why the women operated their escape group away from the police. Your grandmother told us the police couldn't or wouldn't help. Now we know why."

She grabbed her laptop and started the search engine while Colton pulled out his phone.

"I'll put it on speaker," he said, setting the phone on the bed between them.

A moment later, a woman's voice came over the line. "Hey, Colton, what's up?"

"I need a favor."

"I figured. What do you need?"

"Information on a residential fire that occurred in the mid to late seventies."

"That's a long time ago."

"There was a fatality—Stan Harper, Molly Harper's husband."

"Molly Harper? Does this have something to do with that book that's being talked about?"

"Possibly. Do you think you can pull up the case file on that fire?"

"It might take me some time. We still have a lot of older records in storage, but I will do my best."

"Great. And Em, as fast as you can get the info…"

"I know—you need it yesterday. I'll be in touch, and then you'll tell me why you need it."

"Deal." Colton clicked off the phone. "If there's anything to be found, Emma will find it."

"She sounds nice."

"She can be a pain in the ass, but she is also nice."

Olivia smiled. "I like that you're close to your family. It's sweet."

He groaned. "Sweet—just what every man wants to hear."

She could have told him he was a lot of other things besides sweet, but that would take them down a road that would send them completely off course, and right now she needed to focus.

She turned her attention to her computer search. Stanley Harper's name was unfortunately very common, and she skimmed through pages and pages of Stan Harpers that were clearly not the one she was looking for.

While she was doing that, Colton began going through the rest of the papers in the box. For almost twenty minutes, they worked in silence. She grew more frustrated with each passing minute. She couldn't come up with anything on Stan Harper and the fire that had taken his life.

"This is interesting," Colton said, interrupting the quiet.

"Thank goodness. I've got nothing over here."

He held up a piece of paper upon which was a name and a phone number. "I don't know if this is Molly's handwriting, but the name is Keith Fletcher and the area code is for a San Francisco number. Keith and Donald both said they knew Stan but they weren't friends. I wonder why Keith's number would end up in this box. Is it possible Molly reached out to the police for help?"

"If she did, it doesn't appear she got any help, although there could be any number of reasons why she has that number, Colton."

"True."

"We really need to ask your grandmother."

"Not today. She freaked out when we mentioned Stan and the fire."

"I know, you're right. But it's frustrating not to be able to talk to someone who probably has all the information we need."

"Let's take a break, Olivia."

"And do what? If I keep taking breaks, I'm never going to get answers."

"This will be a working break. We need to take Molly's hairbrush and toothbrush to Shayla, and at the same time you can get your cheek swabbed for a DNA sample."

"All right." She could use a minute to think. She knew she was running too fast and jumping to too many conclusions that weren't supported by facts, so she would regroup. And as Colton said, she would still be working on the story, just through another angle.

—➤➤◄◄—

Colton's twin sister Shayla was an attractive blonde who wore her long blonde hair pulled back and up in a twisted bun. While her white coat over a navy blue sheath dress was very professional, Shayla still looked a little young to be a doctor, Olivia thought, but then remembered Colton telling her that Shayla was an intellectual genius who'd skipped several grades in school.

"I appreciate this, Shay," Colton told his sister who had met them in the hallway outside the third-floor lab. "This is Olivia Bennett."

"Nice to meet you," Shayla said, giving her a friendly smile. "So you think you might be related to Molly Harper?"

"That's what I'm trying to find out."

"I checked in on Molly earlier. She's still unconscious. I've been keeping an eye on her for Grandma," Shayla said, her smile dimming. "The prognosis isn't good I'm afraid. But as long as she's alive there's always hope."

Olivia wondered if Shayla really believed that, or if her words were just a practiced line that she'd spoken dozens of times to other anguished relatives.

"What did you bring me?" Shayla asked.

Colton held up the plastic bags. "I grabbed whatever I thought might provide a sample. But I did have the thought that Molly is in this hospital and—"

"And you can put that thought out of your head," Shayla finished. "Molly's son has power of attorney over her medical care, and I'm not taking a DNA sample from her without his permission. However, if you want to get his permission…"

"I don't think he'd give it," Olivia said. "I spoke to him earlier, and he told me that if I were his niece, I should just count my blessings that I'd grown up far away from the Harper family. He had no interest in confirming whether or not I'm related to him, at least not right now." She couldn't help but feel a little bitter and angry about Peter's reaction. He didn't know her, and he didn't want to know her, and despite the fact that she didn't know him, either, she felt rejected, and it stung.

It probably wasn't surprising that she had a lower threshold for rejection than most people. Her biological mother had given her up, and it didn't matter how good her reason was, she'd still given Olivia away, and that was a fact she'd lived with her entire life.

"Well, we'll see what we can get off of these items," Shayla said, taking the bags from her brother. "I have an exam room available." She walked a short way down the hall and opened a door. "I'll get a swab from you, and we'll be good to go."

"Great," she said, following Shayla into the small room. It took only a second for Shayla to take her DNA sample. How strange that such a simple test could possibly change her life.

"How long until we know the results?" Colton asked. "We're kind of in a rush."

"You? In a rush?" Shayla teased. "Why am I not surprised?"

"Actually, we're on Olivia's timetable," Colton replied. "She's supposed to head back to New York next week."

"And I'd really like to know if I'm related to Molly before then," Olivia put in.

"I have a friend who owes me a favor," Shayla said. "Hopefully, I'll have an answer for you tomorrow. But I have to warn you that it may not be completely definitive depending on the sample and the fact that determining a familial relationship is not as strong as identifying maternity or paternity."

"I understand," Olivia said. "If I could even just rule myself out, that would be helpful."

"I'll do what I can to help." Shayla paused. "Wouldn't my grandmother be able to tell you if you're Molly's granddaughter? I've spent a lot of time with Grandma and Molly over the years, and they are super tight. I feel like there's nothing they don't know about each other."

"Really?" Colton interrupted. "I don't remember spending much time with Molly. How come you did?"

"Well, you liked to take off on your bike and come back at dinnertime," Shayla said. "I liked to listen to Grandma's stories, and go with her when she visited her friends. I really liked Molly, too. She was sweet and she made really excellent peanut butter cookies. She was always so happy to see us. I think she was often lonely."

As Olivia listened to Shayla talk about Molly, she felt sad that she might never speak to her grandmother. To have come so far and to be so close and yet not be able to connect was incredibly frustrating.

"I have to get back to work," Shayla said. "I'll let you know as soon as I hear back from my friend."

"Thanks again," Olivia said.

After Shayla left, they walked down the hall and then waited for the elevator.

"It's strange to think that Molly is lying in a bed just two floors above us," she said.

"Do you want to go see her again?" Colton asked.

She hesitated. "I don't think I can risk another run-in with Peter, not until I know more. He was pretty aggressive with me this morning. And from what I read about him, he's a powerful man in San Francisco. He works for an investment group that apparently finances some very large projects. I found a picture of him with the mayor. They were wearing hardhats and breaking ground for some new hotel." She paused. "I think the building was called the Winthrop, and there was a terrible fire there about twenty years ago."

Colton's expression turned grim. "Yeah, a couple of firefighters died in that fire. The way the fire was fought is now taught at the academy as the way *not* to fight a fire. I remember my dad took me by there one day when I was a kid. The place just sat there wrecked for a long time. I was glad when they finally tore it down."

"It will be good to have something new in its place," she murmured.

"And Peter Harper is part of that," he mused. "Interesting. I had no idea he was a wealthy investor. Molly's house sure doesn't look like she's related to anyone who has money."

"Maybe Peter doesn't share his good fortune with his mother," she said as they got onto the elevator. "It wouldn't surprise me."

"I really want to meet this guy."

"Trust me, it's no treat. I'm not sure what I'm hoping for with this DNA test, Colton. Do I want to be Molly's granddaughter? She's dying and her only son hates me. Maybe it would be better if I wasn't related to them."

"It's pointless to speculate," Colton said, as they got off the elevator and walked out to his car.

"I can't help myself. And part of me is angry that Molly dragged me into this. What if she is my grandmother? What if I find that out right before she dies or right after she dies? I'm going to have to grieve for a woman I don't even know. I probably wouldn't even be allowed to go to the funeral. And then what? I just go on with my life as if nothing changed when everything changed?"

He smiled. "You are spinning, Olivia."

"I know, I'm making myself dizzy."

"Me, too. I'd suggest a run, but you're not exactly dressed for it. However, I do have an idea for how you can burn off some of that excess adrenaline you've got racing through your body."

She gave him a suspicious look as he opened her car door. "Does this have something to do with the bed in my hotel room?"

"Damn. I can't get anything by you," he said with a grin. "But, no, you're wrong. That wasn't what I was thinking. I have a much more G-rated idea. However, we can go with your plan if you want."

"Why don't you tell me yours instead?"

"Why don't I just show you? Do you trust me, Olivia?"

She looked into his blue eyes and nodded. "Surprisingly, yes. Don't let me down."

"I won't."

Nineteen

—➤➤⋘⋖—

"You like to be mysterious," Olivia said, as Colton drove out of the hospital parking lot.

"I'd rather have you puzzling about where we're going now and not stewing about your possible biological family."

"So you're making this intriguing for me. How generous."

He grinned. "I do what I can to help."

"And you're happy to help now because the story has moved away from your grandmother," she said pointedly.

"That is true. Not that I don't feel for you, Olivia."

"Even though there's a good chance my imagination has taken this story to a place it didn't need to go?"

He gave her a sympathetic smile. "I think you have good instincts. And while you don't have concrete proof, there's enough circumstantial evidence to believe there's a connection between you and Molly."

"I do believe that."

"Believing that means your world has just turned upside down."

"That's exactly the way it feels. I don't know which side is up. I do wish that Peter had had a more positive reaction when I suggested that I might be related to him. But looking at it from his viewpoint, I can see where he might think I'm a lunatic."

"I've been thinking about Peter, about how it must have been impossibly difficult to grow up in a house where his father was beating up his mom. I can't even imagine what that would have been like. My parents rarely raise their voices to each other. And I know my mother would have never tolerated my dad hitting her."

"My mother wouldn't have allowed that, either. I'd be out the door if someone gave me so much as a shove. But everyone is different, and I don't want to blame Molly for not leaving Stan. It was a different time, and judging by those horrific bruises we saw, she was dealing with something really bad." She paused for a moment, her thoughts moving back to Peter. "Maybe growing up in that environment is why Peter turned out to be such a cold, unfriendly person. He may have had to find a way to stop himself from caring too much."

"The violence could also explain why his sister turned to drugs and alcohol," Colton said. "They were probably two messed-up kids."

She shifted in her seat to give him a smile. "That's pretty good psychoanalysis for a firefighter."

He tipped his head. "I have my moments."

"Well, hopefully the DNA test will at least shed some light on whether or not I'm a Harper by blood. Until then I'm just speculating. It's a good thing you have so many siblings. I think we have half your family working on this puzzle now."

He shot her a smile. "Big families are good for some things."

"A lot of things, from what I can see. I just don't know how any woman has eight kids."

"Oh. Well, Lynda didn't have eight kids." He shot her a quick look. "I didn't mention that my parents were both married before?"

"No, you didn't."

"My dad's first wife died. He was a widower with four little boys and then he met Lynda. She was divorced and she had two little girls."

"Emma and Nicole."

He nodded. "And together Jack and Lynda had twins—Shayla and me."

"A familiar theme song is starting to play in my head," she teased.

He laughed. "Yeah, I know. You're not the first one to sing that tune. I guess we were a little like *The Brady Bunch*, but we didn't have a housekeeper, and as kids we weren't nearly as nice to each other. I got shoved around pretty regularly by my four older brothers."

"They toughened you up."

"They did. I probably had an easier time handling the firehouse because of them. I learned how to stand up for myself when I was very young."

"Even though they tortured you, I suspect they also watched out for you."

"Yeah. Being on the younger end of the spectrum, I've always had a lot of people in my business."

She thought again how nice that all sounded. While she couldn't complain about her childhood, Colton's sounded a lot more fun.

As Colton took a turn, she caught a glimpse of the blue ocean ahead and realized where they were going. "Ah, the beach. Nice choice for an escape."

"Well, you are a southern California surfer girl at heart. I'm just sorry I don't have a surfboard with me."

"That's fine. I'm sure the water is freezing and neither of us is dressed for swimming."

"You've never heard of skinny dipping?" he teased.

"I've heard of it; I've just never done it."

"Never?" he asked with surprise. "Really? Not even when you were a teenager?"

"Nope. I'm a little boring, what can I say?"

"You can say you might try it sometime."

"I might try it sometime," she echoed. "If I have the right incentive."

He flung a grin at her. "That sounds like a challenge."

She smiled back at him. "You take everything as a challenge."

"It's good to push the boundaries, Olivia."

He was right. She'd just never been very good at doing that. Or maybe she had been good—once. But she'd backed away from life after her dad died. She'd stopped taking chances. She'd stopped wanting to feel anything. She didn't want to care about anything too much or love someone too much or want something too much.

Frowning, she realized how her fear had kept her in the

background of life. She'd also stayed behind Philip for far too long. She'd grown out of that job after a year, but she'd stayed for four years. And she was still there.

Maybe not for much longer.

Even if she couldn't cull together a book out of this San Francisco trip, even if it turned out she wasn't Molly's granddaughter, even if everything about this week was a bust, she'd still changed. And she wasn't going to change back. She was going to find a way to step out of the shadows of her own life.

As she cast a sly glance at Colton, she couldn't help but think that she'd found the perfect partner in crime for just such a journey.

Colton pulled into a parking lot off the Great Highway. They were about a mile and a half north of the beach that faced the senior center, and she thought that was probably deliberate. Colton wanted her to enjoy the beach and not think about his grandmother and her stories of the past.

She got out of the car and walked toward the sand, enjoying the brisk afternoon breeze that made her shiver just a little. But it was a good shiver. She already felt rejuvenated. The beach was deserted, the sun was sinking low in the sky at a little before five. The days were definitely getting shorter, but thankfully the weather was still good.

She couldn't believe how much had happened in the last few days. Every hour seemed to arrive with a new twist or turn. It was no wonder she was spinning, but being out here on the beach did make her feel more grounded. It was easy to get tunnel vision when she was working on a research project but now, looking out over the horizon, she felt her world opening up again.

She turned her head to see Colton grabbing something out of the back of his car. When he came nearer, she could see it was a bright orange plastic disc.

"I promised you some exercise," he said.

"I was thinking we could just walk on the beach, watch the sun set. It should be down in the next hour."

"Then we've got sixty minutes left for fun."

She couldn't say no, not in the face of the irresistible smile that he flashed her. "I'm not good at throwing those things. There's a good chance it will end up in the water."

"I'll give you a few tips." He paused as he joined her. "First tip, we take off our shoes." He kicked off his tennis shoes and pulled off his socks.

She was happy to do the same since she didn't really want to walk in the sand with her ankle boots on. Barefoot, she rolled up her jeans to just below her knees and followed Colton across the sand. He had a lanky, long stride and she had to rush a little to keep up with him.

He stopped about ten feet from the waves and dropped his shoes on the ground. She did the same.

"Okay, so there's a trick to throwing the disc correctly."

"Really? There's a trick?"

"It's all in the wrist."

"I guess I should be glad you didn't break the fingers on your right hand."

"I could still throw it with broken fingers, but I am better right-handed."

"Cocky, too."

"I know what I'm good at."

She laughed and rolled her eyes. "I'm sure you do."

"Do you want me to show you or not?"

"Please do."

"We're going to have to get a little closer," he said with a wicked light in his eyes.

"Why am I not surprised?"

"It's easier this way."

He came around behind her, putting one hand on her waist as he proceeded to demonstrate the proper grip and the way to spin the disc with the throw. His words washed over her in a delicious blurry wave of warmth, her focus more on the feel of his hand on her waist, his chest so solid behind her back, his fingers covering hers as they both gripped the disc. She could actually stay like this for a while.

Or maybe she'd turn around, drop the disc on the ground and kiss Colton the way she wanted to.

That thought got her heart pumping, and she was so very

tempted to make that move, but then Colton stepped away from her.

"Ready to try it?" he asked.

She frowned, disappointed that the lesson was over and annoyed with herself for once again being too chicken to make a move. It shouldn't always be about what the guy wanted. It could be about what she wanted, too, couldn't it?"

"What's the problem?" Colton asked, his gaze narrowing in confusion.

"There's no problem. Let's do it. Give me the disc."

"You seem a little pissed off."

"Not at all. I'm just ready to play."

"Okay, great. Let's play." He handed her the disc. "You can take the first throw." Colton ran down the beach about ten yards. "Let's start at this distance."

"You're not very far away."

"So throw it over my head and prove me wrong."

She adjusted the disc in her hand and then threw it as hard as she could. Her wrist motion was all wrong, and the disc landed several feet in front of Colton.

"So that was a good start," he encouraged. He walked forward, picked up the disc and handed it back to her.

"It was a terrible start. Don't be so nice."

"Okay, then suck it up, throw harder and don't forget to use your whole arm, not just your hand. Try to spin it like a guy and not a girl."

Her frown deepened. "Now you've turned mean."

He laughed. "I can't win with you. Just throw it again and see how you do."

She kept some of his suggestions in mind as she tossed the disc in his direction once again. She was surprised at how much she'd improved with one throw.

Her next throw actually sent the disc sailing over Colton's head but at the last minute he leapt into the air and caught it.

"You're getting the hang of it," he yelled.

She continued to improve over the next fifteen minutes, challenging herself to throw it longer and straighter as Colton continued to lengthen the distance between them.

"Now, let's make it tougher," Colton said. "I'm going to make you run for it. You do the same. First one to let the disc hit the ground loses. Actually, I'll let you have one hit with no penalty since you're a—"

"A woman?" she asked, cutting him off. "I don't need any favors just because I'm a woman." She probably did need a practice point, but she hated to admit that she was not as good as he was.

"I wasn't giving you a favor because you're a woman but because you're a beginner, but suit yourself."

"Game on. What do I get when I win?"

"What do you want?"

"How about winner buys dinner?"

"Let's go."

With a renewed sense of purpose, Olivia found herself scrambling across the sand and sometimes diving for the disc as Colton's throws became increasingly more difficult. At one point, she actually came up with a mouthful of sand. She spit it out as Colton asked if she was okay and jumped to her feet. She wasn't going to wimp out now. He might have made her hit the dirt, but she had another plan in mind.

It was clear to her that Colton didn't just like to compete, he also liked to win. And he'd do whatever it took to not let the disc hit the ground.

Her next throw went sailing toward the sea. Colton sprinted across the sand, his focus so pure and precise that he didn't even hesitate to launch himself into the air. He came down with the disc, but he landed in two feet of water, and a rolling wave took him down on his ass.

He struggled to get up, the disc in his hand but murderous intent in his eyes.

"Good catch," she said, laughing at his sopping clothes and disgruntled expression.

"You did that on purpose, Olivia."

"We didn't have any boundaries." She backed up as he stalked toward her.

"The ocean was an implied boundary."

"You never said that." Another laugh slipped past her lips as he paused for a moment to wring out the edge of his t-shirt.

"You're enjoying this a little too much," he said.

She was enjoying herself. The tension of the last three days had completely disappeared with the crashing of the waves, the salty sea breeze dampening her cheeks, and the occasional squawk of a seagull. The beach had worked its magic.

Or maybe it was Colton, the man who was stomping deliberately in her direction. And judging by the expression on his face, he was about to exact payback.

She took off running down the beach, knowing she was probably only postponing the inevitable. Colton ran every day. He was in excellent physical shape, and while she occasionally made it to the gym and got on the elliptical for an hour, most of her days were spent sitting at a desk and working on her computer.

Flinging a quick look over her shoulder, she saw he was closing in on her. Probably the only thing slowing him down was the fact that his jeans and shirt were soaked and heavy with water.

She tried to speed up, but she couldn't get enough traction in the slippery sand. A second later, Colton grabbed her around the waist, and before she could react he had flung her up and over his shoulder like she was no heavier than a rag doll. Then he headed straight for the sea.

"Don't," she squealed, trying to squirm out of his hold, but the man had a grip on her. He was used to carrying people out of burning buildings, so this was probably nothing for him.

He ran right into the water. She could see it swirling around his ankles, and she put every last ounce of energy and guile she had into staying out of the ocean.

"I'll do whatever you want," she pleaded. "Just don't drop me."

"Whatever I want?"

"Well, within reason," she quickly amended.

"I was going to give in until you said that."

"Colton, you can't throw me in."

"You didn't hesitate to get me wet," he retorted.

Up until the second the icy cold water hit her feet, she thought he would save her, but the next thing she knew she was sitting in three feet of freezing water, her eyes blurred from the spray, her heart almost stopping from the cold, and a pile of seaweed wrapping itself around her hand.

As the current began its pull toward the ocean, Colton grabbed her hand and yanked her to her feet. They half ran, half stumbled to dry land. Once her toes curled in the warmer dry sand, she stopped to catch her breath.

Then she looked at Colton, who had a huge smile on his face. "I can't believe you did that."

"I owed you, and you said you didn't want any favors because you're a woman," he reminded her.

"Yeah, but..." She couldn't really finish that sentence because she had no real defense. She had been cocky enough to say that earlier, and she had been the one to send him into the sea first.

He laughed. "Can't think of anything to say? This must be a first."

She thought for a moment and then realized the plastic disc was no longer in his hands. "Actually, I have two words for you—*I win.*"

"What are you talking about? I caught it before I landed in the water."

"But where is it now? You must have dropped it."

"I didn't drop it. I put it down over there," he said pointing down the beach.

"All I know is that it's on the ground and you didn't throw it to me, so I win. And winner buys dinner, remember?"

He stared back at her, his brows drawing into a frown. "Well..."

"Nothing to say?" she prodded a moment later.

"I think you're winning on a technicality."

"A win is a win." She wrapped her arms around her waist as another chill ran through her. "I need to dry off."

"Let's go back to the car. We can argue with the heat on."

As they started to walk, Colton put an arm around her shoulders, and she couldn't resist snuggling up to his side as they made their way down the beach. She told herself she was only being practical and trying to share some of his body heat, but that was a lie. She liked his arm around her. Liked being next to him. She couldn't remember the last time she'd had so much fun.

She even kind of liked the fact that he'd tossed her into the sea, although she'd never admit that to him. But the action showed that he respected her. He'd treated her like an equal and showed that he could take a prank as well as give it back in return. She'd never liked people who took themselves too seriously, who couldn't be the butt of a joke without getting pissed off or embarrassed.

But Colton didn't care that his clothes were soaked in saltwater and that there was sand now clinging to his jeans in thick clumps. And the truth was, she didn't really care, either, because maybe, just maybe, she'd been taking her own life a little too seriously, and she'd needed a vivid reminder that not every day had to be a battle.

Or at least not every part of every day…

When they got to the car, Olivia was also extremely happy that they had taken Colton's car and not her rental.

"Do you have a towel or sweatshirt or anything I can sit on?" she asked.

He shook his head. "Don't worry about it. A little sand and water isn't going to kill this baby. She's been all over the state in all kinds of weather."

Judging by the weathered interior of his Jeep, he wasn't kidding. "Why do men always refer to their cars as *she*?"

"No idea," he said with a smile as he started the car and blasted the heat. "Maybe because, like women, they can be beautiful, fast and also extremely dangerous."

She smiled at that. "Really? You run into burning buildings, and you think women are dangerous?"

He nodded. "Absolutely."

"Well, I think you're crazy. I've never broken anyone's heart."

"Maybe you just don't know that you did." He pulled out of the parking lot and drove back down the Great Highway.

She thought about his words for a moment and then shook her head. "No, I don't think so. I've really only had two serious boyfriends. One was freshman year of college, and I think I picked him because I was still looking to escape all the grief of my last year in high school. He eventually moved on to someone who was probably in a happier state of mind."

"And the second one?"

"He was after college—a law student. We dated for almost a year. I was a little surprised when it ended. But he didn't like law school and he wasn't crazy about New York, so he dropped out of school and decided to travel around for a year. He asked me if I wanted to go with him, but I had just gotten the job with Philip Dunston, and I wanted to be moving towards something, not living like a nomad in whatever place he wanted to go to. So we broke up."

"Did you ever hear from him again?"

"He sent me a few postcards, but that ended after about six months. I later heard from a mutual friend that he moved to Australia." She paused. "So I definitely did not break his heart."

"It doesn't sound like he broke yours, either."

"No, he didn't. I was a little sad when he left, but not sad enough that I wanted to follow him." She glanced at Colton. "He once told me I was too serious for him. That I needed to loosen up and have some fun once in a while."

Colton gazed back at her. "He didn't know you at all."

She liked his answer. "I know I can be too serious. It wasn't a completely unfair criticism."

"But you can also let loose. Look at you now. And you're not even mad that I threw you into the ocean."

"I wouldn't go that far."

He simply smiled.

"What about you—since we're sharing," she said. "Any broken hearts in your wake?"

"I don't think so. I try not to lead women on."

"What about serious girlfriends?"

"I have the opposite problem of you, Olivia. No one thinks I'm serious about anything."

She thought about that, heard the undertone in his voice, and knew without a doubt that he had far more depth than he let on. She repeated his words. "Then they don't know you at all."

Their gazes met, sparked, clung together. And then he

reluctantly turned his attention back to the road.

He didn't say anything more the rest of the way back to the hotel, which was fine, because she hated to admit that she was a bit shaken by what had just passed between them. She could handle the fun and games Colton, the charming man with the irresistible smile. She could play off his wit and sense of humor, but the more serious side of the man made her pulse race, and her heart couldn't seem to settle into a steady beat. That man could really get under her skin, she thought. That man could be someone worth breaking her heart over.

But maybe their relationship didn't have to be about love. It could just be about fun, about sensual, pleasurable, toe-curling fun. Her nerves tingled at the thought.

Colton pulled into a parking spot in front of her hotel. "I guess I should go home, take a shower, and change clothes."

"I guess so," she said, thinking it might be more enjoyable if they took their showers together. Heat ran through her at the thought.

"What are you thinking about?" he asked.

"Nothing," she said quickly. "I should shower and change, too. I'm sure I'm going to draw some curious looks getting into the elevator."

"Maybe I should come with you, then you won't be the only one drawing attention."

"That would be chivalrous," she said lightly, knowing that she was playing with danger.

"Only if you want the company." His gaze once again held hers.

She hesitated for a long second, then nodded. "Yes, I think you should come up to my room with me. I have a nice shower with great water pressure."

A light flashed in his blue eyes. "Seriously?"

"Didn't I just tell you that I'm almost always serious?" Without waiting for an answer, she got out of his car and waited for him on the sidewalk. For a split second, she wondered if he wasn't going to take her up on her offer. That was the problem with putting herself out there—there was always a risk.

Twenty

—⟫⟪⟪⟪—

Colton didn't know what made him hesitate. But it wasn't until he saw Olivia hit the sidewalk and slowly turn to see if he was following that he jumped out of the car. He knew she didn't hook up with random guys. In fact, that's why he hadn't moved right away. He'd still been thinking she'd retract her offer to come inside, because if he went into her hotel room, he would not be leaving anytime soon.

But her sweet, uncertain smile told him she was okay with that. So he met her on the sidewalk and put his arm around her waist as they entered the hotel together.

The front desk gave them a speculative look, but he was on the phone, and quickly his attention was brought back to his call. They didn't see anyone else on their way up to Olivia's room.

Olivia unlocked her door and walked inside, tossing her handbag down on the table. Then she gave him a nervous look. "Should I turn on the shower?"

He found her hesitancy very appealing. She was an intriguing mix of soft and hard, innocence and sophistication, seriousness and fun, all of which made for a really likeable woman. Not to mention beautiful. Even now with her dark ponytail dripping water on the rug and all the makeup erased from her face, she was spectacularly pretty.

"You're staring, Colton."

"I know. I haven't been able to take my eyes off of you since I first met you—in case you hadn't noticed."

She licked her lips. "I've been fighting a similar battle. You have a smile that's pretty irresistible. And your eyes—"

"Are not as amazing as your eyes." He smiled. "So I guess we're two beautiful people, huh?"

She laughed as he broke the tension. "Yes, and we're both really modest." She paused. "You're good at making me relax, Colton."

"You, on the other hand, have me all wound up," he said, feeling edgy and eager but not wanting to rush her too fast into anything.

Her green eyes darkened at his words. "This—us—it could be a mistake."

"It could be," he agreed. "We don't have to do anything, Olivia. I can leave right now. No harm. No foul."

"No fun?"

He tipped his head. "I think we would be missing out on something amazing."

"I do, too." She gazed back at him for a long moment. "I don't want you to leave, Colton. I want you to stay."

His chest tightened at the look of desire in her eyes. "I'm glad you feel that way, because I didn't really have any intention of going anywhere." He quickly bridged the space between them, putting his hands on her waist and leaning in to steal a quick kiss. Her lips were salty and cool; he was determined to change that. "Let's get you out of these wet clothes."

"You first." She grabbed the hem of his t-shirt and helped him pull it over his head. Then she stepped back, her eyes a little awed.

"My God. You're gorgeous, Colton. I mean, I thought you would be, because you're a firefighter, and you're fit, and you run…" She blew out a breath as she fanned her face with her hand. "I feel a little intimidated, I won't lie. I do not have abs like that."

He liked the look of hunger in her eyes. It made him feel good about all those hours he'd spent working out.

"I'm glad," he said. "Because I like curves—soft, sexy curves." He unbuttoned her blouse and pulled it off of her shoulders. As she slipped her arms out of the sleeves, his gaze fell to the deep red bra hugging a generous pair of breasts and his mouth went dry.

Her skin was a pale gold with a dusting of freckles on her shoulders and along her collarbone. A few errant freckles slid behind her bra straps, beckoning him to come closer.

He flicked open the front closure on her bra, pulling the sides apart and shook his head in appreciation of her beautiful breasts. "Now who's intimidated?" He covered her breasts with his hands, loving the soft globes and the hard peaks, and then he lowered his mouth to first one breast and then the other.

Olivia sighed, her hands running through his hair, holding his head to her breasts as his tongue swirled around her nipples.

His jeans were unbelievably tight now, the fabric already stiff from the seawater. He reluctantly raised his head and stepped back so he could unsnap his jeans and pull them off.

While he was doing that, Olivia stepped out of her jeans and a slinky red thong and then gave him a beautiful view of her lovely ass as she ran into the bathroom.

The heated water was just beginning to steam up the glass door when he jumped into the shower with her. She had her arms crossed self-consciously in front of her breasts, but there was no hiding in the small space. He pulled her arms away, his hands sliding down to grab her fingers. And for a long moment he just held on to her and let his gaze travel down her body.

She'd looked good in her clothes, but naked... His blood boiled as his erection stood up in appreciation. She was flipping awesome. And he wanted to take his time to explore every glorious inch of her. But he was by nature impatient, and tonight was no different. He wanted the ride to be long, but he knew once he touched her, kissed her, things were going to go fast.

So he resisted for one long minute.

"Colton," she said, her voice a husky plea of need and desire. "What are you waiting for?"

"You," he said simply. And in that moment, he realized he'd been waiting for her all his life. He just hadn't known it until this second.

He pulled her up against him, then let go of her hands to slide his arms around her back. As the hot spray of water streamed over their heads, he kissed her, and she kissed him back.

Throwing her arms around his neck, she moved closer to him so that the water was running down her back. Then she parted her lips, her tongue teasing his, inviting him inside.

The hesitancy she'd shown earlier completely disappeared as the passion that had been simmering between them burst into flames. Heat shimmered over him in waves from every kiss, every touch. The mix of water and steam surrounded them, creating an island of need. The rest of the world faded away. All he could see, taste, touch was Olivia.

His hands roamed her body, her breasts, her stomach, and the curve of her hips. He played with the heated core between her legs, his fingers dipping inside, every move making her moan with pleasure.

He liked those little moans, the way she squirmed against him. She was so sensitive, so responsive, so gloriously uninhibited now that she'd let down her guard.

And when her hands cupped him, when she whispered into his ear, *I need you,* he had to fight back the urge to push her up against the shower wall and take her right there.

"Bed," he muttered, his brain having trouble working with his blood racing south. He kissed her again and then pulled her out of the shower, grabbing a big white terry cloth towel to wrap around her body.

They dried off quickly, then moved into the bedroom.

While Olivia cleared off the bed, he picked up his jeans and pulled a condom out of his pocket.

"You were prepared for this," Olivia said as he gently pushed her down on the bed. "Or maybe you are always—"

"Hush," he said, putting his fingers across her mouth. "I was just being optimistic." He replaced his fingers with his lips as she fell back against the pillows.

It felt so good to have her under him, to feel all those deliciously soft curves surrounding him. He tried to breathe through the desperate need to immediately slide into her, wanting to make it as good for her as he possibly could.

But Olivia was impatiently urging him on, sliding her legs apart, gripping his ass with her hands as she murmured the four best words in the entire English language—*I want you, Colton.*

"You have me," he said, sliding into her heat with a feeling of complete and utter joy.

They moved together perfectly, as if they'd made love a thousand times before. And as they came together, he looked into her eyes and saw the happy, smoky passion of release and wanted to do it all over again, just so he could see that expression, just so he could feel so completely right with the world.

Olivia pulled him down on top of her, and he let her hold his weight for a moment, delighting in the scent of her wet hair against his face.

Finally, he rolled onto his side and then pulled her into his arms so they were facing each other.

She gave him a hazy smile. "That was good."

He smiled back at her. "Better than good."

She sleepily closed her eyes as she murmured, "Maybe we could stay here forever."

Watching her fall into a sweet sleep of pleasurable exhaustion, he whispered, "Maybe we can."

It was the first time in his life he'd ever considered *forever.*

Olivia stretched, feeling the sweet ache of sensual satisfaction. As she opened her eyes, she realized how dark the room was. She lifted her head off of Colton's chest where she'd been happily pillowed for the last few hours. Glancing at the clock, she realized it was almost eleven o'clock at night.

They'd been in bed since sometime after six and they'd made love twice. As much as she wanted to stay right where she was, her stomach was rumbling.

Her gaze turned to the man beside her. She smiled as she watched Colton sleep, enjoying having a few moments to really look at him. He had a strong jaw and a sexy stubble spreading across his cheeks. A strand of brown hair fell towards one eye, and she couldn't resist sliding it back off of his forehead.

The gentle movement was enough to make his eyes flutter

open. His arm tightened around her waist as he blinked a few times. Then his deep blue gaze met hers. He really had great eyes, she thought. Sometimes they were a light blue like the morning sky, and other times they were the same color as the deepest part of the ocean. Now, with the moonlight streaming through the windows, they looked almost gray.

"Hi," he said softly, his fingers stroking her back. "You're awake."

"Yes, and I know this probably isn't very sexy to say, but I'm hungry."

His lips parted in the smile she liked so much. "Me, too."

"Shall we raid the fridge? Some of the feast you picked up for lunch is still there."

"That would be perfect, but—" His arm tightened around her. "That means one of us is going to have to get out of bed."

"Is that going to be me?"

"Well, I would like to watch you walk around the room naked."

"I wouldn't mind that show from you," she teased. "And it would be the gentlemanly thing to do."

"You're going to play that card, are you? I thought you believed in equal treatment for men and women, but apparently only when it's convenient to you."

"Guilty. However..." She scooted up his body, letting her breasts graze his chest as she kissed his mouth. "I could make it worth your while."

"You don't really think I'm getting out of this bed now, do you?" He shifted beneath her as he pulled her on top of his body, making it very clear that he was far more interested in sex than food.

"You must be hungry."

"I am—for you." He stroked the side of her face with his hand. "You're amazing, Olivia."

"A girl always likes to hear that after..."

He smiled, his thumb running across her lips. "Before, after, during, a month from now...I don't think my opinion has changed since I first met you, and I don't think it will change any time soon.

In fact, the more I get to know you, the more I like you."

"You've grown on me, too." As she said the words, she felt a little sad, because she knew that this relationship—or whatever it was—couldn't go anywhere. Her life was on the other side of the country and his was here in San Francisco. But she didn't want to think about that now. Colton had shown her the beauty in living in the moment, and that's what she was going to do.

She cupped his face with her hands and gave him a long look, then slowly and deliberately lowered her head and covered his mouth with hers. A moment later, he flipped her on her back and threaded his fingers through her hair and continued the assault on her mouth as their bodies moved together once more.

—➤➤◄◄—

Colton woke up to the sun in his eyes and the sound of the shower running. He sat up in bed and glanced at the clock. It was half past eight. The night was officially over.

What a night it had been. He couldn't remember a better one. After making love for the third time, they'd snacked on leftovers from the deli and then turned on the television and watched the film *Blade Runner* on the movie channel.

He'd always loved science fiction, the possibility of other life forms in the universe, and it turned out that Olivia's dad had also been a big fan and had introduced her to some of the classic sci-fi movies at a young age including *Mad Max 2: The Road Warrior* and *Tron.*

Colton had never met a woman who liked science fiction. Although he'd seen a strange look in Olivia's eyes when she'd realized he had yet another thing in common with her dad.

Would she ever be able to risk caring about someone whose job could be dangerous?

But he was getting way ahead of himself. He'd told Olivia to stop worrying so much about the future, and he needed to take his own advice.

As the shower turned off, he realized he'd missed another opportunity to get close to Olivia, but the ringing of his cell phone was another reminder that today was a new day. He got out of bed, pulled on his still sandy briefs and jeans and then grabbed his phone off the table.

"Emma," he answered, seeing his sister's number on the screen. "Do you have something for me?"

"Yes. I found the file on Stan Harper."

"Great. What did you learn?"

"Well, the fire occurred on September 17, 1973. There was one fatality—Stanley Harper. Origin of the fire was the kitchen."

"Rare for a man to die in a kitchen fire," he commented, sitting down on the edge of the bed.

"I agree, but that's what the report says."

"What about his family? Where were they at the time of the fire?"

"According to the investigative report, they weren't at home. In fact, Molly and her kids were at Grandma's house when the fire happened. Grandma lived around the corner from the Harpers."

His stomach tightened at the connection between the fire and his grandmother. "You're kidding."

"Do I sound like I'm kidding? As I read through the report, I actually got chills, Colton, because the connection between the fire and our grandparents doesn't end there. Molly said in her statement that she sent Patrick down to get Stan, because he wasn't answering the phone, and she and Eleanor were busy making cookies for a bake sale. Stan was supposed to pick up the kids, but he hadn't shown up. When Grandpa got to the Harpers' house, it was on fire."

Now Colton had chills running down his spine. "So Grandpa was the first on the scene?"

"Yes, but he wasn't working that night. He was in his street clothes and he had no equipment. He called 911 and attempted to enter the structure by breaking a window in the back of the house, however, he was unable to get into the kitchen. The fire was too intense. Apparently, cleaning chemicals kept under the sink contributed to the rapid escalation of the fire. Grandpa did everything he could to save Stan but was unsuccessful. In fact, he suffered burns on both of his hands and arms from the attempt."

"I've seen those scars. Grandpa would never tell me where he got them."

"Now we know."

"I have to admit you've surprised me, Emma."

"Me, too. I didn't expect the connection to Grandma and Grandpa when you asked me to look into the fire."

"Was there an autopsy?"

"I haven't found one. It's possible it was misplaced, but Harper's body was badly burned, and we didn't have the same forensic technology then that we do now. I asked Max to see if he can find any files on Stanley's death in the police department records. Since Stan was a police officer, I assume the police would have done a full investigation."

"Good move," he said, still trying to assimilate what Emma had told him.

He looked up as Olivia walked into the room. She was dressed in a pair of white jeans with a long-sleeve peach-colored sweater, and her long hair fell in soft curls around her shoulders. She was so pretty, he thought, momentarily distracted from his call. Then his sister's sharp voice rang in his ear.

"Colton!" Emma said loudly.

"Yeah, I'm here."

"Where did you go?"

"Nowhere. Thanks for your help. Let me know what else you find out."

"Will do, but first I'd like to know what this is all about."

"I will fill you in—I promise," he added. "Just not right this second."

"You're so annoying, Colton. Why the mystery?"

"I need to put things together before I jump to any conclusions. Call me when you know anything more."

As he stood up, Olivia gave him a curious look. "Who was that?"

"Emma." He told Olivia what Emma had just told him.

Olivia's eyes widened with each word. "Well, we're back to your grandparents."

He nodded, his jaw tightening. He'd really thought they were moving away from Eleanor and focusing on Molly, but the lives of the two women seemed to be intertwined at every curve.

"Do you think Patrick knew that Stan was beating up on Molly? It wouldn't seem like he would try so hard to save Stan if he did."

"What kind of man Stan Harper was wouldn't have mattered to my grandfather. He's a firefighter. He's trained to save lives. He doesn't judge whether or not they're worth saving."

"So you would risk your life to save a serial killer?"

"I would," he said, not the slightest bit of doubt in his voice. "I might want to kill him afterwards, but I'd do my job, because that's what I do. And that's what my grandfather would do."

She stared back at him with her thoughtful green eyes and nodded. "I don't know if I could do that. I guess I'm lucky that in my job I'll never have to make that decision." She paused. "We should talk to your grandmother again."

He didn't like that idea at all. "She got upset when we mentioned Stan yesterday. She broke down. I don't want that to happen again."

Her brows drew together in a frown. "Are you trying to stonewall me, Colton?"

"No, but I want to be careful with my grandmother's health. You saw what happened."

"It was scary, I admit that. And I understand why you're concerned, but your grandmother might be the only one who knows the truth, and her knowledge is slipping away every day."

"Maybe that's all right," he said, knowing that Olivia would not agree.

"How can you say that?"

"Because all of this shit happened a long time ago. Maybe we should let it be."

"No. All this shit that you're referring to happened to my grandmother, and I want to know the truth."

"You don't even know if she is your grandmother," he said in frustration. "Why do you care so much, Olivia? Is it just ambition to get a book deal of your own? What is it that drives your relentless pursuit of the past?"

Her green eyes turned cold at his words. "Everything you just said drives me, especially the possibility that Molly is my grandmother. I want to know and understand her life. And, yes, I do have a strong desire to write a really excellent book. I'm not going to apologize for my reasons. I'm not doing anything wrong. You should go now." She picked up his shirt off the chair and tossed it to him.

He reluctantly caught the shirt and slipped it over his head. "I'm sorry, I shouldn't have yelled at you like that."

"You and I have always been on opposite sides, Colton. I just forgot for a little while."

"That's not true, Olivia."

"Goodbye, Colton."

"Not goodbye. You're not getting rid of me that easily. And we're not on opposite sides. We're both just trying to watch out for our families." He paused in the doorway and just to piss her off, he stole a kiss from her irritated mouth. "I still like you, Olivia, even if your feelings have changed."

He was barely across the threshold when she slammed the door behind him.

Twenty-One

Olivia's feelings hadn't changed—at least not in the way Colton thought. She leaned against the door, her lips still tingling from his last kiss, a kiss that reminded her of all the other ones they'd exchanged the night before. She'd never felt so uninhibited with a man. Colton had taken her places she'd never been before. But that was last night, and last night was over.

She was annoyed with him and a little hurt that he'd tried to get in the way of her talking to his grandmother, but she also respected him for his loyalty to his family. She was angrier with herself for getting involved with him at all. She'd let down her guard and started thinking he was on her side when he would always be on his grandmother's side, and she couldn't even blame him for that.

With a sigh, she pushed off the door and moved across the room. The sight of her tangled bed sheets only made her heart hurt. She needed to get out of this room. She picked up the pictures of Molly bruised and beaten and stuffed them into her purse along with the stack of letters. Maybe she'd find a quiet place to work where she wouldn't be distracted by memories of Colton.

Once on the street, she avoided her car and just started to walk. It felt good to play tourist for a bit, and she enjoyed the hustle and bustle of the Union Street restaurants, clothing boutiques, art galleries, and the more than occasional coffee spot or organic juice bar. She'd forgotten how health-conscious people were in California.

When she reached a small park at the end of the block, she sat down on a bench and pulled out her phone. It wasn't Sunday, but she needed to touch base with her mother, with the woman who'd raised her and loved her every day of her life. While she'd thought about waiting to contact her mom until she knew for sure whether or not she was Molly's granddaughter, she needed to hear her mom's voice, to feel the connection to her past and to the real people in her life.

"Hey Mom, it's me."

"Olivia, what's wrong?"

"Nothing," she said, but even she could hear the tremble in her voice.

"Honey?"

"I'm just confused."

"About what?"

"Everything. I've been researching the woman who invited me to come to San Francisco, and I've found some information that's a little shocking."

"What do you mean? What did you find out?" her mom asked, concern in her tone.

She took a minute trying to think of what she wanted to say. "Well, it's kind of a crazy coincidence, but Molly's daughter, Francine, had a baby that she gave up for adoption, and that baby has the same birth date as me." She could hear her mom's quick intake of breath on the other end of the line. "I don't know for sure that I'm related to them, but it would make a lot of sense considering how Molly reached out to me."

Silence followed her words. Then her mother finally spoke. "I don't know what to say, Olivia. Is there any other connection besides the birth date?"

"Not that I've found."

"I know Molly's letter resonated with you, but are you sure you're not jumping to conclusions?"

"I'm not at all sure," she admitted.

"What happened to Molly's daughter?"

"Francine died about a year after her baby was born. Apparently, she suffered from depression and was a substance abuser; that's what her brother told me. He said he did not know who the father of the baby was, but he wasn't all that interested in talking to me. He made a point of telling me that his mother doesn't have any money and there won't be an inheritance to go after."

"That jerk. You would never claim a relationship with someone for money," her mother snapped.

"I told him that, but I'm not sure he believed me. He seems to be a cynical person. I'm trying to cut him a little slack since his mother is dying, but I'm not sure he's any nicer of a person when he isn't in this terrible situation. It's strange to think that I may have found my biological family but the only one who wanted to meet me is unconscious and the other remaining relative just wants me to go away."

It felt strange to be speaking so frankly with her mom. While her adoption had never been a secret, it had also rarely been a topic of discussion, especially after her father died.

"Maybe you should leave it alone," her mother suggested tentatively. "It doesn't sound like you have much to gain, honey. And you might end up getting hurt."

"I just need to know if it's true. I took a DNA test, and it's going to be compared to DNA from Molly's hairbrush and toothbrush to see if there's a familial relationship. I should have the results back today or tomorrow."

"That's quick," Elaine said.

"It's not going to change anything with you and me," Olivia said, feeling the need to address what seemed to be simmering right under the surface. "You're still my mom, no matter whose DNA I share. I hope you know that."

"Of course I do," her mom said. "You're my daughter and you always will be."

"That's right."

"How are you getting the test done?"

"Colton's sister is helping me out. She's a doctor, and she has a friend in the lab who's going to rush the results through."

"Who is Colton?"

She suddenly realized how much had happened since she'd

last spoken to her mom. "Colton is Eleanor Callaway's grandson. Eleanor is Molly's best friend."

"Can she tell you if Molly is your grandmother?"

"She said she didn't know, but she also has Alzheimer's so her memories are suspect."

"All of this sounds very complicated, Olivia."

"It's getting more complicated by the minute."

"I can't fault you for wanting to know your biological roots. I wasn't adopted myself, so I don't know how it feels to not be tied to your parents by blood. But I've always felt like you were mine, Olivia. I never ever regretted that we weren't biologically connected. I know it's different for you. And I want to be supportive, but I can't help but worry where this is all going. I just don't see a positive outcome for you."

She didn't, either, but she also couldn't stop now. "You know how I am when I have a question that needs an answer. I keep searching until I find one."

"I know. What can I do to help?"

"You're already doing it," she said, feeling immeasurably better just talking to her mom. "I'll be okay. I just need to figure things out."

"Are you going to be able to do that before you have to go back to New York?"

"I don't know. New York feels really far away right now."

"There's something else, isn't there? What aren't you telling me?"

"Nothing," she denied.

"Olivia. I know you too well. Does it have something to do with the man you mentioned—Colton?"

"Well..."

"I'm going to take that as a yes. Is he giving you a hard time?"

"Yes and no. The thing is..." She searched for the right words.

"Goodness, I've never heard you so tongue-tied," Elaine said. "What exactly is the *thing*?"

She took a deep breath. "I think I might be falling in love with him."

"Well, that's rather surprising. I've wanted to hear you say those words for a long time. But you never seem to have time to date or fall in love."

"I don't have time now, and I don't think it's a good thing."

"Why not?"

"Because I'm going back to New York."

"You don't have to."

"My job is there."

"There are jobs everywhere, honey."

She picked at a piece of lint on her jeans, then said, "He's a firefighter, Mom. He faces danger every time he goes to work."

"So this is about your father," her mother said with a knowing note in her voice.

"I watched you worry about Dad every time he left the house, and when I was old enough, I worried about him, too. And then the worst came true."

"I did worry about your dad. I loved him very much, and I was always a little terrified that I was going to lose him. After he died, I was angry, and I probably showed you a little too much of that anger."

"You were right to be mad. His job killed him."

"No, Olivia, it wasn't his job that killed him; it was one bad person. It took me a long time to get to the point where I could accept that. But I eventually did. I wish you could get there, too."

"If he'd been an insurance salesman or a dentist, he'd still be with us."

"But that wasn't who he was, and I loved him, Olivia. Every day that I had with him was a blessing. I shouldn't have been angry with him for doing what he loved to do, because what he did was part of him. He accomplished so much in his life. He made the world a safer place for you and for me. It sounds like your friend Colton is trying to do much the same thing."

"He is a good man," she admitted. "Handsome, strong, brave."

"The real issue isn't the fact that you live on opposite sides of the country or that he's a fireman, and you know it. You're scared."

"I am scared."

"Is he in love with you, Olivia?"

Her hand tightened on the phone. "I honestly don't know,

Mom."

"Before you leave town, you should find out."

—➤◄—

After leaving Olivia's hotel, Colton drove back to his apartment, showered, changed clothes and all the while stewed over the way he and Olivia had left things at the hotel. He wasn't great at goodbyes after sex, that was for sure, but none of the previous awkward encounters in his life had felt as bad as this one. Because Olivia wasn't just any woman, she was—Olivia.

There weren't really any words to describe her that felt quite right. She was beautiful, sometimes serious, sometimes funny, and she had a competitive streak and a determination to match his own. She liked to surf and watch sci-fi movies and she drove as fast as he did, which was ironic because she seemed to have a lot of patience for meticulous research but little for getting from one point to another.

She was a strong woman but also vulnerable. She tried to act like she didn't care that much, but deep down she was all heart. She felt a lot—too much probably. She still grieved for her dad. And while she'd long ago accepted the fact that she was adopted, now she was floundering, trying to figure out who she really was if she was in fact a Harper.

He couldn't imagine what it felt like to have been given up at birth and sent to live with another family. No matter how fantastically great that family was, wouldn't you still feel rejected?

He thought Olivia did. In fact, he thought she got her guard up every time she got close to a situation where she might get rejected or abandoned or hurt. Not only had her birth mom rejected her, her dad had died, and as a result she'd felt abandoned by him, too. He didn't want to be the third person to put a dent in her heart, but he had a feeling that might be inevitable, which was probably why they shouldn't have hooked up in the first place.

But it hadn't felt like a hookup; it had felt like a lot more than that, and that thought was unsettling.

He'd been so focused on becoming a firefighter, proving his

worth and living up to the Callaway family legacy that he hadn't put any time or energy toward a romantic relationship. He hadn't been interested in having someone waiting for him when he got home, someone who might worry about him, someone who might ask him for more than just a good time. Those kinds of complications seemed best put off for another day. He'd never met anyone who'd made him reconsider that strategy—until now. And of course he had to like someone who lived on the other side of the country. He'd certainly never done anything the easy way.

Frowning at that thought, he picked up his keys and left his apartment building. After getting into his car, he headed to the doctor for his follow-up appointment. His fingers weren't swollen anymore, and although he had some stiffness in the joints, it wasn't anything that would stop him from doing his job. Hopefully, he'd be released back to work.

After arriving at the doctor's office, he was quickly ushered into an examination room. The orthopedist, Dr. John Robertson, conducted a fairly quick exam, testing the motion and swelling of his fingers and told him the healing was progressing nicely.

"I'd like to get back to work," he said.

Dr. Robertson gave him a knowing smile. He'd been mending Callaway bones for two decades. "I'm sure you would. I can release you for full duty starting Saturday."

"That's four days from now."

"Exactly. Four days, not a lifetime. There's still some swelling around that third knuckle. I'd hate to see you suffer a permanent disability in that hand. I can, however, release you to modified duty if you'd like to start sooner."

He groaned. No firefighter ever liked modified duty, which usually involved checking fire alarms and giving school presentations. "I'll stick with full duty on Saturday. That actually fits in pretty well with my shift rotation."

"Good. I'm going to tape your fingers back up today. But you should be able to go without it by Saturday."

"Thanks, Doc."

"Say hello to the family for me."

"Will do." He grabbed the release form and headed out the

door. He would stop by the station on his way home. His crew was working today, so it was good timing. He'd let Captain Warren know he'd be back at the start of the next shift on Saturday morning.

Fifteen minutes later he pulled into a parking spot behind the firehouse and got out. It felt good to be back. The firehouse was more home to him than his apartment. Even though it had only been a few days, it felt like months since he'd been back. A lot had happened in the past week.

He'd always thought everything important in his life occurred from this base point, the firehouse, the center of his world, but ever since Olivia had come to town, his center had shifted.

Adam and his other friends greeted him with smiles and slaps on the back as he walked into the dayroom.

"Are you back?" Adam asked.

"Next shift."

"Good. Your replacement is an asshole."

Colton smiled. "Hanes?" The man who often subbed in on their crew was a twenty-five-year veteran with an attitude that probably matched Warren's. Hanes didn't think anyone who'd been born after the eighties was worth shit.

Adam nodded. "I can't wait for him to retire. He could barely get his ass up the ladder yesterday. I almost had to save him instead of the victim. But does he admit anything? No, he comes at me like I did something wrong."

Colton was surprised at the vehemence in Adam's voice. His friend was usually pretty easygoing. "Anything else going on?" he asked. "How's your hot redhead doing?"

Adam shrugged. "Doing someone else from what I hear."

He'd just come to the heart of Adam's annoyance. "Sorry."

"Whatever. What about you and the beautiful brunette? She still around?"

"For a few more days," he said, feeling depressed at the reminder.

Adam gave him a thoughtful look. Then a smile spread across his face. "So it's like that."

"It's not anything."

"You sure about that?"

"Not really," he admitted.

"What are you doing here? You should be spending every second trying to find out if whatever you have going on is something."

Adam was right. Olivia might have kicked him out this morning, but that didn't mean he had to stay out of her life. In fact, that was the last thing he intended to do. "I'm going to see her later," he said. "First, I need to tell the captain I'll be back on Saturday." Colton got to his feet. "Has his attitude improved in the past week?"

"He's a rigid boss, but the only person he seems to really dislike is you."

"Great," he said with a sigh.

He left the dayroom and walked down the hall to the captain's office. He could see Warren inside, reviewing what appeared to be incident reports. He knocked on the half-open door.

Warren looked up, his jaw tightening as he saw him. "What do you want, Callaway?"

"I've been released for work next shift. I wanted to let you know." He set the form he'd received from the doctor down on the desk.

"I'm thinking you should start that work somewhere else," Warren said. "A change might be good for you."

"I like it here," he said evenly, his stomach churning at the idea of a transfer.

"Well, I don't like you here," Warren returned pointedly.

"Care to explain why?"

Warren gave him a long, hard look. "Why don't you ask your brother?"

"I did ask him. Burke didn't tell me what's between you two, but he did say that you're a good firefighter." Actually, Burke had used the word decent, but Colton wasn't going to say that.

Warren's eyes flashed surprise at that piece of information. And for a moment, it didn't appear that he knew what to say.

"Look, I can do a good job for you," Colton said, taking advantage of Warren's silence. The last thing he wanted was to be transferred because of his last name. "I'm not my brother. I don't know what went down with you and Burke, and even if I did know, there's nothing I can do to change it. But if you give me a chance, I can prove my worth to you and the team. This is my home. I'd like to stay. I'd like for us to find a way to work together."

Warren stared back at him. "I made the same kind of impassioned speech once—to your brother. Do you know what he did? He turned his back and walked away."

Colton ran a frustrated hand through his hair, wondering again what the hell had happened between Warren and Burke.

"I'll think about it," Warren said grudgingly.

"Great. I'll see you Saturday." He left the office before the captain could have second thoughts.

He'd barely hit the hallway when the alarm went off. It went completely against the grain to not react to the call. He wanted to join his crew on the engine. He wanted to be racing to the fire. But instead he had to stand and watch his coworkers go to work while he walked to his car.

Fighting fire was something he'd been born to do. He realized that more clearly now. While he might have originally gone into the job to follow in his father and grandfather's footsteps, his reasons for staying were completely his own. This firehouse was his home, which was why he'd been willing to beg Captain Warren for his job. He'd gotten a reluctant yes. Hopefully, some good work and a little time would destroy whatever doubts Warren had about him. But he was tired of running in the dark. He needed to find out what had gone down between Warren and his brother.

Twenty-Two

Colton found his brother across town at another firehouse. As a battalion chief, Burke had his own office. Burke greeted him with a more welcoming smile than he'd gotten from his captain. But there was still a wary question in his eyes.

"What are you doing here?" Burke asked.

He deliberately shut the door behind him, then moved into the office and took a seat in the chair in front of Burke's desk. This was probably the chair where rookies got chewed out by Burke, but while there had been many times in his life where he'd been intimidated by his big brother's accomplishments, today was not one of those days.

"I need some answers," he said shortly.

Burke's eyes were a darker blue than his own, and they always seemed to be filled with shadows that hid the nature of his thoughts.

"What about?" Burke asked.

"The problem between you and Mitch Warren. I just came from speaking to Warren. He wants to transfer me out because my last name is Callaway and I'm related to you."

"He didn't say that."

"Actually, he did," Colton replied, meeting his brother's gaze. "So what's between you?"

"You might be better off transferring," Burke said.

"I don't think so. I've never run from a fight, and I'm not going to start now." He paused. "You've never run from a fight, either, so the fact that you'd suggest I'd go along with a transfer makes me even more curious."

"My problems with Warren have nothing to do with firefighting." Burke leaned back in his chair and crossed his arms.

"Keep going," Colton urged.

Burke debated for a minute, then said, "Mitch Warren dated Leanne before I did."

Colton was stunned. Burke never ever mentioned his late fiancé by name, and the fact that Warren had been involved with Leanne was even more surprising.

"He blames me for her death," Burke added.

"How on earth is that possible? A drunk driver killed Leanne, not you."

Burke gazed back at him, his eyes icy cold. "He didn't think Leanne would have been on that road if it hadn't been for me."

"I don't understand." Colton paused. "I guess I don't really know what happened that night."

"It doesn't matter. I told Warren that his relationship with Leanne had ended years earlier and it was none of his business why she was out that night. He flipped out and took a swing at me. Of course he missed. He can fight fires, but he can't actually fight."

Colton stared at his brother, hearing the cold contempt in his voice. He didn't know Burke very well. There was over a decade of years between them, so they'd never been close growing up, but he'd always respected his oldest brother and held him up as the kind of man he wanted to be. Burke had always seemed so up-front about everything, but now he was being deliberately vague, almost as if there were some sort of strange reason for why Leanne had been on the road that night.

"So my advice to you," Burke continued, "is to consider a transfer."

"That's not an option." He remembered Mitch's words to him. *I made the same kind of impassioned speech once—to your brother. He turned and walked away.* Whatever Burke had kept from Warren was still driving the captain crazy, and it had been years since Leanne had died.

"Then I don't know what to tell you," Burke said. "Warren is unreasonable, and you're going to pay for what he considers my sins, whether that's warranted or not."

"Why was Leanne on the road that night?"

Burke's lips tightened. "It's not important, Colton."

"It seems like it is to Warren. That's why he hates you, because you won't give him an answer."

"It won't change anything. Leanne will still be dead." Burke cleared his throat. "And that's all I'm going to say on the subject."

Frustration ran through him at Burke's reticence, and he found himself understanding his captain's frustration as well. "Burke—"

"I'm done, Colton. You want to stick it out with Warren, then you'll have to figure out how to get along with him."

Or maybe he could get Warren to tell him what he thought Burke had done so badly when it came to Leanne. But he wasn't going to tell his brother that. "Okay," he said, getting to his feet. "I guess I'll see you around."

"Yeah. Close the door on your way out."

Burke was back to work by the time Colton stepped into the hallway. Or at least he was pretending to be. He couldn't believe Burke was unaffected by the reminder of Leanne. He'd been devastated after her death.

Colton pondered the rest of their conversation all the way back to his car. He knew next to nothing about his brother's relationship with Leanne. Now he couldn't help wondering what had been going on with them at the time of her death. Perhaps there was more to that story than anyone knew.

As he got into his car, his phone rang, and his pulse jumped as Olivia's name appeared on the screen. He hadn't been sure when he'd hear from her again, but for some reason he hadn't anticipated it being this soon.

"Hello, Olivia?"

"Colton, thank goodness."

He could hear the fear in her voice. "What's wrong?"

"Someone broke into my hotel room. They took all the stuff we picked up at Molly's. I don't know what to do."

"Did you talk to the front desk?"

"Yes. They said they'd send up security, but I don't know how that's going to help. Whoever broke in didn't take anything belonging to me, not even my laptop computer, Colton."

His stomach turned over. He was happy Olivia hadn't been hurt, but he was really disturbed by the break-in. "I'm on my way over. I'll be there in ten minutes. Double lock your door."

"I did, but I think the worst has already been done."

"I hope so," he muttered, as he started the engine and sped down the street.

Olivia sat down on the edge of her bed, still feeling shell-shocked by what had happened. After a happy couple of hours browsing the shops on Union Street and enjoying a late breakfast at an outdoor café, she'd come back to the hotel early Wednesday afternoon to find the boxes containing Molly's diaries and other personal effects missing. Who could have done this?

Only one name sprang to mind—Peter Harper, Molly's son. She'd told him that Molly had left her the journals, although she hadn't told him about the rest. But if he'd broken into her room, he would have taken everything he could find that was tied to Molly. It made sense, but it was still difficult to believe that a middle-aged man, a well-respected businessman, would break into her hotel room.

A knock came at her door, followed by Colton's voice. "Olivia?"

She opened the door, and despite the awkward way they'd parted earlier, she launched herself straight into his arms, needing to feel his protective strength for just a moment.

He gave her a long, comforting hug, then pulled back, his gaze troubled. "Are you all right?"

"Yes," she said, forcing herself to move out of his embrace. "Come in."

He walked into the room and looked around. "Where were you when all this happened?"

"I took a walk down Union Street. I got something to eat and did a little shopping. I was probably gone two to three hours."

"It looks like housekeeping came while you were gone, too."

She followed his gaze to the neatly made bed and couldn't help but remember the night she'd spent under those covers with Colton. He'd left only a few hours ago, but it felt a lot longer than that.

"Yes," she said, realizing she needed to say something to break the increasing tension in the room. "Housekeeping came while I was gone. I just spoke to a hotel security guard. He said he'd interview the hotel staff to see if anyone saw anything, but he didn't sound optimistic, nor did he indicate that the police would be interested in a case that involved only missing personal items and not valuables."

"Probably not."

"So whoever did this just gets away with it?"

"There has to be something we can do."

"Do you have any ideas?"

"Well, I don't think the list of suspects is particularly long."

She met his gaze. "Peter Harper is at the top of my list."

"Mine, too. I think we should pay him a visit."

"I agree, but I wonder what kind of recourse we have. Peter has more of a right to his mother's papers than I do."

"She left you her journals," he reminded her. "The director of the senior center gave them to you."

"I know, but the rest of it we just took."

"True, but I still think we should talk to him, and we should ask him about the pictures of abuse that we found."

She started at his words. "Oh, my God, I still have the pictures."

"You do?"

"Yes. I put the photographs documenting Molly's abuse in my purse as well as that stack of letters from the women she helped. I was going to get coffee and go through them, although I never actually did that," she said, reaching for her bag. She pulled out the photographs and letters. "So we still have these."

"That's something," he said with an approving nod.

"Do you think Peter ever saw these pictures?"

"If he didn't, he's going to now."

"Yes," she agreed. "Although with the amount of bruises Molly suffered in those pictures, I doubt her kids were oblivious to what was going on." She paused. "I'd also like to know what Peter remembers about the fire that took his dad's life."

"I think you should call Peter and tell him you want to talk about some photographs you found that indicate his mother and/or his sister was abused," Colton said.

Olivia raised an eyebrow. "You want me to throw in Francine as well?"

He met her gaze. "Yes. I want you to get his attention whatever way you can."

"There's a good chance he's at the hospital. He's been there the last few times I've gone."

"Let's try his office first. If he's not there, we'll see if he's at the hospital."

She liked his action plan. It felt good to go on the offensive—to act instead of react.

She called Peter's office and told the woman who answered that it was urgent she speak to Peter about a personal matter. When pressed for more detail, she relayed what Colton had told her, then asked if Peter would be available to see her that afternoon. After a brief pause, she was given an appointment for one o'clock.

"We have an appointment in twenty minutes," she told Colton as she clicked off her phone. "You're going to have to drive really fast if we're going to get there on time. His office is downtown."

"Not a problem. I know all the shortcuts."

She put the pictures and letters back in her bag and then followed Colton out the door.

They didn't speak for the first few minutes. She was focused on what she wanted to say to Peter, and she assumed Colton was concentrating on the road as he wove in and out of lanes and darted down alleyways to avoid traffic. They were making good time until they ran into construction.

Colton tapped his fingers impatiently on the wheel. "Damn. I should have taken another road."

"We're not that far away, are we?"

"Only a mile or two, but in this traffic, it could still take a few minutes, and we have to find parking downtown, which is always a joy."

"Well, we'll get there and hopefully Peter won't leave before we do."

"If he leaves, we'll track him down. I want to know if he was the one who broke into your room."

"Even if he did, I doubt he'll admit it."

"I think we'll be able to tell by his reaction to our questions." He let out a heavy breath. "I hate the thought of someone breaking into your room, Olivia."

"I almost threw up when I realized what had happened. To think someone was looking through my things..." She shuddered at the thought. "I don't know if I can sleep there tonight."

"You can stay with me."

The invitation came fast and easily because that's the kind of man Colton was, but he obviously hadn't thought it through. A a frown quickly followed the offer.

"I can always go to another hotel," she said.

His frown deepened. "Olivia, this isn't the time to get into a long discussion, but I didn't like the way things ended this morning. We got off track."

"We just got back to reality. Maybe it was a good thing, a reminder that one night is probably all we're going to have."

"Maybe not. You haven't left San Francisco yet."

She shivered a little as he cast his sexy blue gaze in her direction. "That's true, but—"

"But you don't want to sleep with me again," he finished, an odd note in his voice.

She thought about his question for far too long. Then she gave him a rueful smile. "That's the problem, Colton. I do want to sleep with you again, I just don't think I should."

"Why not?"

"A lot of reasons."

"Give me one."

She knew just the one to shut him up. "I'm afraid I'll fall in love with you."

His eyes sparkled at her words, as if the idea wasn't all that repulsive, and for a moment, just a moment, she thought he might reciprocate the words.

Then a horn honked.

"It's our turn to go," she said.

He swore under his breath and then turned his attention back to the road. Whatever he'd been about to say remained unsaid.

Twenty-Three

Ten minutes later Colton pulled into an underground parking garage and handed the valet his keys. As they waited for the elevator to take them up to Peter's office, Colton gave her a serious look. "Olivia, I want you to know that I heard what you said."

"And?" she couldn't help asking.

"And I can see why you might be worried about that."

She was a little taken aback by his cocky words. "Oh, because you're used to women falling in love with you?"

"No, that's not what I meant," he said with a frown.

"Then what did you mean?"

The elevator doors opened, and they stepped back to let a couple off. Then they got inside, and Colton pressed the button for the lobby. "I meant that things got intense between us last night, and I wasn't exactly expecting that."

"Okay," she said, still a little confused. "What are you trying to say, Colton?"

Before he could answer, they'd arrived at the lobby, and as they stepped off and walked across the hall to another bank of elevators, they were caught up in a swarm of people. There was no opportunity for private conversation on their way to the forty-fifth floor.

Olivia could feel Colton's gaze on her, but she was afraid to look at him. His last few comments had only served to make her feel more unsettled. For a guy who was outgoing and seemed to be able to speak to anyone, he'd certainly had trouble putting a couple of coherent sentences together. She'd like to think that was because he was dealing with emotions he wasn't used to dealing with, but maybe that was just wishful thinking.

When they got off the elevator, she could see that Peter Harper's firm took up the entire floor. They stepped out onto plush carpeting and walked through a beautifully decorated and sophisticated reception area. A woman wearing a black sheath dress gave them a smile as they approached the glass counter.

"I'm here to see Peter Harper," she said. "I'm Olivia Bennett and this is Colton Callaway."

"One moment." The woman picked up the phone. "Mr. Harper, your one o'clock appointment is here." She paused. "Yes, of course."

She hung up the phone. "He'll be with you in one moment. Please have a seat."

"Thanks." Olivia moved away from the desk but didn't take advantage of any of the white leather couches. She felt far too restless to sit.

Colton put a hand on her shoulder. "Breathe," he said.

Sometimes she thought he could read her mind. "I am nervous," she admitted. "It's not that he intimidates me, although he does do that. It's because of who he is—who I might be to him. That's the scary part."

"Just take it one step at a time."

"I'm going to try."

His hand slipped down her shoulder and arm, his fingers lacing with hers. "About what I said before—"

"I can't have that conversation right now."

"I understand, but I just want you to know that just because I haven't been able to get the right words out doesn't mean I don't care about you. I do care, Olivia, probably a little too much."

Her nerves tightened, not just at his words, but at the look in his eyes. He'd told her before he didn't lie, and she didn't think he was lying now. But what it all meant was still beyond her.

"Miss Bennett?" the receptionist said, interrupting their conversation. "Mr. Harper will see you now. I'll take you to his office."

"Great." She took as many deep breaths as she could on her way down the hall. She wanted to be as calm as possible when she asked Peter Harper about the terribly disturbing photos of his mother.

Peter stood up when they entered his office. He had his suit coat off. The sleeves of a white button-down shirt were rolled up to the elbows, and his expensive tie hung loosely around his neck. He looked exhausted, and Olivia couldn't help wondering if it was the toll his mother's condition was taking on him, or if there was more going on.

"You're back," he said with a resigned sigh. "Somehow I didn't think I'd seen the last of you." His gaze turned to Colton. "And you brought a friend—wonderful."

"This is Colton Callaway," she said.

Peter's gaze narrowed. "Callaway? Are you related to Eleanor?"

"I'm her grandson, Jack's son," Colton added. "I think you knew him when you were a kid."

"I knew his brother Michael. So what do you want? You mentioned something about pictures of my mother and sister?"

"Your mother," Olivia said, pulling the photos out of her handbag. Peter hadn't asked them to sit down, and she wanted to face him at eye level, so all three of them remained on their feet.

Peter's jaw tightened as he looked down at the photos. He flipped through them silently, then set them down on the large cherry wood desk that separated them. "Where did you get those?"

"From Molly's home."

"You broke into my mother's house? I should have you arrested."

"Olivia isn't a villain. My grandmother gave her a key," Colton cut in. "There's also a good chance she's your niece, so maybe you should change your attitude."

As Peter's silent glare continued, Olivia didn't think he cared one bit about whether or not they might be related.

"My relationship to your mother aside," she said, breaking the tense silence, "what can you tell me about the photos? Was your father hitting your mother?"

"On occasion," Peter admitted. "But it never seemed as bad as what those photos would indicate."

"Are you saying that the photos might have been doctored?"

"How the hell would I know? I'm not even sure they're of my mother. She used to hang out with a lot of abused women. Domestic abuse became her cause in life."

She couldn't ignore the bitter note in his voice. "You sound angry about it."

"I was angry about it. My mother turned her back on the family to help strangers when she should have been helping her own daughter."

"Francine was being abused?"

"No. But she was struggling to survive after my father died. While my mother was focused on others, Francine was killing herself with drugs and alcohol. By the time my mother turned her attention back to her daughter, Francine was too far gone to be saved."

"Why didn't you save her?" Colton cut in.

Peter's gaze swung to Colton. "I tried—many, many times. But when the substance abuse first began, I was in college, then I went into the Navy. I didn't know what was going on. I was counting on my mother to actually be a mother."

Olivia could see that Peter held his mother responsible for all of Francine's problems. Whether that was fair or not, she couldn't say. "We're getting a little off the point," she said, drawing his attention back to her. "You're angry with your mother, obviously, but don't you feel any compassion for what she went through at the hands of your father?"

"Like I said, it wasn't that bad," he replied. "Yeah, he drank too much, and he'd get pissed off really easily. He slapped her now and then, gave her a shove, tossed her dinner in the trash, but that wasn't all the time. He could be a good guy, too. He'd buy her presents, take her on trips, and he supported her and us. He had a stressful job, and it was wrong what he did, but she didn't have to—" Peter stopped abruptly.

"She didn't have to do what?" Olivia prodded.

He stared back at her for a long moment, the pulse in his neck beating hard and fast. "It doesn't matter."

"It does matter," she said in frustration. She kept getting close and then someone slammed a door in her face. "What did Molly do?"

"Fine. You want to know, I'll tell you. She killed him," Peter said flatly. "She killed my father. She stole him from Francine and me."

She put a hand to her mouth, feeling shocked and a little sickened by his words. "I don't understand. There was a fire—"

"A fire she started when he was too passed out to save himself."

Olivia swallowed a knot in her throat and glanced over at Colton, wondering what he thought of Peter's statement.

Colton's expression was grim as he gazed back at her, then he turned to Peter. "That's not what the official report says. It stated that you, Francine and your mother were at my grandmother's house when the fire broke out. Your mother got worried when your dad didn't answer the phone and sent my grandfather to look for him."

"All bullshit," Peter said. "My parents were fighting in the kitchen. Eleanor showed up in the middle of it. She took Francine and me out of the house and sent us around the corner to her house. She and my mom showed up about fifteen minutes later. Then we heard the sirens. I thought they sounded really close, but I didn't know until the next day that those fire engines were racing to my house, that my father was dead."

Silence followed his words. She didn't know what to say.

Finally, she murmured, "I'm sorry."

"I don't need your sympathy," he said. "Are we done now?"

"Not quite," she said quickly, sensing he was about to end their conversation. "Why do you think the report was filled with lies?"

"Because the Callaways wanted to protect my mother from going to jail. Maybe they thought it was for the best. My father was dead, and my mother was the only person we had left. I was a kid when it all went down. I didn't know all the ins and outs of it. It wasn't until much later when I started piecing things together that I realized the truth."

"Your father was a cop," Colton interjected. "Why wouldn't the police have investigated his death and discovered the truth?"

Peter shrugged. "I have no idea. Maybe my mother played the sympathy card."

"You mean maybe she told someone your father was abusing her?" Olivia asked, unable to understand why Peter was so determined to sweep that part of the story under the rug.

"I don't know what she did."

"You've never asked her? In all the years since then, the subject never came up?" she challenged.

"Not once. I think my mother felt guilty at what she'd done. I, frankly, don't know how she sat through the funeral services. My father's fellow officers spoke of him as a hero. They told the world of all the good he'd done. And my mother just sat there silently. She didn't even cry."

Peter's words resonated deeply within her. She'd sat through the same kind of service when her father died, all the pageantry, all the stories of heroism. In her case, she'd never had reason to doubt those stories, but she'd taken a path different from Peter's. She hadn't revered her father in his death, she'd just been angry that he was gone. But she could see that Peter's adoration had only grown in the intervening years. He'd obviously convinced himself that his father was good and his mother was very, very bad.

"Why do you go to see Molly—if you hate her so much?" she asked. "I've seen you at your mother's bedside twice."

He didn't answer right away. "I don't know. Duty, I guess."

"Did you ever consider that you might not know the whole story of your parents' marriage?"

He shook his head. "I was there. If I didn't know it, who did?"

"Your mother. And those photos paint a very different picture of your father than the one you've drawn for us. Those horrific bruises don't come from a few slaps and shoves. Are you telling me you never saw your mom in that condition?" She picked up the picture and held it up in front of his face. "Look at her. Look at how hurt she is. Was it really a hero who did that?"

"I—I don't think that's her," he prevaricated.

"Of course it's her." She met his gaze head on. "And you know that. You just don't want to let go of the lies you've told yourself all these years."

"What do you know about it? You don't even know her."

"I know what she wrote to me in her letter. I know that she felt silenced by the men in her life and that she had been too cowardly to tell her story. And I know that she was abused, because those pictures don't lie, unless you want them to."

Silence fell between them. "I don't know what you want from me," Peter said. "My mother will probably be dead soon, and I doubt she'll ever regain consciousness. So even if I were inclined to speak to her about it, it's too late. My family is just about gone, Miss Bennett." He paused. "And even if you are Francine's daughter, there's nothing I can do for you."

"I don't want you to do anything for me; I just want the truth." She took a breath, changing the subject. "Do you know who the father of Francine's baby was?"

"I already told you I didn't."

"Even if she didn't give you a name, she never told you anything about him?" Olivia asked, feeling like this was her last chance to get any information on who might be her father.

"She said he was a musician and that she loved him, but he wasn't interested in being a father. As soon as I heard that, I got worried. She'd been doing pretty well for about a year. She hadn't been using and had been going to AA. I'd hoped that her life was on the upswing. She kept it together during the pregnancy, didn't do any drugs, took her vitamins, tried to be healthy. She kept hoping that the guy she was in love with would come back and they'd live happily ever after. That's the kind of girl Francine was; she was always living in a dream world."

Olivia wasn't surprised. It sounded like Francine had had a lot of reasons to want to escape her life. "When did she decide to give her baby up?"

"The day after her daughter was born. She'd been thinking

about it for a while. When her baby daddy didn't show up at the hospital, reality set in. She called the social worker and told her she was going to do the right thing for the first time in her life and make sure her daughter had a good home."

Olivia felt a wave of emotion rush through her. She still didn't know the DNA results, but she believed she was Francine's daughter and Molly's granddaughter. And she liked the idea that her biological mother had chosen to give her a better life than the one she had.

"My sister was a good person," Peter continued. "She was just a lost soul after my father died. After I went to college, she got into all kinds of trouble. She needed someone to save her, but my mother wasn't up to the task. She encouraged Francine to give the baby up. She could have helped Francine instead, but she didn't make that offer."

Olivia sighed, not knowing what to think about Molly. "Did Francine tell you anything about the adoptive parents?"

He stared back at her. "She told me that the father was a cop."

A shiver ran down her spine. More evidence that she was Francine's daughter. "My father was a cop."

"Was?" he queried.

"He was killed on the job when I was in high school."

Peter drew in a quick breath. "Well, I guess it's true that the good die young."

"He was good." She wished she could say the same for *his* father—her biological grandfather, but she couldn't.

"So that's it," Peter said. "That's all I know."

"One last question," Colton interjected. "Why did you break into Olivia's hotel room and steal your mother's journals?"

Peter's jaw dropped. "What the hell are you talking about? I don't even know where she's staying."

"I told you I had your mother's journals," Olivia said. "And it probably wouldn't have been that difficult to track me down once you knew my name. This morning, someone broke into my hotel room and took the journals that Molly left behind for me to look through."

"I don't know what you're talking about. I've been here in this office all morning."

Peter didn't appear to be lying. And he'd been pretty forthcoming up to now, so she didn't know what to think. "Who else would be interested in your mother's memories?" she asked. "I can't think of anyone but you."

Peter looked back at her. "I can't, either. I just know it wasn't me. You can take those pictures with you."

"No," she said. "You keep them."

"Fine, whatever." He glanced down at his watch. "I have another appointment. Are we done?"

"For now," she said, unwilling to commit to forever, even if it was very clear that Peter hoped he would never have to see her again.

Twenty-Four

—→≫≪←—

"Are you okay?" Colton asked, as they waited for the valet to bring their car around.

"I don't know," Olivia said with a helpless shrug.

"Peter wasn't what I expected."

"What did you expect?"

"Someone who didn't hate his mother, for starters. I don't understand how he could blame her for the abuse or discount the pictures we showed him."

"He's obviously living in a world of denial."

"You should have hung on to the pictures, Olivia."

"Perhaps. I wanted him to really look at the bruises on his mother's body, and I didn't think he'd do that with us standing there."

"He probably threw them into the trash. He doesn't want to hear or see a different story than the one he made up in his head." Anger ran through him at the memory of the excuses Peter had made. Molly deserved a son who would stand up for her, not blame her for being a victim.

"You might be right. What I'm more concerned with now is who broke into my hotel room. I no longer think it was Peter. But with him off the list, I don't know where to go next."

"Who else knows you've been staying at the hotel?"

"I gave my information to Nancy at the senior center; that's how you found me originally. So I'm sure any of the seniors at that center could get my address if they wanted it." She paused for a moment. "Your grandfather isn't back in town, is he?"

"No. He's out of town," Colton said with a frown, his muscles tightening at her words. "He wouldn't break into your hotel room, Olivia. For God's sake, he's eighty-four years old."

"I wasn't accusing him. I was just going down the list of people I've spoken to who don't want me around. And your grandfather is definitely at the top of that list. Besides, most of our suspects are old, so your grandfather's age doesn't make him special. I understand that you're protective about your family, Colton, but I can't let your feelings get in the way of the facts."

"That's harsh," he retorted.

The air sizzled between them, and it wasn't the good kind of electricity.

Olivia gave him an apologetic look. "I'm sorry. I didn't mean it the way it came out."

He hoped she didn't, because her words had stung.

"Sometimes I get a little tunnel vision when I'm focused on a problem," she added. "Your feelings do matter to me, Colton."

He nodded, cutting her a little slack since she was under a lot of stress. "Thank you. I understand that you're frustrated. I am, too. And I know that the next logical step is to talk to my grandmother."

"She is the common denominator, Colton."

"Yeah, I wish she wasn't." He paused as the valet brought his car around. They got inside, and a few minutes later they were driving out of the parking structure. He was happy to see the sun again. It lightened the tension of the last hour.

"What I also don't understand," Olivia said as they stopped at a light, "is why Peter would lie about the night of the fire? I get that he's trying to rewrite history when it comes to his mother's abuse. It makes sense that he doesn't want to remember his father as a monster. But why does he have a different story about that night than what is in the fire investigation report?"

"Someone is obviously lying or not remembering it the way it happened." He gave her a quick glance. "Do you think Molly killed Stan as Peter suggested?"

"If she did, it was in self-defense. Do you think your

grandparents would try to cover it up to protect her?"

"No." He shook his head, considering the facts. "Molly had those damning photographs of abuse in her possession. We know that they didn't burn in the fire, so she would have had proof that her husband was hitting her. It's doubtful anyone would want to prosecute her for defending herself."

"That's not always true," Olivia argued. "If a jury didn't think it was self-defense but rather that Molly got angry and killed her husband, she could have gone to jail."

He hated to think that the justice system could go wrong like that, but he knew it sometimes happened. "I guess that's possible."

"And a trial would have certainly put a lot of dirty laundry in the spotlight," she added. "Molly might not have wanted to go through that or put her kids through that. I do wonder why Peter never said anything to anyone, though. If he truly thinks his mom is a murderer, why did he stay quiet all these years?"

"Maybe he didn't think anyone would believe him, or perhaps it was part of his desire to live in denial. He was a kid when it happened. He was confused and grief stricken. He'd lost his father and I'm sure he didn't want to lose his mother, too."

"True." She paused for a moment. "You know I've been thinking that there's another angle to this that we haven't considered."

"Really?" he asked, both surprised and hopeful. Because he felt like they were rats running around on a never-ending wheel of frustration. "What's that?"

She shifted in her seat so she could look at him. "The letters that I still have in my purse. Maybe someone is trying to locate one of those women, or what if one of those women is back in town and has heard about me wanting to write a book and wants to protect her secret past?"

"Well, that's a thought, but all of this happened so long ago, Olivia."

"Okay. What about this—what if Ginnie or Constance had a friend that was saved, someone they've stayed in contact with over the years? They might have mentioned I was writing the book and that Molly had left me some of her things. Maybe they got nervous about their part in the railroad. Perhaps someone in one of their families doesn't like the idea of a book any better than your grandfather did. It doesn't have to be Ginnie or Constance; it could be one of their kids or a sibling or anyone tied to them."

He tipped his head. "I can't argue with your theories, but all you're doing is lengthening our list of suspects. What we need to do is narrow it down."

"I know," she said with a sigh. "I'm just trying to come up with a plan of attack."

He thought for a moment as he drove through the city, and there was really only one plan that made sense. "We'll go see my grandmother."

"Really?" Olivia asked, doubt in her voice. "I thought that was your last resort."

"I think we're there. You could be in danger."

"I don't know that I'm in danger," she said slowly. "No one tried to hurt me."

"Not yet," he said heavily.

"Okay, now you're scaring me a little."

"I don't like that someone was in your room. How did they get in there? How did they know you weren't there? I don't like it. And since I don't know who we're dealing with, I don't know what they're capable of doing next. Obviously, your presence and the secrets you're stirring up are making someone nervous."

"Now you're scaring me a little more."

He flashed her a quick, reassuring smile. "Don't worry. I'm going to protect you, Olivia. Nothing is going to happen to you on my watch."

She smiled back at him. "I do feel safer with you I must admit."

"Good. That's the way I want you to feel." He changed lanes and sped through a yellow light. "We'll talk to my grandmother. Let's just be careful about how we bring up Stan's name. That seemed to be the trigger the last time."

Ten minutes later, Donna let them into his grandmother's house with a welcoming smile, saying that Eleanor was feeling good and was in the living room.

He was happy to see that his grandmother looked as good as she apparently felt. She was wearing a blue dress with big white flowers. The blue brought out her eyes, and flowers reminded him of her sense of fun.

"Grandma, you look pretty today."

"Thank you, Colton," she said with a warm smile. "Hello, Olivia. It's good to see you again. I was at the senior center earlier, but you weren't there. I wondered if you'd gone back to New York."

"I was planning to go, but I got sidetracked," Olivia said.

"Lynda tells me I upset you both yesterday."

Colton sat down next to his grandmother while Olivia took the chair across from them. "We upset you," he said.

"What were we talking about when I slipped away?" Eleanor asked with her sweet, loving smile.

His heart turned over as he wondered how many more times he'd be able to talk to her like this, to see the real her, and not just the scary shell he'd seen the day before. He really didn't want to do anything that would send her over the edge again. But he also wanted to help Olivia.

"You're conflicted about something." Eleanor tilted her head to one side as she gave him a sharp look. "That's unusual for you, Colton. You're usually so sure of what you want. It's something I've always admired about you. In fact, in that way you remind me very much of your grandfather. So what's the problem? Is it something I can help with?"

"I don't know if you remember our last conversation," he said slowly. "We told you that we thought Olivia might be related to Molly."

"I do remember that," Eleanor said with a nod. "And wouldn't that be lovely? I always felt so badly for Francine. She was such a troubled girl. She didn't want to give her child up, but she knew she couldn't be a good mother, and I respected her decision."

"I got the impression that Molly encouraged Francine to give up her baby," Olivia said.

"Who told you that?"

"Peter."

"Oh, Peter." Eleanor's voice changed dramatically. "That boy grew up to be a hard, cold man. Molly used to tremble when he came by. I think she was almost grateful when their estrangement kept him away from her."

Colton suddenly wondered if Peter had turned out to be a wife-beater like his father. But he didn't want to bring the conversation around to Stan just yet.

"No," Eleanor continued. "Molly told Francine she'd help her with the baby, but it was Peter who suggested adoption. He wasn't wrong when he said that the baby would probably be better off. Francine had made a lot of poor decisions in her life, but I still felt badly for Francine, because she was very sad after she gave the baby away."

"Wasn't she sad before that?" Colton asked. "Peter said she was a mess after her father died."

"I suppose that's true. It was a terrible time. Molly was devastated after Francine's death. Poor thing. Every few years she seemed to lose someone else."

"Speaking of Molly," Olivia said slowly. "I want to talk to you about some photographs that I found in Molly's things. She'd had someone photograph some horrific bruises. I'm assuming that those bruises were the work of her husband."

Colton held his breath as Olivia brought Stan into the conversation, although she'd deliberately not mentioned him by name. His grandmother had paled a little at her words, but her eyes showed she was still present.

"Yes," Eleanor said. "It's a hard thing to say out loud even after all these years, but Molly was abused by her husband."

"When did you know?" Olivia asked.

"It took some time. I had my suspicions for a while, but Molly always had an excuse. One day the bruises were too bad to ignore, and I confronted her. That's when she finally told me the truth. It had been going on for quite some time, and the beatings were usually triggered by Stan's drinking."

"Were you the one who took the pictures of Molly?" Olivia asked.

"Yes. Molly had gone to talk to a police officer before that particular beating. She went to a station where her husband didn't work hoping that she could get someone objective to look at her situation and to help her, but the man she spoke to was not at all helpful or even kind. He said he would look into her complaints but that her husband had a stressful job and perhaps she should consider taking him on vacation rather than trying to get him arrested."

Olivia shook her head in disbelief. "That's absurd. I can't believe a police officer would react that way, even if it involved his coworker."

"I told her to talk to someone else, but she said she needed proof, and that's why we took the pictures."

"Grandma, are you doing okay?" Colton asked, as his grandmother began to twist her fingers together. "Can I get you some water? Do you want us to stop talking about this?"

Eleanor hesitated, then shook her head. "No, I knew this was coming. I thought I was ready for it. I've certainly had a long enough time to get ready." She drew in a deep breath and let it out. "I know what you both want to ask me."

"You do?" Colton asked, drawing her gaze to his.

She nodded, her lips tightening. "You want to know what happened to Stan."

His gut clenched. "Only if you're up to it."

"I promised your grandfather a long time ago that I would never speak of that night." Her gaze moved from Colton to Olivia. "But I know that Molly wanted you to hear her story, Olivia. I didn't realize it was because you were her granddaughter. I thought she just wanted to get the truth out, because it had been eating at her for decades."

"What is the truth?" Olivia asked.

"Molly and Stan had a terrible fight one night. I had been worried about Molly all week, because the violence had been escalating. Stan had problems at work, and he was taking them out on Molly. She was going to make him a special dinner to try to put him in a good mood, but I had a bad feeling about it. I tried calling her on the phone just before dinnertime. I didn't think Stan would be home yet. He didn't like her taking calls in the evening, so we always spoke during the day."

"Did she answer the phone?" Olivia asked, edging forward on her seat.

"Yes, she did," Eleanor said. "She was upset. I could hear Stan yelling in the background. I knew it was bad, so I went over to their house. I left my son Kevin in charge of my kids. I thought I'd be back in a few minutes. But when I got to Molly's house, I entered into the middle of a terrifying battle. I had never seen a man hit a woman before. Stan was out of control. He was drunk and in a rage. He was screaming obscenities and storming around the kitchen throwing pots and pans against the walls and at Molly. I saw sparks flying. I thought he was going to kill Molly and burn the house down."

Eleanor took a breath, then continued. "Molly yelled at me to get her children out of the house. I didn't want to leave her alone in the kitchen with Stan, but I had to do what she asked me to do. So I went upstairs and I found the children hiding in the closet of Francine's bedroom. Peter had his arm around Francine, and she was crying. I took them outside and told Peter to go to my house and then I went back into the kitchen."

Colton slid closer to his grandmother, putting an arm around her trembling shoulders. "You can stop, Grandma. If this is too much—"

"No. I can't stop. Molly can't speak for herself anymore. I was always going to leave it to her to tell the truth, but now she can't do that. So I have to do it for her. She's my best friend in the world, and I know she would want her granddaughter to know the truth."

"What is the truth?" Olivia asked, her voice edged with worried anticipation.

He held his breath, as it seemed to take forever for his grandmother to speak. When she couldn't find the words, he jumped in.

"Molly killed her husband, didn't she?" he asked.

Eleanor stared at him, her eyes wide and a little afraid. "No," she said, meeting his gaze. "Molly didn't kill her husband—I did."

Twenty-Five

"What's going on here?" Patrick demanded.

Colton jumped to his feet as his grandfather entered the living room, fury in his eyes. He'd obviously heard at least part of their conversation.

Patrick moved quickly to Eleanor's side, sitting down on the couch next to her, taking her hand in his as he searched her face for any sign of distress. "Are you all right, Ellie?"

"I'm okay," she said, giving him a tight smile. "I'm sorry, but I had to tell them the truth."

Patrick glared at Colton. "What the hell do you think you're doing?"

"Don't yell at him," Eleanor said. "Olivia is Molly's granddaughter. She's the child that Francine gave away. She needed to know what happened to Stan."

"What?" Patrick echoed in shock. He looked at Olivia. "Do you have proof of this?"

"I—I'm getting it," she said.

Olivia had also jumped to her feet when Patrick came storming into the house, and Colton now moved next to her, feeling she needed a little support in the face of his grandfather's icy glare.

"Shayla's friend is running a DNA test," Colton explained. "But we're pretty certain of what the results will be."

"I asked you to do one simple thing, Colton—to keep your grandmother away from this woman. You gave me a promise."

There was massive disappointment in his grandfather's voice.

"I couldn't keep it," he said, not really feeling any regret. "And this woman that you're referring to has a name. It's Olivia. She's an amazing person, and she's Molly's granddaughter. She's not trying to hurt Grandma. She's trying to figure out what happened in her family."

"Don't blame Olivia or Colton, Patrick," Eleanor said to her husband. "You know how I get when I'm determined to do something. I wanted to talk to Olivia, because Molly wanted it, and she's my very dear friend who is quite possibly dying."

"You've already done more than enough for Molly," Patrick said tersely. "When does it stop?"

"I think it stops now," Eleanor said.

"Is it true then?" Colton asked. As he looked at his grandparents, he almost felt as if they were strangers. Had his grandmother killed a man and then covered it up? Had his grandfather known the truth all along and kept silent? It seemed impossible to believe.

"Yes," Eleanor said.

"No." Patrick's sharp answer drowned out his wife's affirmative.

"Well, what is it?" Colton asked in frustration.

Patrick looked at Eleanor and took her hand in his. "You didn't kill Stan, Ellie. You're not remembering it right."

Eleanor frowned. "I feel very clear-headed, Patrick. I don't have that hazy feeling I usually get right before things go black."

"If Grandma didn't kill Stan, then who did?" Colton asked. "Was it Molly?"

"It wasn't Molly or your grandmother," Patrick said, shushing his wife when she started to speak. "It was me."

Colton sucked in a quick breath. "What?"

"You heard what I said. It was me." His grandfather's voice was unwavering.

"I don't understand," Colton said, his heart beating so fast he thought he was going to pass out.

Olivia put her hand in his, and he squeezed her fingers, grateful for her touch. He needed to steady himself.

"I killed Stan Harper. What don't you understand?" Patrick asked defiantly.

"I don't understand why the fire report tells a different story," he said, finally finding his voice. "You were burned trying to pull Stan out of the house. You have the scars on your hands to back that up."

Patrick looked down at his weathered hands, the freckled skin so thin his veins stood out. And on those hands were the white scars of fire.

"These scars serve to remind me of what I did that night." He lifted his gaze to Colton's. "The truth is that when I got to the house, Stan was crazy with rage. We got into a fight. He was throwing pans around the kitchen. One of them caught fire. I tried to stop him. We struggled. He slipped and hit his head on the counter, and he was knocked unconscious. By then the kitchen was burning around us."

"It couldn't have been that bad."

"It was spreading quickly. There were cleaning chemicals under the sink and in the pantry. Things were exploding, escalating fast.

"You had time to save him," Colton said, picturing the incident in his mind.

Patrick gave him a hard look. "Maybe I did, but I didn't try to save him. I burned my hands fighting my way out of the fire. That's how I got the scars."

"I don't believe you," Colton said, shaking his head. There was no way his grandfather, a firefighter, would walk away from an unconscious man.

"It's true," Patrick said. "Stan was evil, sick. He was never going to pay for what he was doing to his wife. His kids were starting to show signs of bruises, too. I was worried that he'd turn on Ellie and the rest of our family. I couldn't let that happen. I did what I had to do to protect my family. I'm not sorry."

"You should be sorry. You're a firefighter. You've spent your entire life living by a code of honor. You taught me to live up to the highest standards and those standards require you to save whoever needs to be saved," Colton said. "We don't make judgments. We don't decide who gets to live or die. What you did was wrong. It wasn't just wrong; it was criminal."

"Colton."

He heard his grandmother's plaintive cry, but he was too caught up in the shock of what his grandfather had done to listen. He had to get out of this house. He had to get the hell away from the two people he'd thought he could trust over anyone in the world.

He stormed out of the living room, throwing open the front door and letting it slam shut behind him. He thought about getting into his car, but he was too angry to drive. So he ran. He took off down the street at a dead sprint. He had no idea where he was going, but he wasn't going to stop until his world started making sense again.

It was going to be a long run.

"You should go after him, Patrick," Eleanor said.

"He doesn't want to talk to me," Patrick said gruffly. His gaze moved to Olivia. "Did you get what you wanted?"

She didn't know how to answer that question. She was still trying to process what they'd each said, and while they'd both made lengthy explanations, she still felt like she was missing something. "Molly's son Peter thinks that Molly killed Stan. Eleanor says that she did it. And you now take responsibility for it." She paused. "I honestly don't know who to believe."

"You can believe me," he told her forcefully. "I was there that night. I was the last one to see Stan." He glanced back at Ellie. "You know that's true, sweetheart."

"I know you went there after me," she said, her gaze troubled. "But—"

"That's all you need to know," Patrick said, cutting her off. He looked back at Olivia. "What are you going to do with this information?"

"I don't know." She licked her lips. "I understand that in the terrifying, adrenaline-charged moments of that night that decisions were made in a split second, and fear was driving those decisions, but I don't understand how no one asked any questions later. A man was dead. He was a horrible man, apparently, but he was a police officer, and surely someone cared that he'd died under what it sounds like were suspicious circumstances."

"The police were satisfied with their investigation," Patrick said. "So was the fire department. Molly and her children were safe, and Stan wasn't going to hurt anyone ever again."

She wondered if that made everything all right in his mind. It certainly sounded like it. "I have more questions," she said.

"They'll have to wait," Patrick said. "We're not going to speak any further about any of this without consulting our attorney."

"I'm not the law; I'm Molly's granddaughter."

"Until you have proof of that, I don't really know who you are," he said.

"Olivia, you should go after Colton," Eleanor said. "He's upset, and he needs someone. He needs you."

"I don't know about that," she said softly. "I'm the one who started all this, who ripped his world apart." She stared at his grandparents, seeing guilt and pain in Eleanor's eyes and anger and frustration in Patrick's gaze.

"Then help him put it back together," Eleanor said.

Patrick stood up. "I'll see you out."

The last thing she wanted was another private conversation with Patrick Callaway. "No need. I know the way out."

When she got to the street, she looked around for Colton. His car was still there, but there was no sign of him. She called his phone, but he didn't answer. She waited another five minutes, then decided to catch a cab back to her hotel. Who knew how long it would be before Colton came back, and she didn't want to stand in front of his grandparents' house all day. She needed to do what she'd told Patrick and Eleanor she would do—figure out the truth.

Despite Patrick's claims, she wasn't buying his story. There were holes in it, for one. Eleanor had said that sparks were flying when she got to the house. By the time she and Molly would have run down the street and sent Patrick back, a few minutes would have had to have passed. Yet Patrick claimed the fire had started while he was there. Maybe it was a small thing. Perhaps the fire didn't really take off until Patrick arrived, but her instincts told her that tiny hole in the story would rip the fabric of lies apart.

She was inclined to believe Eleanor's side of the story. It made far more sense that Patrick was just covering for his wife.

But she also couldn't discount the possibility that Eleanor was covering for Molly.

It always came back to Molly.

—➤➤◄◄◄—

Colton finally arrived back at his car, sweaty, tired, and a little less crazed after his hour-long run. He pulled out his phone and saw the missed call from Olivia. She hadn't left a message, but he was quite sure she'd found her own way back to the hotel. He felt guilty now for leaving her with his grandparents and taking off without a word.

He punched in her number. She answered a moment later.

"I'm sorry," he said.

"Are you feeling better?"

"Not really." He leaned against his car and looked back at his grandparents' house. "But I shouldn't have ditched you."

"I understood, Colton. You were in shock."

"Now I know how you've been feeling the last few days."

"We can spin together," she said lightly.

His hand tightened around the phone. "You're pretty amazing, you know that?"

"Well, I like to think I am, but what have I done that's so amazing today?"

"You stood by me," he said.

"You've been standing by me all week," she replied. "It was my turn to pay it back."

"You do realize that my grandfather killed your grandfather?"

"I know that's one of the scenarios."

"Well, if it wasn't him, then it was my grandmother, which doesn't make it any better."

"Or it was Molly," she reminded him. "And that doesn't make

it any better, either. It's weird that the one person who's dead was a horrible person and all the people suspected of killing him are good. It doesn't seem right."

"No, it doesn't. Did my grandparents say anything important after I left?"

"Your grandfather said he wouldn't speak any further with me until he consulted an attorney."

"Great. That's just great. Calling an attorney certainly implies guilt."

"Your grandfather is not trying to *imply* anything, Colton. He's falling on his sword. He's quite willing to go to jail for Stan's death."

"Well, maybe he should."

"You don't mean that."

"I might," he said, wishing he'd actually said he was sure he did mean that, but as usual Olivia was reading him a little too well. "I always thought he was an honorable man. He was the person I shaped my life around. How stupid was that?"

"It wasn't stupid. And your grandfather is obviously a complicated man, a man I don't think you know very well."

"That's very true. And what I thought I knew is a lie."

"You need to talk to him again. You need to talk to both of them."

"I can't right now. I'm too wound up. I need to calm down, get some perspective. I need to see you, Olivia. Where are you now? I'll come and meet you."

"I just got to Molly's house."

His nerves tightened. "What are you doing there? We already know what happened the night of the fire. In fact, we have too many suspects. Why go looking for more?"

"Because I'm not entirely convinced that any of our suspects is guilty. We have three people willing to take blame or give blame, but I don't think we've gotten to the truth yet."

He ran a hand through his hair and wished he could disagree, but he couldn't. "I'll come and meet you then. I don't think you should be there alone."

"I'll be fine."

"I'm still coming. Be careful. I'll see you soon."

As he ended the call, his grandfather walked out of the house and down the steps. He could have met him halfway, but he decided to let his grandfather come to him for a change.

"You're back," Patrick said, stopping a few feet from him.

Looking at his grandfather now, Colton felt like he was seeing the man through new eyes, and he wasn't sure what he saw. His grandfather had always been his hero, right up there with his father—maybe even higher than Jack, because Patrick had been a legend in the fire department, the kind of man who would push every boundary to the limit, who risked his life over and over again to save people from the worst kind of death.

But he hadn't saved Stan.

Colton blew out a breath and said, "I don't think we should talk right now. I'm angry."

"I know you are. I'd feel the same way in your shoes."

He'd said he didn't want to talk, but he couldn't stop the question from slipping through his lips. "Why didn't you save him, Grandpa?"

Patrick looked him straight in the eye. "Because I couldn't. If he'd survived, the repercussions would have been horrific for Molly and her kids, your grandmother, our whole family."

"You don't think the law could have handled Stan Harper?"

"He *was* the law."

"No, he was only one man. You had power. You had friends who were cops. Why didn't you talk to them? Why didn't you go to them before the whole thing escalated? You must have had some idea what was going on. Grandma would have told you that Molly was being hurt."

"Actually, she didn't tell me for a long time. She'd made a promise to her friend, and she'd kept it until she realized Molly was in a lot of danger. That was only two weeks before the fire. We were talking about a way to help Molly, but she was not being cooperative. Molly would go back and forth about what she wanted to do. Sometimes she wanted to send Stan to jail. Other times she was worried about how she'd survive without her husband. She was a homemaker with two kids and no job."

"You would have helped her I'm sure."

"I would have, but that opportunity didn't present itself in time."

Colton gave his grandfather a hard look. "You don't seem particularly upset about what you did. Did you have no remorse whatsoever?"

"Well, it's been a long time, Colton—over forty years. I learned to live with what happened. And I know in my heart that I did the right thing at that time, the only thing I could do. Maybe if I'd had more time to think about it..." He shrugged. "But I only had seconds."

He was disappointed in his grandfather's answer. "You have always been so sure of what is right and what is wrong. Growing up, you were the benchmark for all of us kids. We had to live up to you. That was our duty—the Callaway tradition."

"And now you've discovered that your hero is just a flawed man," Patrick said, resignation in his voice. "There's nothing I can say to change that. But I want you to know one thing, Colton. Your grandmother was incredibly brave that night. She stepped into the middle of a battle zone without a second thought. She put her own life on the line for her friend. If you want someone to live up to, live up to her."

With that, Patrick walked back into his house and shut the door.

Twenty-Six

—➤➤◄◄◄—

Olivia wandered through Molly's house with a weary frown. She'd rechecked the upstairs bedrooms and closets but found no other items of interest. Done with the upstairs, she returned to the first floor, using the flashlight feature on her phone to illuminate her way. She didn't want to turn on a lot of lights and broadcast her presence in Molly's house—just in case anyone was watching. And she really hoped no one was watching, but she was a little nervous being in the house alone, especially after what had happened at her hotel room.

But she had to believe that anyone could have gotten into Molly's home at any time, so there was no reason for someone to come now. Whoever had wanted what she'd taken from the house could have just taken the information to keep it out of her hands, afraid that she might use the information in a book. And she couldn't help remembering the dissenting opinions among the ladies at the senior center when Eleanor had first offered her the key to Molly's house.

As she went down the long narrow hallway on the first floor, she entered the laundry room to take a quick look. She opened a narrow door, thinking it would lead to a pantry and was surprised when she saw stairs going into a basement.

Her heart sped up as she turned on an overhead light and went down the stairs. When she got to the bottom step, she felt a surge of excitement. A very old sewing machine was in one corner of the room and next to it was a rack of costumes. On the floor were clear plastic bins filled with material, pins, buttons, zippers, sequins and other accessories.

She wondered why Molly had moved all of her supplies down here instead of using the extra bedroom upstairs, unless she didn't sew anymore?

As Olivia walked around the room, she saw dozens of framed photographs of men and women in beautiful costumes. These had probably come from Molly's community theater days, and there were a few familiar faces: Ginnie, Eleanor and Constance, all dressed up for whatever part they were playing.

They'd been beautiful, courageous women, she thought again. And hardly anyone had known that.

She turned away from the wall of fame and her gaze fell on another box upon which one word was scrawled in green marker—*Francine*.

Her heart skipped a beat and her breath caught in her chest as she squatted down in front of that box. For some reason, she felt almost afraid to open it. She'd been concentrating so much on Molly being her grandmother and Peter being her very cold and unwelcoming uncle that she hadn't spent a lot of time thinking about the woman who might be her mother.

She pulled apart the edges of the box and looked inside. The first thing she saw was a beautiful music box. The tarnished silver was engraved with Francine's name, and swirls of hearts were etched on the lid. She opened it up and a tiny ballerina popped up as the music began to play.

She looked at the dancer for a long minute, letting the melody of the song wash over her. She felt inexplicably close to Francine right now, knowing that this was her music box, that she'd probably played this song and watched this dancer a million times.

The music box reminded her of one she'd had as a little girl. There had been no dancer, but it had played a lovely tune, and having that box had made her feel very grown up. It was where she had stashed her first pieces of costume jewelry.

With that thought in mind, she lifted the velvet platform and saw a bunch of girlish rings and bracelets and a heart necklace. At the bottom of the box was a thick square piece of folded paper.

She carefully opened it, feeling as if she was about to get another glimpse into the past.

The note was written on two pages of lined paper, and her heart skipped a beat as she read the first few words.

I'm sorry baby girl. I had to give you away. I didn't want to, but I had to do it. I knew in my heart that I couldn't give you the life that you deserved, a life that I hope will be much better than mine. I know you're with a good family now and that they can take care of you. But I still miss you terribly. I hope that one day you'll find me, and I'll be able to give you this letter, so that you'll know how much I loved you.

You'll probably have questions about your father. And I won't have the answers you want. His name is Rex Coleman. Right now he plays bass guitar for a group called Night Wolves. But the band name has already changed twice, so I don't know what it will be years from now or even if Rex will still be playing. Actually, that's not true. I'm sure he'll still be a musician, because the only thing he loves in his life is music. I wish he loved me the way I loved him. And I know you're thinking right now that he didn't love you either, but he didn't know you baby girl. When I told him I was pregnant, all he heard was responsibility, and he took off. I'm still trying to forgive him for that.

I guess I'm a lot like my mother when it comes to men and bad judgment. I hope you'll break the chain, because you won't be raised by us. You won't see what we had to see or live through what we had to live through. At least I pray that you don't.

You probably want to know something about me, too. I hope I'll be able to tell you, that we'll share lots of long talks, but there's a part of me that is afraid that won't happen, because I'm a lot like my dad, I get restless and afraid and I drink too much. I don't hurt people like he did—except maybe myself. Which is another reason I had to give you away, because I never ever want to hurt you.

So if we never meet, and that might be the case, because only the Lord knows where I'll end up, I want you to know a few things about me. I love to dance. I wanted to be a ballerina when I was a little girl. I like puppies; I don't care for cats—don't tell my mom. She's a cat lover. I like mint chip ice cream and my favorite hour is midnight. Sometimes I go down to the beach just before midnight and watch the ocean as one day turns into another. I wait for the sun to come up, and I hope the new day will be better than the last.

I'm at the beach right now. I wish you could see the moon playing off the waves. It's so beautiful. When I look out at the sky and the sea, I feel like I'm close to heaven. And it calms me. I know everything will be all right. You'll grow up happy and loved. I wish I knew what your name was. I told the social worker that I wanted them to call you Olivia, but she said I couldn't tell your parents what to name you. Olivia is my middle name, and I'd love to have a piece of me with you. But whatever your name is, I'm sure it's as beautiful as you are.

With all my love,
Your Mama

Olivia sat down on the floor as she pressed the letter to her chest. Only then did she realize that she was crying. The words of her mother—and she now knew without a doubt that Francine was her mother—ran around in her head. She felt both sad and angry that the only contact she would have with the woman who gave birth to her was this letter.

But Francine had predicted that that might be the case. At least she'd had the foresight to leave this note behind—a note she might never have found if Molly hadn't reached out to her. And she didn't even know if Molly knew about the letter since it was hidden away in Francine's music box.

She folded the letter back up and put it in the pocket of her jeans. She knew she'd reread it a million times in the upcoming days, weeks and years.

As she got to her feet, she wiped the tears from her eyes. She blinked against the stinging moisture and as she did so, she realized that the air was smoky and thick. She'd been so caught up in the letter, she hadn't smelled anything until just now.

She ran up the stairs and into the laundry room. The smoke was much thicker, the heat intense, and along with smoke, she smelled gasoline. She stumbled to the door, her way now lighted by bright orange flames.

The house was on fire!

She reached for her phone, but she realized she'd set it down on the floor in the basement. She had no light anymore. But she didn't want to take time to go back and find it.

She felt her way toward the hallway door with one hand outstretched. With the other hand, she tried to pull her sweater up over her mouth and nose.

When she entered the hallway, she saw a wall of flames between her and the front of the house. And then she saw a male figure come out of the dining room. He had on dark clothes and a hood over his head, but when he saw her, he stopped abruptly, staring at her in shock.

At first she'd thought it was Peter, but as the flames leapt higher she realized it was Keith Fletcher, the police officer she'd met at the bar, the one who'd been having drinks with Colton's father.

"What the hell are you doing here?" he shouted. "No one was supposed to be here."

"Why did you do this?" she asker, her eyes watering as she stumbled down the hallway.

"I couldn't take the chance there was anything else here to find."

His words weren't making sense, but she didn't have time for questions. She started coughing as the heat and smoke began to make her dizzy. She put her hand toward the wall as a horrible rumble ran through the house, and then everything exploded.

She was knocked off her feet and six feet down the hall by a blast of fire. As she landed on the ground, she put her hands in defense as the ceiling came crashing down on top of her, revealing more fire coming from the upstairs. He'd obviously started the fire on the second floor.

It took a moment to get her wits about her. Then she felt intense pain running through her ankle. She tried to move, but a heavy piece of wood had pinned her to the ground.

"Help me," she cried. She tried to see down the hall, but everything was black and smoky now. She didn't even know if Fletcher was still in the house.

Then she felt a rush of air that was both welcome and terrifying as the fire around her inhaled new oxygen.

She'd never thought of fire as loud before, but everything was crackling, popping, breaking. And in that moment, she realized there was a good chance she was not going to make it out of this house.

"Oh, God," she whispered. "Please help me."

She thought about her mom, about Colton, about her friends, all the people who would miss her, all the things she would miss.

And then a voice came through the darkness. *"Hang in there, baby girl."*

She looked around, but she couldn't see anyone.

The voice came again. *"Fight. Don't give up like I did."*

She reacted to the words, to the challenge. She wasn't going to give up. She wasn't going to die in Molly's house. She had to find a way to get free. She twisted and strained and tried to slip out from under the beam, but it wasn't moving and the fire was getting worse.

Then she heard another voice—male this time, and very familiar. She looked up as a man appeared on the other side of a curtain of fire that hung halfway down the hall, the flames licking angry paths up and down the melting wallpaper as they came closer to her.

Colton!

She was both relieved to see him and terrified that he was now in danger, too.

"Hang on," he yelled. "I'm going to get you out of there."

She wanted him to do just that, but how could he get to her without being caught in the fire? He had no gear with him, no protective clothes or mask.

Colton disappeared, then reappeared a moment later with a towel around his head and chest. Another second, and he barreled through the flames, batting the sparks away as he reached her.

He dropped to his knees. "Can you move, Olivia?"

She shook her head. "My leg is trapped."

"It's going to be okay."

She'd appreciated his calm confidence before, but she liked it even more now.

He grabbed the beam with both hands and tried to move it off of her, but the weight of the ceiling bearing down on the upper portion was too much for him. He tried again, and she could see the strain in every muscle of his face.

The fire was getting worse. Not only was she going to die, Colton was going to die as well. "You have to leave, Colton. Get help."

He looked into her eyes. "Help is coming, and I'll never leave you, Olivia. You just have to hang on."

Another man appeared behind him. At first she thought it was a firefighter, but was shocked to see it was Keith Fletcher. She would have thought he'd be long gone by now.

Like Colton, he pulled his hoodie over his head, then made a dash through the fire. His sleeves were flaming when he reached them. Colton helped him beat out the fire.

"You came back," she said in amazement.

He gave her a hard look. "I once had a chance to save Molly, but I didn't take it. I can't do the same tonight. I can't let her granddaughter die."

"How do you know I'm her granddaughter?"

"I've been researching you ever since you showed up in town. You've got her eyes, eyes that once pleaded with me to arrest her husband."

"We can do this later," Colton interrupted. "Help me lift this beam."

With Keith's help, Colton was finally able to move the heavy wood enough for her to wiggle free. She tried to stand, but more pain shot through her ankle. "I can't walk."

Colton didn't hesitate. He grabbed the towel and wrapped it around the upper part of her body. Then he swept her up in his arms. "Hold your breath. We'll be out of here in a second."

She squeezed her eyes shut and didn't allow herself to breathe as he took her through the fire. The heat was intense. And for a minute she didn't think they would be able to escape the flames, but somehow Colton got her through them.

His speed increased as he hit the front door, and he didn't stop running until he got to the sidewalk. As he set her down on the ground, a fire engine came screaming around the corner.

"It's about damn time," he muttered. Then he looked back at her with grave concern in his eyes. "Are you all right?"

She nodded. "Thanks—to you," she coughed.

He cupped her face and gave her a quick kiss. "Don't try to talk. I'm going to go find Fletcher."

"Wasn't he right behind us?"

"I don't know where he went. Stay here."

"Don't go back in there, Colton." She couldn't bear the thought of him going back into that fire. But she saw the resolute gleam in his eyes and she knew nothing she could say would dissuade him from doing what he considered to be his job.

"It's going to be okay, Olivia. I promise."

She didn't know how he could make that promise, but he'd once told her he never lied, so she was going to trust him to come back to her.

Robin, the EMT she'd met in the bar a few days earlier, was at her side a moment later, insisting on slipping an oxygen mask over her face and putting her leg in a splint. Then Robin and a male EMT helped her onto a gurney and loaded her into the ambulance.

"We're going to take you to the hospital," Robin told her.

"Wait, where's Colton?" she asked, straining to see through the swelling crowd. Not only were there a dozen or so firefighters at the house, there were now also neighbors milling around.

"Colton is fine," Robin said, giving her a smile. "Don't worry about him. This is what he does, Olivia. I'm sure he'll be your first visitor in the E.R."

As the ambulance left the scene, she tried to relax, to tell herself the worst was over, but she knew she wouldn't be able to relax until she saw Colton again.

She slipped her hand into the pocket of her jeans, her fingers curling around the letter her mother had left her. Everything else in Molly's house might be destroyed by fire, but the note had survived, and she would have at least one special link to her mother.

She closed her eyes and as she did so, she heard the same

female voice she'd heard during the fire. "*You're going to be fine baby girl.*"

She was going to be fine. "*Thanks*," she whispered.

Twenty-Seven

It was almost an hour and a half before Colton could get to the hospital. He knew Olivia was in good hands and that her injuries were not serious, but he was still worried. She'd inhaled a lot of smoke. She could have damage to her lungs. She could have gone into shock after leaving the scene.

All kinds of negative scenarios ran through his mind, shocking him with their intensity. He wasn't a man to imagine the worst. He'd always been able to compartmentalize, to be optimistic, to believe he could overcome any obstacle, but when it came to Olivia he was one big mass of nerves.

When he'd arrived at Molly's house and smelled the smoke, terror had run through his body. That fear had increased when he'd seen Olivia trapped under a pile of debris, the flames within a few feet of her.

In his mind, he'd been taken back to the week before, when he'd lost a man in a similar circumstance. But he couldn't lose Olivia, not now, not when he'd just realized that he was falling in love with her.

Thank God, he'd been able to get her out.

He probably wouldn't have been able to do it if Keith Fletcher hadn't come back to help him. While the man had been willing to commit arson, his conscience wouldn't let him commit murder. Colton was grateful for that.

After striding through the E.R. doors, Colton quickly located a nurse who took him to Olivia. When he walked into the exam room, he found Olivia sitting on the table, her back supported, her left leg stretched out in front of her, her ankle covered by an ice pack.

She gave him a bright, happy smile and pulled the oxygen mask away from her mouth to say. "Colton, I am so glad to see you."

"Likewise, babe."

Her lips trembled and her eyes filled with tears. "I was so afraid—"

He wrapped his arms around her and gave her a tight hug. He could smell the smoke in her hair and on her skin, reminding him of how close he'd come to losing her. But he hadn't lost her.

He pulled back so he could see her face. And gently, he wiped the tears from her cheeks with his fingers. "You can't cry now. It's all over."

"I think that's why I'm crying," she sniffed. "Sorry."

"Don't apologize. You've been through a lot tonight. How's the leg?"

"The x-ray showed a hairline fracture. The doctor wants to put me in a boot cast."

"Sorry about that." He gave her a sympathetic smile. "But I'm glad it's not worse. How are your lungs?"

"I'll be okay."

"Put the mask back on," he ordered.

"In a second. I want to thank you. If you hadn't come in when you did, I don't think I'd be alive."

"But you are alive; that's all that matters."

"What happened to Fletcher? He got out, didn't he?"

Colton nodded. "He got out, and he's been arrested."

"Well, at least he's not dead."

He marveled at the fact that Olivia didn't wish him dead after the man had almost killed her. "No, Fletcher will survive, and he'll pay for what he did tonight."

"What about what he did in the past? He was the one Molly went to for help. He turned her away."

"Because he owed Stan money, and he was afraid of him, too," Colton said, realizing he needed to update Olivia. "I just got off the phone with my brother-in-law Max. The cops have been interviewing Fletcher for the past hour."

"What did he say?"

"Fletcher told Max that Stan was running a bookie operation back in the day, and a lot of cops were in debt to him."

"Really?" she asked in surprise. "That's the first we've heard of that."

"Yes, it was all very hush-hush. When Stan was killed, the police didn't investigate his death, because they thought one of them had killed Stan."

"That's why the investigation was so short. Just when I start to think I know everything, I realize I don't."

"When you started digging into the past, Fletcher was afraid that somehow his part in what had happened would come out, not just the gambling, but the fact that he'd turned the other way when an abused woman came to him for help. He thought it would screw his chances of being Chief of Police, something he's worked for his whole life."

"He has no chance now that he's committed arson. I can't believe he was desperate enough to burn Molly's house down."

"He was also the one who broke into your hotel room. You told him at the bar the other night that Molly had left you her journals. He was afraid of what she'd written about him. However, after taking the journals from the hotel room, he also started to wonder if there might be more evidence against him back at Molly's house. He was terrified that this book you wanted to write was going to reveal all of his past wrongdoings."

"If he was worried about evidence, why didn't he try to find it before now? It's been so many years, Colton."

"He thought he was safe. After the fire Molly didn't want an investigation into Stan's death. She didn't press the cops to keep going when they stopped. She didn't tell them Stan abused her. She wanted it all to just go away. "

"I guess that makes sense," she said slowly.

"It was your book project that made him realize he might not be safe after all. And he didn't just turn Molly away, he broke laws gambling with Stan, and he helped cover up what he was sure was

Stan's murder."

"Did he think Molly did it?"

"He wasn't sure. He suspected Molly, but he also knew that a couple of cops were in a lot of debt to Stan, and if Stan died, so did their debts." Colton took a breath, then added, "Fletcher didn't think anyone would be in the house tonight. He knew Molly lived alone and that she was at the hospital, probably dying. In his twisted rationalization, he didn't believe anyone would care if her house burned down."

"Until he realized I was in the house."

"He claims he never intended to hurt anyone."

"Well, he did help you free me, so I guess I have to believe that."

"I wouldn't let him off the hook so easily. You wouldn't have been in danger if it hadn't been for him," he said sharply, the memory of his terror when he'd seen Molly's house on fire running through him again. "He could have killed you, Olivia. I want him to pay for that."

She gave him a soft smile. "Hey, now who's thinking about something that didn't happen?"

He blew out a breath. "Guilty. Anyway, I guess we have all the answers now. Fletcher didn't help Molly and the cops didn't investigate because of Stan's bookie operation. And my grandfather killed Stan."

"Colton," she said.

He didn't like the gleam in her beautiful green eyes. "What?"

"It wasn't your grandfather."

"He told us how it all went down."

"It was a good story, but it wasn't the truth, and you know it."

Her words rang through him, and as he looked into her eyes, he realized he did know the truth. "Yeah, I know it. I just don't know what to do. I can't turn my grandmother over to the police."

"It was self-defense, Colton. She hit Stan to save Molly."

"She'd have to prove it in a trial. She can't go through something like that. She's sick, Olivia. You've seen what happens to her when she gets agitated."

"Which is probably why no one would ever put her on the

stand." Her gaze softened in sympathy. "But you don't have to turn her in. You don't have to do anything."

"And that would be all right with you—considering that you may be Stan's granddaughter?"

"I *am* his granddaughter. I didn't get to tell you, but before the fire broke out, I found this in Francine's music box. It's a note she wrote to her baby girl after she gave her away." Olivia pulled some paper out of her pocket. "Francine said that the only thing she asked of the adoptive parents was they call the baby Olivia, because that was her middle name."

He smiled as Olivia got teary-eyed again, but this time there was a smile on her face.

"It's a beautiful letter," she said. "I want you to read it."

"I will, but not tonight. Tonight that letter is just for you to savor."

She nodded and slipped the note back into her pocket, then gave him a smile that made his heart turn over. "Thanks for being so understanding. You've been amazingly wonderful the past few days. I don't think I would have gotten through them without you."

"I feel the same way." His heart began to beat faster as he gazed at her, as emotions he'd never felt before, words he'd never said before threatened to spill out.

"Colton? Is there something you want to say?"

"Yes." But before he could say it, the door opened and the doctor walked in. He told Olivia that he would put a cast on her leg and that the pulmonologist wanted her to spend the night so they could keep an eye on her lungs and provide several breathing treatments over the next twelve to twenty-four hours.

Olivia tried to argue, but the doctor was firm, and Colton wasn't about to help her get out of the hospital. He wanted to be sure that she was completely fine before she walked out the door.

"I really hate this," Olivia told him when the doctor stepped out for a moment.

"I know, but it's only for a night. Do you want me to call anyone for you—your mom maybe?"

"No, I don't want to worry her. I'll talk to her tomorrow when I'm not in the hospital."

He brushed an errant strand of hair off of her face. "Olivia, I know I could pick a better time to say this. I'm sure the doctor will be back in any second."

"Then maybe you should speak quickly," she said with a smile. "Instead of all this rambling, which is so un-Colton-like. You're usually very confident."

He smiled back at her. "Not when it comes to something this important."

She groaned. "It's a good thing I'm in the hospital, because you're killing me."

"I've fallen for you, Olivia. I think it happened the first time I saw you when you literally knocked me off my feet."

Her smile lit up her eyes. "That was not my fault. You were checking your phone."

"And you were intensely curious about what was in your mystery box. Who knew it would all end up here?"

"Or what would happen along the way," she said quietly. "I've fallen for you, too, Colton. I just don't know what we're going to do about it."

"We're going to figure it out," he said, and this time he was confident. Because as long as he knew she felt the same way, he was going to make it happen.

The nurse came into the room and began setting up instruments for Olivia's cast.

Olivia gave him another smile. "You should go home, Colton."

"I don't want to leave you here alone. I can stay with you tonight."

"I'll be fine. I'm just going to be sleeping. I'm kind of exhausted. It's been a really long day. But if you want to pick me up in the morning..."

"I'll be here in the morning." He leaned over and gave her a loving kiss. "Don't get into any more trouble without me."

"I won't," she said with a smile. "I'll miss you tonight."

"I'll miss you, too, babe."

Olivia slept through the night, exhaustion and pain medication sending her into a dreamless sleep. While the cast was uncomfortable, and she still had an ache in her leg, when she woke up a little before eight o'clock in the morning, she felt quite a bit better. She nibbled on some food the nurse brought her, wondering when she'd see Colton again. She hoped the pain medication hadn't made her imagine things, and that he had in fact told her he was falling in love with her, because she was definitely falling in love with him.

The man had literally walked through fire for her. His courage and strength were amazing. But those weren't the only traits that made her like him. She appreciated his loyalty to family and friends, the way he protected the people he cared about, and his ability to be completely honest and up front. He didn't play games.

She smiled to herself. That wasn't exactly true, but the games he did play she liked very much. She found her cheeks warming at the memories of being in bed with him. It seemed like a long time ago. And a part of her wished she hadn't sent him home last night, but he'd been as tired as she was, and she couldn't stand the thought of him trying to catch a nap while sitting up in the hard, uncomfortable chair next to her hospital bed.

Glancing at the clock, she felt impatient and restless. The nurse had told her that the doctor probably wouldn't be in to discharge her until ten, so she had two hours to kill. Impulsively, she pressed her call button. When the nurse appeared, she asked if she could be taken upstairs to see her grandmother. The nurse said she didn't see why not, and a few moments later, Olivia was wheeled into her grandmother's room.

Molly looked smaller, thinner, paler…She was clearly slipping away, if she wasn't already gone.

Olivia stared at her grandmother for a long time, wanting to soak up what might be the last few minutes she ever had with her. She wheeled her chair a little closer to the bed and put her hand over Molly's.

"I don't know if you can hear me or feel my touch," she said. "But it's me, Olivia. I know now that you wrote to me for a reason.

I think you wanted to meet me, and you wanted me to meet you. Maybe at some point you would have told me the whole story and revealed our true relationship, or maybe not. I just wish we'd had the chance to speak to each other. I wish I could hear your voice, see your eyes—the eyes that people say look just like mine."

Sorrow filled her at a loss she'd never expected to feel.

"It's not fair that we should have come so close and not been allowed to connect," she continued. "But if this is all we get, then I'm going to take it." She swallowed hard and pushed through the heavy weight of emotion as she thought about what she wanted to say.

"I want you to know that I've had a good life. My parents were wonderful people. I have no complaints about where I grew up. Francine wanted the best for me, and I got it. So thanks to her, I had a good childhood, probably a better childhood than Francine had."

She squeezed Molly's fingers. "I know what you went through. I've been piecing together your story, and I have it pretty straight now. I don't know if you really wanted me to tell it, or if you just wanted me to hear it." She thought about that for another moment, then said, "But I know what I want to do now. And while I still hold out hope that you'll open your eyes and say hello to me, even if you don't, I'm going to do right by you. I promise you that."

She let out a sigh. "I wish you could hear me, Molly. I wish you could feel the connection between us, the love I have for you. I know that sounds strange, because we've never met, but I do love you. And I'll never forget you."

As a tear dripped out of her eye, she felt Molly's fingers move beneath hers. She started, looking at Molly's face. There was absolutely no movement there, and now her fingers weren't moving either. Had she imagined it?

"You're back again," a male voice said with resignation.

She didn't have to turn around to know it was Peter.

He moved around to the other side of the bed. "So I hear you narrowly escaped getting burned to death in my mother's house."

"You could try to sound a little happier about my escape," she retorted.

"I've been at the police station and at my mother's house for most of the night, so I'm a little tired."

He did look exhausted. There were dark shadows under his eyes. "I guess you know what happened."

"I know enough." His gaze moved to his mother and then back to her. "Those pictures you showed me yesterday; they were horrible."

She nodded. "Yes, they were."

"Her bruises were a lot worse than I remembered. I told myself for a long time that it wasn't that bad. My father could get mad, but he could be a good guy—sometimes—once in a while." He paused for a long moment. "I was lying to myself. I didn't want to have a father who beat his wife. After he died, it was easier to pretend that the fire was just an accident, that everything that had happened before didn't matter anymore."

"You were a child," she said gently. "You tried to protect yourself the only way you knew how. But you're not a child anymore."

"No, I'm older than my father was when he died. I wish I could tell my mother that I was sorry for downplaying what she went through, for blaming her for what happened to Francine. In many ways I treated my mother with the same disdain my father once did. I wish I could go back and change it all, but I can't."

"Oh, my God," Olivia murmured, distracted by Molly once again.

"What?" Peter asked.

"Her fingers are moving." She lifted her gaze to his. "You have to feel this."

He reached across the bed and put his hand on his mother's wrist as Molly moved her fingers. The action was unmistakable this time.

"Mom," he said. "I'm here with you. And..." He looked at Olivia. "And I'm with Francine's daughter. We need you to come back to us."

Olivia held her breath as Molly's eyelids began to flicker and then finally her eyes opened, and Olivia was looking at eyes as green as hers.

"Mom," Peter said with excitement. "You're awake. I can't believe you're awake." He looked back at Olivia. "Can you get the nurse? I don't want to leave her."

She reluctantly let go of Molly's hand long enough to wheel herself into the hall and motion for the nurse to come. "She woke up," she said, still not sure she could believe it was true.

But it was true and thirty minutes later after being examined by two doctors, Molly's breathing tube was removed and she was breathing on her own again. Her eyes were also open and aware, although she had yet to speak, and the doctor had told them all to go slow, that her speech and brain might need time to recover.

As the doctor left the room, Peter and Olivia moved back to the bed, this time side-by-side.

"Hello, Molly," she said quietly. "I'm Olivia, your granddaughter."

"Olivia," Molly's response was hoarse but clear.

"Don't try to talk, Mom," Peter said quickly, putting his hand on his mother's arm. "We've got time. Olivia isn't going anywhere." He looked back at her. "Are you?"

"Not anytime soon."

Molly's eyes fluttered closed, and Olivia wondered if they'd already lost her again, but the nurse who had been hovering nearby said, "It's okay. She's just sleeping."

"But she's going to wake up again, right?" Olivia asked.

"I think so," the nurse said.

"I think so, too," Peter said confidently.

"What's going on?" Colton asked, as he entered the room.

"Molly woke up, Colton. She looked right at me and said my name."

"That's great," he said with surprise in his eyes.

"My eyes are just like hers."

He gave her a smile. "That's what my grandmother said."

"We have to tell your grandmother that Molly woke up."

"We will."

Olivia looked back at Peter, who was quietly watching their exchange. "I know you don't like me, but do you think we could call a truce, at least when we're with your mother? I don't know how much time we'll have with her, but I don't want to waste it in tension and anger."

"I agree," he said.

"Good."

"I'm going to make a call," Peter said.

As Peter left, she turned back to Colton. "It feels like a miracle just happened."

He nodded. "It does feel that way. I know you're convinced that you're Molly's granddaughter, but I want you to know that I just spoke to Shayla, and the DNA test confirms that fact."

"I knew it would. From the first minute I read Molly's letter to me, I felt an irresistible pull to her. I had no idea what I was getting myself into, but I knew I had to come to San Francisco."

"I'm certainly glad you did."

"Have you spoken to your grandparents again?"

"No, but I will—soon. Are you ready to get out of here?"

"I'd like to stay with Molly for a while. I hate to leave her now that I've met her."

"Then I'll stay with you," he said, pulling over a chair so he could sit next to her.

She smiled, her heart overflowing with love for him. "You're a good man, Colton Callaway."

"I am, and when we eventually get out of here and get away from our family problems, I'm going to show you just how good I can be."

Her nerves tingled at his words. "I'm going to hold you to that."

Twenty-Eight

---➤➤◄◄◄---

The next day the Callaway family gathered in the lounge at the Sunset Senior Center just after five o'clock on Friday. Seated on the couches were Eleanor and Patrick Callaway along with Eleanor's friends Ginnie, Constance and Tom. Peter Harper and the rest of the Callaway family were sitting in chairs brought over from the card tables.

Peter looked awkward and uncomfortable, Olivia thought, but she was beginning to think that was just his natural demeanor. He'd obviously put up a wall a very long time ago, probably when he was a small child and had begun to witness the violence between his mother and father. She didn't know if they would ever be close or even friends, but in the past twenty-four hours they'd managed to keep a quiet truce between them, and on a few occasions he'd even let something positive slip about Francine. With Olivia's presence, he was starting to remember some of the good times that had come before Francine's tragic death.

As Olivia looked around the room, she felt as if the whole scene was somewhat surreal. A week ago the family had been celebrating Eleanor's birthday in this very same room, and she'd just arrived in San Francisco, eager to meet a group of women who could possibly jumpstart her writing career.

But how quickly her goals had moved beyond a book and had turned toward unraveling an old mystery, and a series of secrets that had made her the center of a story she had never expected to hear.

"Ready?" Colton murmured, leaning in close to whisper in her ear.

She shivered a little as his breath grazed her cheek. Colton had been another unexpected but wonderful surprise. "I think so," she said. She and Colton were sitting on the couch next to Eleanor and Patrick and while she had an idea about what his grandparents might say, she wasn't completely sure. Colton had tried to speak to his grandparents several times the day before, but Patrick had always cut him off, saying they would talk when they were ready. Apparently, they were ready.

She slipped her hand into Colton's, knowing he was feeling stressed about what might come, but the truth needed to be told, no matter how difficult it would be for everyone to hear it.

Glancing over at the elderly couple, Olivia saw that Eleanor and Patrick were also holding hands. They'd been together more than sixty years. Theirs was an amazing love story. She couldn't help but hope she'd have that same story to tell sixty years from now.

Eleanor gave her a steady smile, her bright blue eyes alert, with the light of battle clearly evident. She was definitely ready to speak, and Olivia smiled back at her encouragingly.

Patrick cleared his throat. "Thank you all for coming. I wasn't going to do this here, because I thought it was a family matter, but Eleanor insists that you are all family, especially when it comes to what happened a very long time ago—to Molly and her husband." His gaze drifted to Peter. "And her children," he added.

Peter inclined his head in acknowledgment.

As Patrick paused, Olivia saw Ginnie and Constance exchange a look. She couldn't help wondering what the others in the theater group had known. Perhaps the secret hadn't been as well kept as everyone thought.

Patrick looked at Eleanor. "Shall I do the honors?"

"No, I want to tell the story, Patrick, because I know what Molly would want me to say. First, before I go back to the very distant past, I want you all to know that I spoke to Molly yesterday. She's doing a lot better. She's going to need some help getting full control over her speech and some of her movements, but she's very aware and alert and quite happy to have her long-lost granddaughter here in San Francisco." She smiled again at Olivia. "None of us had any idea that you were Molly's granddaughter when she told us about a writer she wanted to invite to hear our story. Now, it makes perfect sense.

Eleanor looked back at the group. "I told Molly yesterday that I was going to tell the truth about what happened to her husband Stan. It was a secret that we kept for forty years, not just to protect ourselves, but also to protect Molly's children." Eleanor took a deep breath and lifted her chin as if she were about to go into battle, and perhaps she was.

"Molly was very much in love with her husband, but Stan had a terrible temper, and he drank too much," Eleanor said. "When he drank, he got violent, and his target was always Molly. She tried to do everything she could to prevent him from going into a rage, but her efforts were rarely good enough. Some of you may wonder why Molly stayed with Stan. Her parents had died when she was a teenager. She was left to live with an uncaring aunt. She felt very alone in the world, and when she fell in love with Stan and had her children, she felt like she had a family again, and she didn't want to break that family up."

Eleanor moistened her lips with her tongue, her gaze moving to Peter. "Molly told me that one day she saw Stan grab Peter and shove him against the wall and that she knew then she was going to have to do something, because she couldn't let him hurt her children. She started sending the kids to sleepovers on the weekends when Stan was more likely to be drinking. She tried contacting the police at a station where her husband didn't work, but the man she spoke to, Keith Fletcher, was unwilling to help her."

"After one particularly violent night, Molly asked me to photograph her bruises. She wanted to have proof of what Stan was doing to her, so the next time she went back she would have evidence. Unfortunately, before she could do that, Stan came home in a rage one night. Molly was making Stan a special dinner. He'd been in a bad mood all week, and she wanted to do everything right. She probably had every burner on the stove turned on as she was making all his favorites. She was trying so hard to please him."

Eleanor's voice turned grim. "But Stan came home early and drunk. Dinner wasn't ready, and he was furious. He started hitting Molly. I happened to call during the attack, and she managed to get to the phone. She had barely said my name when he disconnected the call. I knew she was in trouble. Patrick wasn't home from work yet, and I thought about calling the police, but after what they'd told Molly, I didn't think I could wait for them to come."

"What did you do, Grandma?" Emma asked as Eleanor paused to take a sip of water.

"I ran down to Molly's house and barreled into the kitchen. Molly screamed at me to get the kids out. She was bleeding badly from her nose, and one eye was already swelling. Stan had a bottle in his hand, and I was pretty sure he was about to hit her over the head with it. I didn't know what to do. Molly yelled at me again to get the kids. So I ran up the stairs."

Eleanor's gaze turned to Peter.

Olivia followed that look, seeing her uncle turn pale as Eleanor took them all back to probably the worst night of his life.

"We were in Francine's closet," Peter said. "Francine was crying. She was terrified. She had her arms around her favorite stuffed rabbit, and I had my arms around her," he said slowly. "It was the worst fight I'd ever heard. My mom's screams rang through the house. My dad sounded like an angry bear. I kept hearing things break. I couldn't imagine what the house was going to look like when they finally stopped."

Olivia was shocked at how much Peter had to say. He'd been so reticent about the past until now.

Peter shook his head in bewilderment. "I don't think I remembered any of that until just this second."

"You were so young," Eleanor said sympathetically. "I grabbed your hands and took you both down the stairs."

"And you told us to run to your house," Peter finished. "Then you went back inside."

"What happened then?" Emma asked, always the impatient one.

"The kitchen was in shambles," Eleanor said. "Stan must have tossed the pans around the kitchen, because there were little sparks starting to flame all over the room. He couldn't even see that he was setting fire to his own house. He was too focused on Molly. He had his hands around her throat, his big, red, beefy hands," she added. "He was choking her to death, and I really believed in that moment she was going to die. I grabbed an iron skillet. It was the closest thing to me, and I hit him over the head. He immediately fell to the ground."

Eleanor paused, her gaze back on Peter. "Your mother was shaking and gasping for breath. I knew I had to get her out of the house. So I took her to my house."

Peter stared back at her. "All these years, I thought my mother killed my father and was just afraid to admit it."

"But the story doesn't end there," Colton interrupted. "Tell the rest of the story, Grandma."

"Let her get to it in her own time," Patrick snapped at Colton. "Don't push her."

Eleanor hushed her husband. "It's okay, Patrick. I can do this. When I got Molly back to my house, Patrick was home. I told him what had happened, and he ran down the street. About ten minutes later, I heard the sirens. I didn't know what was happening at Molly's house. I was tending to her injuries and trying to comfort the kids." She looked at her husband. "I guess this is where you take over."

Patrick nodded. "When I got to the house, Stan was back on his feet, stumbling around the kitchen. We fought as the kitchen burned around us. When I finally knocked him out, the fire was huge. I looked at him on the ground, and I thought about saving him..." His voice trailed away as he took a deep breath. "But I didn't."

"That's not what the fire report said," Emma interrupted. "You told the investigators when you got to the house the fire was too big. You couldn't get to Stan. You burned your hands trying to save him."

"I made that up," Patrick said. "But I didn't try to save him. I let him die."

"No, you didn't," Jack said, stepping forward to face his father.

"That's not what happened. I've never believed that."

"You knew about this, Dad?" Colton challenged, rising to his feet as he looked at Jack.

"I was at the house when Mom came back with Molly and the kids. I knew that Stan died in the fire." Jack looked at Patrick. "But I don't believe you let him die."

"Well, I did," Patrick said, also rising.

The air bristled between the men. Some of Colton's brothers also stood up. Burke seemed particularly shocked. "I don't believe it, either," Burke said. "You're a firefighter. You don't leave people behind."

"Everyone sit down and stop talking," Eleanor said sharply. "I mean it," she added, when no one moved. "Look, I may not have more than a few minutes before I forget who I am and why I'm here. While I still have my wits about me, I want to come clean about everything."

Slowly, reluctantly, the Callaways sat down.

Eleanor turned to Patrick. "I'm not going to let you take the blame for me anymore. You promised me that tonight we would tell the truth."

"I've told the truth," he argued. "You just don't remember it right, Ellie."

"I do remember that night, Patrick. And I've let you lie to me for forty years. It has to stop now, because we're running out of time, and I can't bear to keep the secret any longer. We've both known all these years that I killed Stan with that frying pan, and you covered it up."

"Is that true, Grandpa?" Colton asked.

Patrick's eyes reflected his anger and frustration, but Eleanor's pointed glance was weakening his resolve. "Yes," he said finally.

Olivia let out the breath she'd been holding. She'd thought that Patrick was protecting Eleanor, but she wasn't sure she'd ever hear him admit it.

Eleanor also looked a bit surprised that her husband had finally spoken the truth.

Patrick shifted in his seat, taking both of his wife's hands in his. "I couldn't let you live the rest of your life feeling guilty for killing Stan, Ellie. And I couldn't let you go to jail for killing a man who would have killed you and Molly and anyone else he could get his hands on."

She nodded. "I knew that's why you told me that you killed him in a fight, but I always knew in my heart it wasn't true. I saw Stan when he fell to the ground. I knew he was dead. I kept thinking that when the police started asking questions, the truth would come out, and I would speak up, but they never came around. Colton told me earlier that that was because Stan was doing some illegal things at work and other cops were involved. They thought that one of them might have killed Stan. Of course I didn't know that at the time."

"I've always wondered," Peter broke in, "why the cops didn't look at my mother's beaten-up face and ask how she'd gotten so badly hurt when she was supposedly baking cookies with you."

"I can answer that," Eleanor said. "I kept Molly away from the police the night of the fire. I said she was hysterical, and she'd taken a sleeping pill. By the time she spoke to the detectives, a good twenty-four hours had passed. Her swelling had gone down, and we were able to cover a lot of her bruises. The truth is the police officers didn't look her in the eye, and the interview was very short."

Eleanor took a breath and then continued. "Molly didn't want an investigation. She didn't want the community to know what kind of a man Stan was. She didn't want to have to put you and Francine on the stand, Peter."

"So everyone had a reason to keep silent," Olivia said, very aware now that she was the center of attention. "The cops, Molly, and the two of you," she said, turning toward Eleanor. "I understand why you did what you did back then—both of you," she added, including Patrick in her statement. "But I guess the question is—what are you going to do now?"

Eleanor and Patrick looked back at her. "I'm going to tell the police what I did," Eleanor said.

"Absolutely not," Patrick said.

"I've actually already told the police," Eleanor said, looking at Emma's husband Max, who was now shifting uncomfortably in his seat.

"I'm just Emma's husband tonight," Max said.

Eleanor smiled. "You're such a good man for her, Max."

Max turned a little red at the compliment and then muttered, "Thanks."

"But I do want to do the right thing," Eleanor said. "I know I might not even remember this decision tomorrow, but I feel I should step up. I should have done it a long time ago. I took the easy way out."

"No, you didn't," Peter interrupted. He got up from his chair and walked over to Eleanor. Then he dropped to one knee so he and Eleanor were at eye level. "You saved my mother. You saved me and my sister." He gave a heavy sigh. "When Olivia came to me and asked me about the fire, I was so sure I remembered it exactly the way it happened, but after I thought about it, other memories started coming back into my head. Hearing your story tonight took me right back to that night."

"I'm sorry, Peter," Eleanor said.

"No, I'm sorry. I did what every other man in my mother's life did—I blamed her instead of the real villain, my father. And that night when he was choking her to death, I was hiding in the closet."

"You were a boy. Please don't blame yourself. Your father is the only one to blame."

"Exactly. He deserved what he got. He started that fire all by himself. And you only hit him because you were defending my mother. The people who needed to know the truth now know it. You're not going to the police. You're not going to put your family or mine through any more pain."

"If that's what you want," Eleanor said slowly.

"It is. I don't want my father to ruin any more lives. This ends tonight."

Eleanor nodded and then opened her arms to Peter.

Olivia was shocked to see her crusty, cold uncle give Eleanor a hug, and for just a moment she saw the boy he'd once been and the loving neighbor who had quite literally saved his life.

As Peter stood up, he said, "I'm going to see my mother now, and I'll reassure her that the past is going to stay in the past—just the way she always wanted." He looked around at the other women and added, "I realize now that the theater group was my mother's way of giving back and doing something good in her life. I didn't like it at the time. It took her away from me and my sister, but now I realize that she needed the group to save her from sinking into depression and guilt. By doing something good for someone else, she had a reason to keep going. Thank you all for that. Goodnight."

Murmurs of *goodnight* followed his exit.

"So that's it," Patrick said, getting to his feet. "You now know the secret your grandmother has been trying not to say for the last few years."

"I knew you weren't just rambling, Grandma," Emma said, coming over to give her grandmother a kiss on the cheek. "I thought you were amazing before, but I'm even more impressed now. I think I know where I get my courage."

"That's a sweet thing to say," Eleanor replied.

Olivia looked at Colton as chatter broke out among the various groups in the room. "What do you think?"

"Peter showed incredibly good judgment just now, and I'm glad my grandparents told the truth."

"Your grandfather didn't let Stan die in that fire, Colton. He's still the man you always thought he was."

"No, he's not, because I always thought of him as a hero, but now I realize he's just a man."

"A good man," she said.

He nodded. "Yes, he is."

"He would give his life for your grandmother. I've never seen a man so devoted to the woman he loves."

"Then you aren't looking at me."

Her breath caught in her chest at the intense look in his blue eyes.

"Let's get out of here, Olivia."

"You want to leave your family now?"

"Yes. I've had enough family to last me for a while. I want to spend some time with you." He helped her to her feet and handed her the crutches she would have to use for the next few weeks.

"Should we say goodbye?" she asked.

"Everyone is caught up in conversation. Let's just slip out."

"Okay, lead the way."

He forged a path through the crowded room and then made sure she made it down the stairs on her crutches. Once in the parking lot, he paused. "Instead of going home, let's go across to the beach."

"I don't know how well my crutches will do in the sand."

He gave her a smile. "I'll carry you."

"Well, I can make it across the street. Then you can carry me."

"Deal."

They waited for a car to pass, then walked across the highway. Colton set her crutches to the side and then swept her up into his arms and carried her to a lovely spot on the sand about ten yards from where the waves were landing on the beach.

The sun was sinking below the horizon and the moon was already on the rise, sending dancing lights off the shimmering waves. The wind blew in her face, and as she felt the salty spray on her lips, she remembered Francine's letter and how she'd said she always loved the beach at night.

"I wonder if this is the beach Francine came to when she wrote my letter," Olivia mused as Colton sat down next to her.

"Maybe. She didn't grow up too far from here."

"It's weird that two pages of handwriting can create a connection that will last forever."

"I'm sorry you didn't get to meet her, Olivia."

"Me, too, but I had a good mom, and I actually want you to meet her," she said.

He gave her a speculative look. "You've told her about me?"

"Yes. I told her I was terrified that I was falling for a man who was going to make me worry every time he left the house."

Colton's smile dimmed. "Olivia, about my job—"

"No, wait," she said, putting her fingers over his lips. "Do you want to know what my mom said back to me?"

"Do I?" he countered.

"She said that I should follow my father's lead and live my life with no fear and no regrets, that real love was worth any risk." She paused. "She was right, and everything she said reminded me not only of my dad but also of you. You live with the same sense of fearlessness and passion for life that he did. More importantly, you've made me want to live my life the same way. No more planning and worrying and playing it safe. I don't want to be someone's assistant anymore. I don't want to always be the passenger. I want to drive my own life." As she spoke, she felt a wave of absolute certainty for the direction she wanted to go. "I've decided to quit my job and write my own books."

"That sounds like a good plan," Colton said approvingly.

"I can write anywhere," she said.

"Even San Francisco?"

"Even San Francisco. And you know what else I have planned?"

"Tell me."

"I'm planning to spend a lot of my time dating a really sexy firefighter."

"Now you're talking."

She laughed. "Do you have any plans you want to share with me?"

"Well, I'm more the live-in-the-moment kind of guy, remember?"

"How could I forget? You've shown me some pretty wonderful moments." She tilted her head as his gaze turned serious. "What are you thinking?"

"That you're changing a lot of your life for me."

"Not just for you. For me, Colton, for us. And I don't want you to think that I'm expecting a proposal. I want to spend time with you, to see where this goes. I think we could be good together."

"I know we could be good together. You can move in with me. We'll watch sci-fi movies and make love all night long. And in the mornings we'll go surfing, and maybe you'll learn to love running as much as I do."

"Or maybe you'll enjoy a lazy morning spent reading a good book," she suggested.

"Maybe I will. So you'll move in?"

"I don't know about that. Your apartment is kind of boring. I might want my own place."

He laughed. "I can decorate."

"All evidence to the contrary," she said, smiling back at him. "We'll see. I know I'm going to need some space to write my book."

"Wait. Hold on. Are you going to write Molly's story or my grandparents' story or both?"

She could see the sudden tension around his eyes. "Relax, Colton. I'm not going to spill anyone's secret. I know now that Molly just wanted me to hear her story not to write it. And your grandmother and her friends don't really want to tell the story of their underground railroad, but I can't just let it all pass. I want to do something that will help. I want to pay homage to the bravery and the sacrifice of these women."

He gave her a curious look. "So what are you going to do?"

"Take a page out of your grandmother's book. I'm going to use what I do to help raise money for a women's shelter. I'm going to write a novel or a biography or whatever I can come up with and donate at least half the proceeds to a place that helps women. It will be my way of continuing on with what our grandmothers started."

He nodded approvingly. "I like it. It's a wonderful, generous plan."

"I still have to write something that will sell or my generosity will be very small."

"You will. I believe in you."

"I believe in me, too." She let out a breath. "Anyway, that's the plan. I feel good about it and everything else. I love knowing who I am, even though my biological family is probably not what I would have ordered up, at least I know where I come from. Molly is great. Peter may loosen up, who knows? But most of all, I'm glad I met you, Colton." She paused, thinking that she wanted him to know how she really felt. "You're an amazing man."

He cupped her face with his hands. "And you're an amazing woman. Remember when I told you I never lie?"

"Yes."

"Then you'll know I'm telling the truth when I say I love you." He paused. "And I do love you, Olivia."

She swallowed hard as emotion tightened her throat and chest. "That's a serious statement for a lighthearted guy."

"I know. I've never told a woman I loved her. I knew when I did, I would want it to mean something."

"It means everything," she said, her heart overflowing with love for this man—this man who had literally run through fire for her. And he hadn't just saved her life—he'd changed it completely. "I love you, too, Colton. Will you take me home now?"

"I thought you'd never ask."

He gave her a long, loving kiss, and then they headed for home.

THE END

Keep reading for an excerpt from

the next book in the Callaway series

SOMEWHERE ONLY WE KNOW
(Releases December 2015!)

One

---→→→←←---

The cold wintry night was eerily similar to the one three years ago when thick clouds of fog had swept into San Francisco just after dusk, shutting out the last bit of daylight, holding the city in the icy fingers of late January. And just like that night, Burke felt a chill run down his spine, an uneasy feeling that was heightened by the sirens that suddenly lit up the air.

As a firefighter, he was used to sirens, to emergencies, to the unthinkable happening in a second, but nothing had prepared him for *that* night.

He tried to force the horrific images out of his mind.

It wasn't the same, he told himself, but three years had done little to erase the memories, which was why the last thing he wanted to do was attend yet another memorial dinner in honor of his late fiancée Leanne Parker. But Chuck and Marjorie Parker insisted on remembering their only daughter's death every year since the tragic car accident had taken her life. As Leanne's former fiancé, he could do nothing but support them. It was his duty to attend, and he'd never been a man to shirk his duty.

As a cold blast of wind rocketed through the tall buildings that surrounded him, he zipped up his jacket and proceeded up the steep hill to the Hanover Club. Originally a private gentlemen's establishment started by one of San Francisco's first families, the Hanover Club now catered to high-powered executives and politicians of both genders interested in holding parties or meetings. Tonight was something in between…

"Burke, wait up."

He stopped, surprised at the sound of his sister's voice. He turned around to see Emma and his younger brother Sean walking quickly up the hill behind him. Emma was a slender blonde with snapping blue eyes that reflected her sparkling, often stubborn personality. A fire investigator for the San Francisco Fire Department, she'd obviously come straight from work, wearing her navy blue slacks and matching jacket.

Sean wore dark jeans under a black wool coat, and like all the Callaway men, he had brown hair and blue eyes. But while Sean looked like everyone else in the family, he was in many ways the odd man out: the musician, the soulful, emotional singer/songwriter in a family of overachievers, many of whom were firefighters.

"What are you guys doing here?" Burke asked.

"Supporting you," Emma said with a purposeful smile, as if she was expecting to get an argument from him. "You should have told us about the dinner, Burke."

"I didn't tell you, because I didn't want you to come." Bluntness was the only thing that worked when it came to his stubborn younger sister. "How did you find out?"

"Mrs. Parker called Mom to see who from the family would be attending. You can imagine how thrilled Mom was that you hadn't told her."

Now he knew why he had four voice messages from his mother that he had yet to listen to. He'd also been avoiding his text messages, which had been pinging away all day. He glanced at Sean and frowned. "And you—this is what you decide to show up for? The guy who misses almost every family event? This one you have to make?"

Sean gave him an understanding look. "Emma insisted. Drew and Ria are on their way as well as Aiden, Sara and Mom. Jessica and Nicole send their regards, but they had a school function with Brandon and Kyle tonight. I'm not sure what's up with Shayla or Colton."

"They're both stuck at work," Emma put in. "And Dad had a dinner meeting he couldn't miss."

"Thank God for that," Burke muttered. While he was close to his father, Jack Callaway had a huge personality, and Jack had never gotten along that well with Leanne's dad. Chuck was a white-collar investment banker and staunch conservative. Jack was blue collar all the way, although he now served as Deputy Chief of Operations for the San Francisco Fire Department.

"How are you doing, Burke?" Emma asked, her blue eyes filled with worry.

"I'm fine, and you really didn't have to come."

"We all loved Leanne. She was going to be part of the family."

"It seems like a long time ago now."

"There's Mom." Sean tipped his head toward the top of the hill where his mother, his brother Aiden and Aiden's wife Sara were getting out of a car. "Don't fight it," Sean advised. "We're going to be here for you whether you like it or not. It's the Callaway way."

He knew it was the Callaway way. Usually, he was the first one to support a sibling or parent or cousin in need, but he wasn't used to being on the receiving end of the attention, and he didn't like it. As the oldest of eight siblings, he'd always been the one to take care of everyone else, to be the strong, independent leader of the family. It was a role he both loved and hated. It was tiring to always have to set the bar high. On the other hand, as his brother Aiden liked to remind him, he did have the chance to set the bar while the rest of his siblings had to follow.

They walked up the hill together, meeting up with his other family members outside the entrance to the club.

His mom Lynda gave him a hug. Aiden nodded, concern in his eyes, and Sara sent him a warm smile and told him that Drew and Ria were on the way.

"Great," he muttered. "I guess we should go in."

As they walked through the lobby and into the private dining room, he saw Leanne's family and friends chatting around tall cocktail tables while waiters served champagne and appetizers. Despite the party set-up, there was a somber air in the room, and Burke felt better having some members of his family walking behind him.

Chuck saw him and immediately came over to shake his hand.

Dressed in a dark suit, Chuck had aged in the last few years, his gray hair now completely white, and the shadows under his brown eyes had become permanent fixtures.

"Burke, I was beginning to think you might not make it," Chuck said.

There was a hint of censure in his voice, but that was Chuck. He was always demanding and often disappointed in the people around him. Leanne had told him many times that she just couldn't seem to make her father happy.

"Don't give him a hard time," Marjorie interrupted with a smile that was very much like her daughter's, and that smile made his heart squeeze a little tighter. "It's nice to see you, Burke. It's been a long time."

"Yes," he admitted. "I like your hair." Her normally brown hair was now a deep rich auburn.

She gave him a dimpled smile. "I decided to go red. Leanne always used to tell me I should change things up every once in a while, so today I decided to finally do that." Her gaze swept across the rest of his family. "I'm so glad you could all come. It means so much to us."

Burke stepped back as his mother and Marjorie exchanged a hug and Chuck shook hands with the rest of his siblings.

As he looked around the dining room, he saw four of his coworkers at one of the tall tables. Apparently, they'd also heard about the event. Since his cousin and fellow firefighter Dylan Callaway was at the table, Burke wasn't surprised they'd found out about the event. Next to Dylan was Frank Harding, who'd been friends with him since the fire academy, Rachel Briggs, a paramedic at their firehouse, and Shelby Cooper, one of their long-time dispatchers who also worked out of the firehouse.

He was touched by their attendance and not that surprised by their presence. His firehouse family was as close as his Callaway family.

Rachel and Shelby both gave him hugs while Frank slapped him on the shoulder and Dylan gave him a nod.

"Thanks for coming," he said.

"No problem," Dylan replied. "I remember last year the

Parkers put on a good spread."

"You're always looking for your next meal," he said, appreciating Dylan's attempt to lighten the mood.

"Are you all right, Burke?" Shelby asked.

Shelby was a dark-eyed brunette in her mid-thirties who worked dispatch with a calm coolness that always kept them on track. Since Leanne's death, Shelby had offered him a friendly ear on more than one occasion. She'd also been friends with Leanne, so it was easy to share memories with her, not that they spent much time talking about Leanne anymore. It had been three years, but tonight it felt like yesterday.

"I'm fine." He wondered how many more times he would say those words tonight.

"Are you?" Rachel challenged. A tall, slender blonde, Rachel could have been a model if she'd had any interest in posing in front of a camera. But she was a tomboy at heart, a girl who loved action sports and pushing herself to the limit.

"I'd just like to get this over with," he told her.

She nodded in understanding. "I'm sure."

"We're going to Brady's after this," Shelby added. "You should come with us after you pay your respects to the Parkers."

"I'll think about it."

"Looks like the buffet table is open," Dylan said. "Anyone want to get some food?"

"You guys go ahead." He wasn't the least bit hungry.

As his friends moved over to the buffet, Aiden crossed the room and put a bottle of beer into his hand.

"Thanks," he said, taking a long swig of cold beer.

"What do you figure? Give this a half hour, then say goodbye?" Aiden asked.

"Definitely not longer than that." He looked towards the front of the room and saw Leanne's smiling face gazing back at him from a large poster. Her parents had set up the same photos that they'd had at the funeral—a display of Leanne's life in photographs. He shook his head in bewilderment. "What are they thinking? When does this end? When do we stop celebrating the worst day in all of our lives?"

"They're thinking that they don't want anyone to forget their daughter," Aiden said quietly.

"I don't need a poster to remind me of Leanne."

"Maybe they do," Sara suggested, joining them. "Sometimes memories start to fade and people worry that they'll forget. I remember feeling that way after my mom died. As the years went by, I couldn't see her face as clearly. I couldn't hear her voice in my head. I couldn't remember her laugh. To tell you the truth, it scared me. I felt like she was slipping away. Perhaps the Parkers feel like that, too."

Sara's words rang true in his head. Leanne had been fading in his mind. While he hadn't been in a serious romantic relationship since then, he had dated other women. He had gone on with his life. Maybe that was why he hadn't wanted to come tonight. He felt like the Parkers were trying to pull him back into the darkness, and he didn't want to be there anymore. He'd gone through the anger, the guilt, the sadness and the multitude of *what ifs* that could have changed the outcome if only he'd done something different. He was over all that.

He looked away from the pictures, his gaze coming to rest on the newest arrival to the gathering—Mitch Warren. His heart sank. This was not going to go well.

Mitch was in his mid-thirties and was a fellow firefighter. Mitch had also been a good friend of Leanne's long before Burke had met her. In fact, Burke had always thought that Mitch had felt a lot more than friendship for Leanne, but Leanne had always dismissed that idea with a laugh, saying they were just good friends.

As much as Mitch liked Leanne, he did not care for Burke. And that dislike had only grown after Leanne's death. Mitch was convinced that Leanne's death was not an accident, that somehow Burke was to blame. He could understand that Mitch needed someone to blame, because he'd looked for a scapegoat himself, but some accidents were just that—unexpected, unexplainable and tragic.

Next to Mitch was Burke's youngest brother Colton.

Burke could see the worry in Colton's eyes. His brother

worked under Mitch at a firehouse on the other side of the city, but he was caught in the war between Burke and Mitch, and there was nothing Burke could do about it. Colton would have to find his own way to a relationship with Mitch Warren.

He stiffened as Mitch saw him and headed in his direction. The last thing he wanted was a confrontation here, but there was nowhere to run, and it seemed obvious from the aggressive look in Mitch's eyes that he wanted to make a scene. He was itching for a fight.

"I can't believe you had the nerve to show up," Mitch ground out, anger burning in his eyes.

He told himself not to react. Mitch's anger came from a place of grief, and that was something they had in common. It wasn't something to fight over.

"Let's get something to eat, Captain," Colton suggested.

"Not yet. I'm done letting your brother act like he had nothing to do with Leanne's death, when we all know he did."

As Mitch spat out the words, Burke could smell the liquor on Mitch's breath. There was no question that alcohol was fueling his fire.

"Why don't we go outside?" Burke suggested calmly, seeing Chuck and Marjorie approaching, tense looks on their faces.

"I'm not going anywhere with you," Mitch replied. "You and I are going to have it out. I'm tired of playing your games. You don't want to answer my questions, but tonight you're going to have to do just that."

"Captain," Colton began again.

"Get out of my face, Callaway," Mitch said forcefully, shoving Colton away.

"What's going on?" Chuck Parker asked.

"It's Burke's fault, Chuck," Mitch said, looking at Leanne's father. "I know you don't want to hear that, but it's true."

"I don't understand." Chuck sent Burke a sharp look. "What's he talking about?"

"I'll tell you what I'm talking about," Mitch answered, not giving Burke a chance to explain. "Ask Burke why Leanne was on the road that night. Ask him why she was so close to the firehouse.

Ask him why there didn't happen to be any security cameras in that particular neighborhood. Go on, ask him."

"Leanne was going to her yoga class," Marjorie cut in. "We already know that, Mitch. She went there every Thursday night."

"And it's not far from the firehouse," Chuck said.

"She wasn't going to yoga. That wasn't the way to the studio."

"She took a shortcut," Marjorie interrupted. "Leanne was always cutting through back alleys."

"I don't believe that. Leanne was upset with him." Mitch pointed an accusatory finger at Burke. "Leanne left me a message that day. She was crying. She said she had to talk to me about him."

Marjorie put a hand on Mitch's arm. "Mitch, we understand that you're upset. You and Leanne were so close. But this isn't going to solve anything. We'll never know what Leanne wanted to talk to you about."

"We'd know if he'd talk," Mitch said, glaring at him again. "But he just stands there and says nothing."

Burke had more than a couple of reasons for why he'd never responded to Mitch's questions, but there was no point in trying to explain that now...or ever. Nothing would bring Leanne back or change the past.

"Let it go," Chuck said firmly.

Mitch shook his head. "So he gets a free pass? No, he needs to pay. He needs to feel some of the pain that the rest of us are in."

Burke saw Mitch pull his hand back a split second too late. He tried to duck, but he was pinned in. Mitch's fist connected with his jawbone, the force of the man's anger making it a solid, purposeful punch.

He stumbled backwards, his head spinning, and knocked into one of the waitresses handing out glasses of champagne. He tried to stop himself from falling, but he got tangled up with the woman, and the next thing he knew he was on his ass on the floor with champagne splashing into his eyes and across his stinging face.

"Oh, my God," the waitress said, on her knees next to him. "I'm so sorry. Are you all right?"

He looked into a pair of emerald green eyes framed by thick

dark lashes and felt like he'd been punched again. "Maddie Heller?"

"Burke Callaway?" she asked, the same amazement in her voice.

As he stared into Maddie's face, he didn't know whether his night had just gotten better or a whole lot worse.

Somewhere Only We Know releases December 2015!

About The Author

Barbara Freethy is a #1 New York Times Bestselling Author of 42 novels ranging from contemporary romance to romantic suspense and women's fiction. Traditionally published for many years, Barbara opened her own publishing company in 2011 and has since sold over 5 million books! Nineteen of her titles have appeared on the New York Times and USA Today Bestseller Lists.

Known for her emotional and compelling stories of love, family, mystery and romance, Barbara enjoys writing about ordinary people caught up in extraordinary adventures. Barbara's books have won numerous awards. She is a six-time finalist for the RITA for best contemporary romance from Romance Writers of America and a two-time winner for DANIEL'S GIFT and THE WAY BACK HOME.

Barbara has lived all over the state of California and currently resides in Northern California where she draws much of her inspiration from the beautiful bay area.

For a complete listing of books, as well as excerpts and contests, and to connect with Barbara:

Visit Barbara's Website:
www.barbarafreethy.com

Join Barbara on Facebook:
www.facebook.com/barbarafreethybooks

Follow Barbara on Twitter:
www.twitter.com/barbarafreethy

CPSIA information can be obtained
at www.ICGtesting.com
Printed in the USA
LVHW110047201218
601166LV00002B/6/P